A Little More Than Kin

Also by Ernest Hebert

The Dogs of March

Ernest Hebert

A Little More Than Kin

THE VIKING PRESS   NEW YORK

A portion of this book appeared originally
in *Yankee* Magazine.

Library of Congress Cataloging in Publication Data
Hebert, Ernest.
   A little more than kin.
   I. Title.
PS3558.E277L5   813.54   81-24135
ISBN 0-670-43209-1   AACR2

Printed in the United States of America
Set in Fototronic Caslon

FOR MEDORA

ACKNOWLEDGMENTS

I would like to thank the National Endowment for the Arts for a grant that helped make the writing of this book easier. I would also like to thank Terry Pindell, who suggested the line from Shakespeare, "A Little More Than Kin," as the title. Finally, I want to say thanks to my wife, Medora, for her support.

Contents

God chose those whom the world considers absurd to shame the wise; he singled out the weak of this world to shame the strong. He chose the world's lowborn and despised, those who count for nothing, to reduce to nothing those who were something; so that mankind can do no boasting before God.

The First Letter of Paul to the Corinthians, 1, 27-29

A Little More Than Kin

Ollie and Willow

Old Man Dorne gathered the phlegm in his throat and spat it into a handkerchief, and that was how the storekeeper knew he was getting ready to launch into a speech.

"The Jordans are no kin of mine, no kin of yours, no kin of God almighty himself," he said. "They ain't even a family exactly, not like you and I think of as a family, anyway. Just a collection of like-minded individuals, like communists or participants in modern art. Course the blood bond is there, right from the line of Cain, if you don't mind me speaking a little in a religious vein here. Not that I have anything personal against the Jordans, except maybe against Willow, who upset my missus over the matter of some petunias. I don't bear him any malice, however, not as Harold Flagg would. How that man could hold a grudge, God rest his soul. God rest all our souls. I wouldn't admit this in front of a bunch of strangers, but I'm getting a little atheistic in my old age. A man gets more impressed by the evidence and less by the arguments, older he gets. You could get mad at Willow Jordan, but you couldn't hate him. It's hard to hate an idiot. It's something that takes practice, and I never had the time.

"As I say, Willow Jordan is an idiot, but his father Ollie is another matter. There is something brooding and figurative about the man. A mind like his is dangerous to society, dangerous to itself, but there's an admirability about it too. That's why I think Flagg hated him so. Flagg was a big law-and-order man, and he was a smart man, but he didn't have much admirability. So, you see, he had double grounds to hate Ollie Jordan: philosophy and jealousy. It's not generally known, but Flagg's the one that got Ollie and his kin run off from that piece of land they were living on. I'm for private property and all that but they were on that land so long they had a claim to it.

"The land is owned by some feller from down-country. He rents out space for the Basketville sign that you can see from the Interstate across the river in Vermont—God bless that state and its crippled deer herd. He also rented to the Jordans. Nobody else would want to live up there, on that lonely road that the town don't—won't—plow. The Jordans arrived there maybe twelve, fifteen years ago, and through it all Flagg built up this animosity against Ollie Jordan. Flagg gave him credit, you know. Wanted the man to owe him something, so that when he took back from him, he could take back everything and call it interest. He bided his time. A man with a grudge don't like swift retribution. Then about in March, Flagg got the planning board to write the feller from down-country and tell him he couldn't rent his land no more, and Flagg called him up, all sweet, you know, and said hush, hush. The next week Flagg died of a heart attack but the wheels were set in motion. Last month the Jordans were evicted. Now I don't say that Flagg knew he was going to die, but I say each man has certain, er, call 'em cognitions, when his time is near, even if he don't see them for what they are, and he tries to put his house in order, or bring down somebody else's house, if he's the kind.

"Course nobody really likes the Jordans. But I don't go with those who say they don't belong in Darby. I say every town has its Jordans and moreover needs its Jordans so the people can take their mind off their troubles. Give a man somebody lower than himself to compare himself to, and I'll show you a man with a strong belief in his own being. Even Willow, I'll admit, was put here for some purpose. Your average Congregational minister will tell you that, of course, but I mean to say I know the purpose: somebody to wear the fun hat. Every man needs somebody to laugh at that he ain't related to, and there's no one on this earth more distant a relative to you and me than Willow Jordan. On the whole, I'll argue the town's poorer without the Jordans. I'm not saying I was happy to see Ollie and his idiot son this morning. I'm speaking theoretical here. Anyway, as Professor Blue would say, 'It's purely academic,' because I don't imagine they'll stay. When Ollie Jordan sees what's been done to his land, he'll run like any other lonely heart fleeing the scene of his hurt . . ."

A call on the storekeeper's CB from Mrs. McCurtin interrupted Old Man Dorne. The cops were headed for the Jordan place, she said. Heard it on the scanner. No confirmation. A code 9. Unfamiliar to her. Therefore, must be something considerable. She signed off temporarily to listen some more to the scanner. The old-timers in the store fell silent, waiting for more news.

Mrs. McCurtin was the town reporter, that is, the town gossip, but she lacked tenure, just as the storekeeper did. Old Man Dorne had explained the situation. The former longtime town gossip, Arlene Flagg, the old-maid sister of Harold Flagg, had committed an unpardonable act: She had mocked the town with her own secret. After her brother died suddenly, she sold the store through the Stout Realty people and then left town without telling anyone where she went. Someone said she had run off with Lancelot Early, the milk salesman from Walpole, but no one in Darby was sure. The fact was no one knew where Arlene was or why she'd done what she'd done because there was no one in Darby with the sources that Arlene herself had. Mrs. McCurtin had spirit, curiosity, persistence, and a darned good scanner, but she was inexperienced. She got overexcited. Her speculation was not put forth logically. Nonetheless, the town was giving her a grace period while she got some on-the-job training. The position of town gossip was an important and difficult one. It took time to break in.

Old Man Dorne was about eighty, slow-talking, with a heavy up-country dialect. His yarns revealed him as one who had read much but had had little formal education. He was the kind of man who could use the words "ain't" and "incur" in the same sentence and make it work. Others in the store included a teenager with a horse laugh, an out-of-work wallpaper hanger who made vile speeches against plywood paneling and women's liberation, and Dr. Hadly Blue, a college teacher, who was the only person in Darby, New Hampshire, with a Ph.D. Never mind that, of the customers, only Old Man Dorne was old. As far as the storekeeper was concerned, if someone came into his store and lingered a moment to chew the fat, he was an old-timer.

The storekeeper had few regrets about leaving Pennsylvania, but he was subject to a peculiar malaise. Back in Hazleton, he had nurtured his soul with a dream of running a country store in New England. Now he had the store. The dream, which had brought him some moments of ecstasy, was now an ache. He was homesick for a place in his mind that he had left. Back there in Hazleton he had created the old-timers, a composite mental picture of people he'd read about in *Yankee* magazine and heard about from his cousin Richard, who had settled in Claremont, New Hampshire, and who, ironically, had returned to Hazleton, divorced and alcoholic, about the time the storekeeper had moved himself and his family to the store in Darby. That had been the first hint that the dream could not be brought forth in anything like its entirety. The full realization came down on him shortly after he took over the store. Most of the people in town were like people anywhere else. As he had sought to regard them as quaint, so they were seeking to regard him. Everybody is part of everybody else's dream, he thought, and it's when we get to know each other that we get let down. Still, he was settled here, and he would not return to Pennsylvania.

Gloria, who had held up his move for ten years, now was saying it had been her idea. As wife of the storekeeper, a junior college graduate, and an obviously concerned parent, she had automatic status in Darby, and she was feeling surges of power. In fact, she was thinking about running for the school board. The kids were getting on after a period of moping. Nancy was crowned spelling champion of Darby. Victor was learning how to trap muskrats from Old Man Dorne. People came to his store and hung around to chew the fat, as they never had done when Flagg was running the place. The storekeeper figured he had awakened in them some long-forgotten pride in self and place by the interest he took in their town, by the reverence he showed for their ways.

He had never heard of the Jordans until Old Man Dorne said that he had seen Ollie and his idiot son Willow this morning driving up the road to where their shacks had been. The storekeeper sensed that in the Jordans was something both pure and tainted, and out of the heart of this region. Even now he felt kinship with this man he did not know who was returning to a place he had once called home.

The Sign

Ollie Jordan stepped from the family truck onto the soil where once his home had been, turned to his son Willow, and said, "Wiped clean." A bulldozer had scooped out a cavern in the hardpan and buried his shacks. All that was left were the caterpillar tracks of the dozer. Already some wild grasses had taken hold in the soil. Willow tugged at the chain that bound him to his father. Willow was looking at the back of the great sign—BASKETVILLE EXIT 8—in whose shadow the Jordan shacks had sprouted. He wanted to climb the sign, swing among the steel struts, holler, exercise what his father called his mysterious sense of humor. Someday, thought Ollie, I'm not going to be strong enough to hold him, and he'll drag me where he wants as now I drag him.

Ollie began at the north corner of the sign and walked thirty-two paces southeast. Here had been the sleeping shack, which he had built for Helen and himself and which he called the "boodwar." He had overheard the word "boudoir," and deciphered that it meant a place for lovers. He had analyzed the word and found it a good one. The meaning of the "-war" part was clear enough, for what were lovers but ceaseless battlers? As for "bood"—he figured that was one of the less ugly terms referring to copulation. He walked twenty more paces. Here his cousin Tooker had settled with his family in a converted schoolbus. To the right was the shack he had built for Adele and her baby, and behind that the room that his children, Turtle and the twins, had fixed up so that they could call it their own. Now, as the wind quieted and the early summer sun fell upon the earth—his earth—Ollie Jordan caught a remnant of his home that the bulldozer could not remove: the smell of his clan.

Ollie's place sat on half an acre on top of a hill. It was bounded by steep ledges and hemlock trees whose roots gripped the granite with all the determination of dying millionaires clutching their money. Here, where the porch had been, a man could sit in a rocking chair, drink a beer, smoke a pipe, hold forth. Here he had said to his friend Howard Elman: "A man fishes to catch his natural-born self. You'll see a banker casting a fly to a rainbow trout, a mailman throwing plug at a smallmouth bass, and a man like me offering a worm to a horn pout . . . You can keep your trout. I don't want no fish that walks on water when it feels the hook." If the sign blocked his view of the Connecticut River valley below and the Vermont hills beyond, at least he could listen to the music of the Interstate highway, which ran beside the river, and to the bitching and moaning of the wind like a woman too long without comfort.

Although the sadness of the loss of the place had settled in him before, and although he knew that later he would feel even more deeply the knowledge of its complete annihilation, Ollie Jordan did not bother to puzzle over why he had been evicted and why his works had been buried because Ollie, like nearly all the Jordans in Cheshire County, did not bother himself with causation. Perhaps this was all for the better. If Ollie had known that one man, Harold Flagg, had plotted to get him evicted simply because he didn't like him and then, as if to prevent any possibility of revenge, had died, and that another man, Alfred Rizzo of Cranston, Rhode Island, had demolished his works because it was the cheapest way to prepare the property for the real estate market—if Ollie had known these matters, he might have gone mad on the spot. As it was, he said to his idiot son, "Willow, there ain't no place left here for a man to sit civilized."

Willow tugged at his chain. He wanted to climb the sign.

Ollie's mind went blank for a moment and then, responding to an urge outside his consciousness, he hit the boy in the face with the flat of his hand. Willow dropped to his knees and began pawing at the earth. It used to be that Ollie would hit Willow when he did something wrong, but the boy learned nothing from discipline, and so now Ollie only hit him to relieve his own tension. Someday, he thought, my temper will lead to murder, either his or mine.

Ollie sat on the ground and put his arm around Willow. The earth was warm. It was going to be a hot day. He was grateful. He knew there were places where it was summer nearly year round, but he could never live there. He had not the will to move, nor—somehow—the right to such a luxury.

"What to do next?" he asked, bringing his mind to bear on the immediate problem, which was the only kind of problem that he considered. To Ollie the only truth of a clock was the ticking, and that was how he took life, tick by tick. Ollie Jordan had returned to his former home in the vague hope that he might sneak back onto his land with Willow. He never imagined that there would be nothing here but the sign.

After he and his family had been evicted, they had been offered succor by Ollie's half-brother, Ike. A professional man, in the Jordan sense, Ike was a successful burglar. Ike's wife, Elvira, introduced Ollie's common-law wife, Helen, to a social worker, and thus was born a great tension. Ollie was a traditionalist, in the Jordan sense. He feared welfare because he was afraid it would change him and change his family's ways. Not that he was proud of himself or the family, but he did believe in the rough integrity of distinction among creatures; and the Jordans, whatever else they were, were as distinct from the run of society as mongrels were from poodles.

Matters reached a crisis when Ollie learned that the "Welfare Department," which was Ollie's phrase for any social service agency, had found a place for them to live in Keene. Helen urged him to move with her. Ollie was about ready to go along with the idea, partly because, as he would say about certain women, Helen could always "cast a spell over this frog," and partly because he was willing to sacrifice a philosophical point to get away from Ike's succor. But then Helen said that the Welfare Department wanted to examine Willow. They said, she said, that Willow might not be as dumb as he looked, might even be "educable," a word that Ollie translated as a marriage of the words "edible" and "vegetable." No one was going to examine Willow as long as his father was alive. He couldn't explain it so it made sense, but he held a deep conviction that in his son's apparent stupidity and odd behavior there was a seed of genius that someday would sprout, provided it was kept away from meddlers such as the Welfare Department. Willow's place was with him, and that was that. As was his wont, Ike entered the argument. "It ain't good for a man's spirit to have an idiot chained to him," Ike said.

"Everybody's got an idiot chained to him," said Ollie. "Only difference is mine is here to see."

Ike smiled. He had the narrow-minded confidence of a successful man. Furthermore, while he was generous with his advice, he was cheap with his beer, which to Ollie demonstrated a poverty of style. That night Helen walked out on him with nearly all the family belongings and the children, save Willow of course. Ike drove the pack of them to Keene in his auctioneer's moving van. Ollie knew Ike's motives in helping Helen, and indeed in providing his family with succor in the first place. Ike meant to gain ascendancy over him. Ollie Jordan might allow his woman of many years to leave with everything they had made together, but he could not allow Ike, his inferior half-brother, to enjoy ascendancy over him. Therefore, the next morning Ollie absconded with Ike's considerable beer supply. He fled with Willow in the family pickup, an ancient four-wheel drive International that Ollie had outfitted with a salvaged church pew, where the kids would ride in warm weather. Besides the beer and his son, Ollie took only his tools, a few personal items, and the knowledge that he had prevented Ike from gaining ascendancy.

Now, broke and angry, and knowing that as soon as the anger wore off he would be sick with loss of his family, Ollie drove at random on the back roads of Cheshire County, like a bandit with no hideout to go to.

Ollie Jordan had never traveled more than one hundred miles from Keene, the hub of Cheshire County. The farther he got from the county, the more uneasy he became, like some sailor of old fearing he might fall off the edge of the earth. Once he had been to Hampton Beach, getting his first and last look at the ocean. He had been appalled by its immensity, which seemed designed specifically by the Creator to diminish humans. On a practical level, he couldn't understand why men and women would want to strip to their undies and lie on gritty sand under a harsh sun, unless it was that the ocean air had disturbed their minds. Certainly it had disturbed his, and he had rushed home.

This morning, every time he had approached the borders of the county, he had found a reason to turn around. He had had no destination, no plan, only Willow and the beer. By accident, it seemed, they had arrived at the narrow dirt road that wound up the mountain from Route 63 to the Basketville sign. For a second, he had thrilled to the thought of returning to the shacks he had built. Now the truth was upon him. All that was here of home was an old scent that the rain eventually would wash away.

Willow tugged at his chain, making a sound like a puppy.

"Oh, all right," Ollie said, and he slipped the key in the padlock that kept the chain around the boy's waist and released him. No doubt trouble would follow. It always did when Willow was loose, but at this point trouble seemed better than nothing.

Willow headed for the sign. At six feet, he was taller than his father by a couple of inches, but he seemed shorter because he walked hunched over like an ape. Ollie stood ramrod straight, except that he held his head bent sideways on occasion. Ollie Jordan smiled little, but when he did he revealed a mouth of black, jagged teeth. Willow smiled often, and his smile was white and empty. Both Ollie and his son had dark hair, slicked by their own body oils, coated with dust. Ollie kept his hair short, so that his hat would always fit correctly. He hated to shave, mainly because no one had explained to him when he was a young man the benefits of hot water, and he hated a beard out of a vague philosophical bias. He groomed himself with a pair of scissors, so that his face had a permanent stubble. He fancied he looked distinguished.

Willow, as his father had said, was "late getting a beard and he's late getting brains," and he sported sparse whiskers which his father would trim. Ollie's skin was pale because he wore a felt hat everywhere and stayed out of the sun as much as possible. The hat was Helen's idea, but Ollie had taken to it and considered the hat part of his uniform. Willow's skin was darkened by the sun because he kept his head up, looking at the sky. Most of the Jordans had pale blue eyes, but both Ollie and his son had drab, brown eyes, which up close revealed wormy markings like pinto beans drying in a musty pantry. There was only one other person in the Jordan clan with eyes like that, and that was the woman they called the Witch.

Willow paused before the sign to sniff the treats wafting on the air currents of morning. Satisfied that at the moment the world was good, he grabbed one of the steel supports on the rear of the sign and, with monkeylike grace and monkeylike foolishness, swung from strut to strut until he was nearly at the top. There he rested, draping himself in the crook made by two pieces of steel. Ollie watched Willow's performance, proud as any father would be before the athletic exploits of his son.

Ollie now prepared to make himself comfortable. He fetched a quart of Ike's Narraganset beer from the truck,

searched about for a patch of ground just the right temperature, sat cross-legged, and lit his pipe to await developments.
He figured that Willow, who like himself had not eaten breakfast, would realize he was hungry in about an hour and then
would come down from the sign. How they would eat with no
food and no money Ollie didn't know. He'd solve that problem
when the hunger came. He had nothing but contempt for men
who held full-time jobs, ate regular meals, and showed any
other evidence that they sought to order their lives in space
and time. "There ain't no other time but now," he would say.
Thus, his despair at seeing his works destroyed lost hold for
the moment, as the comfort of the day, the comfort of the
beer, the comfort of his thoughts settled in.

He watched white clouds gamboling in the sky, and they
reminded him of his dogs. God, he missed them—their wet
tongues and bad breath, their ridiculous insistence on protect-
ing him from nonexistent threats. Dogs were loyal to undeserving men, as men were loyal to their own undeserving
ideas about how to live. He supposed that after he had abandoned them, the dogs had stayed around until the bulldozer
came. Some would raid garbage pails and thus would get shot.
Others would attach themselves to humans, and thus stood a
fifty-fifty chance of survival and a fifty-fifty chance of being
gassed by the county. Ollie imagined that such a death would
be without pain and also without the sweetness that follows
pain. Perhaps one dog, say the shepherd, would learn to hunt
alone again and return to the wild life to live in unacknowl-
edged glory until his teeth went bad and he slowly starved to
death or until he succumbed to his own parasites, eaten inside
out as a man is by his beliefs. The dogs stood no chance with
men, he thought. And men stood no chance at all. Men, like
the dogs that they made over as their own dark inferiors, were
neither wild enough to go it alone, nor civilized enough to get
along together.

To survive, the world needed some improved versions of its
creatures. He had worked on this idea long ago, when he had
sensed the strangeness in himself and had sought to give it

dignity and importance by contriving a theory around it. Soon, however, he realized he was not better than most men, nor fitter, but merely different. But in his son Willow, Ollie saw possibilities. Indeed, he had concluded that Willow's idiocy was a departure point. He had gotten the idea by observing caterpillars immobilize themselves in silky webs, to emerge later as butterflies. He had seen hints in Willow of the butterfly, in the boy's inscrutable and dangerous adventures, what Ollie called "his sense of humor." Lately, as more and more people—even Helen—had called upon him to shuck off the burden of his son, Ollie Jordan recognized the love he had for him as an instinctive, brainless duty, the human equivalent of a salmon swimming upriver to fertilize some eggs and die. But also he saw in Willow his own shadowy love of self.

For almost an hour, Ollie's thoughts passed in review like the clouds above, to thicken into meaning and then dissolve into nothing. He had finished his beer, his pipe had gone out, and he was starting to doze when he was startled by a thump at his feet: Willow's shoes and pants. Moments later the shirt, then the undies came fluttering down. The clothes, all in a bunch at his feet, reminded Ollie of a parachutist whose chute had not opened. He looked up to see Willow hoist himself to the four-inch-wide header at the top of the sign, stand, and— baldacky bareass—face the Interstate highway below.

"When you come down here, I'm going to beat you blue," Ollie said, but even as he spoke, even as he proceeded to give Willow holy hell, even as he shook his fist and jumped up and down at his own frustration, even so, Ollie Jordan thrilled at the sight of his mad son. "You stupid bastard," he shouted, but added under his breath, "My what a sense of humor that boy has got."

After a few more minutes of perfunctory ranting, Ollie fetched another beer, reloaded his pipe, and considered the situation.

The worst, and unfortunately most likely, thing that could happen next would be that someone on the highway would report seeing a naked man on the Basketville sign and in no time flat the Welfare Department would arrive and take Willow away in a white van with a red light and a siren that said *wup-wup-wup*. The second worst thing that could happen—and now Ollie was hearing himself voice his thought—"is that the little bastard will fall off and break his head on the ledges."

What to do? If he could go around the front of the sign, perhaps with a long pole—say a young maple sapling—he might be able to knock Willow off so he would land on the softer earth at the rear of the sign. "It won't work," he said to himself. "The little bastard is too quick." He calculated it would take a motorist twenty minutes to get off at the exit in Putney and find a phone. It would take the Mutual Aid dispatcher another ten minutes to get somebody to the scene of the crime. Let's see, he thought, twenty and ten is thirty minutes—half an hour, that ain't bad. Unless of course a state trooper saw Willow and radioed ahead. But Ollie, operationally optimistic if philosophically pessimistic, wouldn't consider that possibility. Half an hour, not bad, not bad at all. He had, oh, fifteen minutes to enjoy this show before he had to do some serious thinking. He took a swig of beer and watched Willow.

Willow, arms outstretched, tiptoed along the top of the sign, like some creature half-ape, half-dancer. He'd walk to one end of the sign, pivot, and walk the seventy-five feet to the other end. Through it all, he seemed to be keeping time to a music heard only by himself.

Suddenly Ollie Jordan heard a car churning up the dirt on the road that led to the sign. Moments later, Godfrey Perkins, the part-time constable of Darby, N. H., stepped out of his cruiser, paused to adjust his stomach, and with studied nonchalance said, "I see Willow's got himself in a pickle again."

"It's his pickle," said Ollie.

"Not quite. It's a public pickle. He's disturbing the peace of the good people down there on the highway."

"Do 'em some good to have their peace disturbed."

"If you won't get him down here, the law will," said Godfrey.

"Be my guest," said Ollie.

"He won't come down for you?"

"Nope. Got any ideas?"

"Not at the moment," said Godfrey.

The two men settled in, hands meditatively on their chins, like a couple of stand-up comics mocking intellectuals. Willow continued to perform. Occasionally, he would do a handstand on the top of the sign while giggling loudly at the upside-down world, and then, almost faster than the eye could follow, he would spring back to the world of right side up, and continue his walking. Or he would imitate Constable Perkins hoisting up his stomach by the gun belt. "If you could get a pair of pants on him, you could put him on the Ed Sullivan Show," said Perkins, who would have been surprised to hear that Ed Sullivan was deceased.

Godfrey Perkins was a passably tolerable man, for a cop, thought Ollie, who envied the constable for his stomach. It was a magnificent thing, a soft, basketball-sized, man's answer to pregnancy, especially remarkable in that it resided in the frame of an otherwise thin man.

As for himself, Ollie had never been able to cultivate an impressive gut. "You have to have good teeth to make good fat," he would say, and spit. His own blackened teeth punished him like a grief with a constant dull ache, unless he was drinking. They hurt him outright if he ate sweets, and they failed to serve him at all in chewing anything tougher than ground meat. Eating was such trouble he often skipped meals. But now, in the flush of noticing Godfrey's stomach, he was reconsidering his past ways. If he really wanted a nice-sized stomach, he said to himself, he would have to grind his food, and force himself to shovel three meals down the hatch. Was the product worth the labor? He glanced at Perkins, whose belly swayed to and fro, as if inside a lazy baby lolled. The sight inspired Ollie. He vowed silently to amend his life. The vow lifted his spirit for about thirty seconds, and then it vanished forever as he again heard the sound of a vehicle on his road.

A government car leading a cloud of dust came to a halt just behind Godfrey's cruiser. Ollie feared the worst—the Welfare

Department had come to get his boy. A woman driver and a male passenger stepped out of the car. Ollie watched them walk the hundred feet from where the cars were parked to the sign. To Ollie they looked like vacationers: tanned, pretty, dressed in colors instead of garments, it seemed, more ideas of people than actual people, the woman walking like a man, the man walking like a boy.

"Good morning," said the woman. "We're Kay Bradford, social worker, and George Petulio, intern, from the I-I? Independence for Independents in Keene?" Her voice traveled up-slope, so that it appeared she was asking a question instead of introducing herself. She glanced at Ollie, taking in his circumstance, he figured, like a loan company manager watching a stranger approaching his desk, but it was Perkins that she had addressed.

"Ma'am, you're talking to Constable Perkins and this is Mr. Jordan," said Godfrey, "and I must warn you that we've got a naked subject on top that sign."

The woman smiled. "Have you tried talking him down?" she asked.

"Not really; I just got here," said Godfrey.

Ollie could see that the woman was going to run the show. So it goes, he thought. Men talked big and fought big, and ran governments like fancy sportsmen's clubs, but when women chose to step in, they had their way. Women told you where to put the back door, what pan to spit in, and what pot to piss in, took, really, complete command of the important things. He believed that women were tough as oak knots on the inside, and that displays of tears and hysteria were more techniques of control than emotions. As for Polio, which was how Ollie heard the name "Petulio," there was something peculiar about him, and it took Ollie a moment or two to realize what it was. He was big, not bear-big or bull-big like some men, but merely unnaturally outsized, as though in the universe in which he lived, things came bigger.

"Mr. Jordan," said the woman. "We want to help your son, and we want to help you help yourself . . ." She knew him somehow, Ollie sensed, and he was alarmed. They had papers on him, he guessed. These government people knew everything and they knew nothing. They were more dangerous than Christian ministers. "We're going to try to talk him down, and you can stand by and help," said the woman.

She walked over to the sign, placing herself just below Willow, cupped her hands, and said to Willow in a strong voice, "Your mother and your brothers and sisters miss you. They want you to come home."

The word "mother" jarred Ollie into a fear that seemed for just a moment to transport him into a time past, and he saw Willow the infant playing in a pool of blood, if that's what it was, and then he was back into time present in the brightness of the day, the fear gone, and he was wondering how the woman had gotten on to him and Willow. Although, of course, she hadn't entirely. Willow had a mother, but she would not miss him. The woman must mean Helen, he figured; she must have talked to Helen, who had given her some of the facts of their life, but not all, of course, for Helen did not know all. He felt mildly disappointed. He had the idea (foolish, he realized) that the Welfare Department, if it did not know all, at least *could* know all. An idea came to him now that if the extraordinary events surrounding Willow's conception, birth, and upbringing were written down as official government record, the curse that had been put on his memory by the Witch would be lifted. ("I want to know," he had said to the Witch. "You don't want to know," she said. "I was there and you made me forget," he said. "You made yourself forget. All for the best.") How she could taunt him. Somehow, through her black magic, she had drawn curtains across his mind. ("You cut off parts of me. Makes a man lonely for his own self," he had said. "All for the best," she said.) Could the government help him? he asked himself, and he looked at the woman speaking to his son, and at the giant young man with the note pad, and he knew that they could not help. His past resided only in the mind of the Witch and in the region of his own bad dreams.

"Have you had anything to eat today?" the woman asked

Willow. "If you come down we'll buy you a biiiiig hamburger."

Willow continued his business on the sign, ignoring the woman.

"Willow . . . Willow . . . Willow," she called, but Willow seemed not to hear.

She continued for a few more minutes, but she had to step back when Willow turned toward her to urinate. Not that there was anything personal in his action. He just needed to take a leak.

Constable Perkins was disturbed. He had a daughter just a couple of years younger than the social worker, and it bothered him that there was not a trace of shame on her face at the sight of a naked man. The crazy idea was forming in his mind that himself witnessing the social worker watching Willow would somehow influence his own daughter toward depraved ways.

"Damn your soul, Jordan, get that subject down here," said Perkins to Ollie.

The woman turned a stern look on the constable. Clearly, she didn't like his approach, but then again hers wasn't succeeding. She seemed to consider the situation, and then she asked Ollie, "Why did he climb up there in the first place?"

"His reasons," said Ollie.

"Crazy reasons," said Perkins, as Petulio continued to scribble.

"He looks frightened to me," said the woman.

"He ain't, but he ought to be," said Ollie.

Kay Bradford thought she understood now. "Mr. Jordan, is that boy up there because you abused him?"

"I'm going to abuse him when he comes down," said Ollie. His voice was rough as granite. He was shocked by what he considered to be the woman's familiarity. It was clear to him before that they wanted to take his son away from him. Now it was clear that they also were looking for an excuse to put him in jail. They want everything, he thought. It wasn't the armies you had to fear. It was the truant officers and welfare people.

The woman caught hold of her emotions and said with a smile, "Mr. Jordan, you haven't been able to get the boy down. Why not give us a chance—alone? You just melt away. Maybe when he sees you're gone, he'll come down on his own."

"He always did like that sign. Course he never went up it bareass before." Ollie stood his ground. The smile on the woman's face demonstrated to him a lack of cleverness that heretofore he'd thought she possessed. She was dangerous, he said to himself, but ignorant as a stump. No way she could gain ascendancy over him.

It was Godfrey who worried Ollie now. The constable had lost his sense of humor; he was beginning to become professionally annoyed by the situation. Minutes later, Perkins summoned the woman and the note taker to the vehicles for a conference. Ollie could see that they were having a spat, and he could also see that Willow was not about to come down from the sign. When the woman returned, Ollie could tell by the urgency in her voice that something important had transpired at the vehicles.

"Willow, we don't have much time," she shouted. "Willow, it's hot today. You must be getting thirsty. If you come down, we'll buy you a . . . [she turned to Ollie] what does he drink?"

"Moxie." Ollie lied.

"Willow, we will bring you a Moxie," said the woman; then she turned to Petulio and said, "Go to the store and buy Willow a Moxie."

Petulio seemed uncertain whether she really meant what she said—as well he should be, thought Ollie—and his uncertainty seemed to shift from mind to body, so that he swayed like a tree sawed through but undecided which way to fall.

Ollie sidled up to Constable Perkins and launched an exploratory mission for information. "She ain't doing too good," he said.

"It don't matter," said Perkins. His hands were cupped under his stomach; his manner was distinctly self-satisfied.

Ollie moved off. He had no doubt now that Perkins had

called for help. He eased down to the vehicles, and there he heard the dispatcher speaking on the two-way radio in Perkins's cruiser. They were sending a fire truck with a hook and ladder from Keene, presumably to go get Willow. Ollie figured he had only minutes to act.

Back at the sign, Kay Bradford stood with her arms folded beside the sign. She had given up.

"A sad case," she said to Perkins. "Child abuse, parenting without goals or objectives." She spoke as if to implicate Perkins in the sadness of the case.

"He ain't no child, ma'am, he's as grown as you and me," Perkins said, defending, it seemed, himself.

"Mentally, still a child. Look at him," she said.

Perkins's small anger, small smugness had left him unexpectedly, and now he found himself blushing for the social worker, blushing because she could not blush herself. He simultaneously felt warmth for her, and revulsion. He didn't like this scene one bit. Too shifty. Give me a good accident, he thought, somewhere where I can be of service to the public. Oh, well, soon it would be over. "Retarded, I guess," he said.

"Possibly not. Possibly his development was arrested by a traumatic childhood experience."

Why, Perkins asked himself, did he get the feeling he was being implicated in Willow's problems? "Whatever—still an idiot," he said.

The social worker breathed a sigh that obviously was an accusation, and Perkins for the life of him couldn't understand what she thought he had done wrong.

At this point, Petulio, the assistant, put his note pad in his pocket and spoke for the first time. "Is that gas I smell?" he asked.

Constable Perkins was alarmed. It struck him that he had made a mistake in not keeping an eye on Ollie Jordan. Then he heard, or perhaps felt, a *wump!*—a thing of substance that seemed to engage him with a cloud of black smoke full of orange light and lift him off his feet and carry him into the sky. So this is death—not bad, he thought. Seconds later he came to his senses. The social worker and her assistant each had a hold of one of his ankles and they were dragging him along the ground. He could feel heat in the air. The indignity of being saved by a woman and a college student hastened a return of his manly bearing, and soon he was on his feet. The faces of his saviors—and his own, he guessed—were blackened. He thought about his brother, Andy, and how he would imitate Al Jolson singing, "Oh, Mammy, oh, Mammy . . ."

"He's taking him." That was the voice of the social worker and Perkins turned to see Willow scrambling down the un-burning end of the sign, saw his father corral him in some kind of rope getup with one hand, beat him with a stick with the other, until off they went like a couple of guys in old movies being chased by cops. Perkins, too, found himself running—dead last. Ahead of him were the social worker and the assistant. He saw the Jordans get in their vehicle and peel out. Seconds later the social worker reached her car, but Perkins knew somehow that this chase would not amount to anything. Sure enough, Ollie Jordan had taken the time to slash the tires of his cruiser and the government car.

Perkins turned to look at the burning sign. It was a pretty fire. The people on the highway would thrill to it. He deduced that Ollie Jordan had siphoned gas into a can, crept along the ledge, and doused the front of the sign with the gas while he and the social worker were busy yacking at the rear. Perkins now could hear the fire truck that he had summoned pulling off the hardtop onto the dirt road. There was a good chance it would be too big to negotiate the steep turns. Oh, well, that was of little importance. What was important was that the world, as he saw it, was becoming faintly orange around the edges. He began to taste the hot dog he'd had this morning from Joe Begin's lunch wagon. Nausea—sign of shock, he thought. He touched his face. It was numb, and left a dark, greasy smudge on his fingers. Under the black on his face would be red like a bad sunburn. Blow up a white man to make a Negro, he thought; wash a Negro to make an Indian. The social worker and the assistant had gotten out of the car, and they were moving toward him, floating it seemed on a carpet of orange light.

"Oh, my God, what's happened to our faces," said the social worker.

"Oh, Mammy, oh, Mammy," said Perkins.

The Charm

The first thing that Ollie did when he pulled his truck onto the main road was open the last quart of beer and with it salute the fire truck as it sped by. He drove about five miles and turned off a dirt road that led to a sandbank on the Boyle property, where he stashed his truck in some pucker brush. He tried to concentrate on what he should do next, but instead he remembered that as a boy he had conducted evening eavesdropping missions at another sandbank at the end of another road. High school boys in hee-haw voices came in packs to drink beer there, smash bottles, and talk about automobiles. Lovers parked in cars and struggled agonizingly for an hour to do what the young Ollie could do in two minutes. From his observations, he gained in knowledge. He concluded that people tried to imprison one another and in so doing imprisoned themselves. He was warned, and it wouldn't happen to him, he had told himself. He realized now that he had been wrong. Knowledge of error tended to make one error-prone instead of error-shy. Show a man the destruction a gun can bring, and the first thing he wants to do is fire it.

Undecided as to the proper course of action, Ollie walked his naked son through the woods a short way to Boyle's barn. He found an old army blanket in a stall and he wrapped Willow in it and took him up a ladder to the hayloft. Willow had drifted off into a walking-doze that sometimes came over him following his adventures. He'd be easy to handle until the next morning, when he'd awaken frisky and hungry. Ollie drank the remainder of his beer in the hayloft, but he dared not light his pipe. Farmers had good noses for smoke, especially in their barns. When the beer was gone, Ollie shackled Willow to himself and took a nap. Ollie preferred daytime sleeping because the demons stayed away. When Ollie woke, farmer Boyle was milking his cows below. "What's a matter with you?" he asked them. "Moon gotcha?" Ollie hungered for food, drink, and tobacco; his bladder cried for relief; and he was afraid that Willow might reveal their position at any moment. Guess I must be desperate, Ollie thought to himself, and was reassured by the idea since he didn't feel all that bad.

When night fell, Ollie tied Willow to a post in the barn and foraged outside. He swiped a pair of coveralls and a shirt from Mrs. Boyle's clothesline, dressed Willow, returned with him to the sandbank, and drove off in the truck. Time was running out. He had no money, no food, no drink, no place to dwell, no good ideas, and he was running low on tobacco. There was only one thing to do, what he always did when he was desperate: visit the Witch. He faced the prospect with loathing and excitement. It was as if he deliberately got himself into situations where he must turn to her. Oh, well, she'd have liquor, and she'd offer them succor. Had to.

The Witch lived in the tiny town of Dubber, N.H., named after Alexander Dubber, the founder of what is now the Boston law firm of Dubber, Dubber, Dubber, Grosbeck, and Dubber. The central feature in Dubber was Dubber Lake, which commanded a magnificent view of Mount Monadnock, which was only about 3186 feet high but gave the illusion of being higher because it was surrounded by smaller hills and because its peak was bare of trees. Dubber was dominated by a class of people who had lived the American dream in reverse. During the 1920s, the progenitors of this class had come to Dubber, drawn by the lake and the mountain, to build a couple of dozen mansions that lay hidden in the spruce and birch forests like mortal sins deep in the souls of clergymen. When the 1930s came, the money slowly evaporated; by the 1940s, all the servants had gone to war and returned affluent and arrogant; by the 1980s, the sons and daughters of the builders found themselves with huge real estate holdings that they could not afford to own or maintain. The town was also pocked with small populations of shacks and trailers, and in one of the trailers, on the edge of a bog, lived the Jordan Witch.

Ollie and Willow arrived under the blue light of a full moon. Stumps poked up through the stagnant water of the bog and immediately were transformed in Ollie's mind into the petrified remains of slouching, stunted men carrying sacks of their young to be drowned, the men rooted in the mud as punishment by the granite god of the mountain that loomed in the background. He could smell the cesspool as they approached the trailer. The edge of a swamp was a crazy place for a home, he thought. It would be windy and cold in the winter, stifling and hot in the summer; it would be infested by mosquitoes and birds that ruined a man's sleep first thing in the morning. And yet, the place had a beauty that took hold of him. The stars were so numerous overhead that he could feel a lifting of the weight of his own isolation. The Witch had gotten the place a couple of years ago from an old man whom she had screwed to death, or so Ollie imagined. The property included a trailer up on blocks that seemed to be sinking slowly into the soft earth, a shed that perhaps had been there before the trailer, a tiny lawn and garden. There were no other of man's works to be seen; the area was dominated by the immensities of swamp, forest, mountain, sky. A light was on in the trailer, but Ollie could see no sign of life. The Witch would be in the shadows, like a spider or a dirty book, or perhaps she was in the bedroom entertaining. He wouldn't put it past her. The idea suddenly outraged him. "And at her age," he heard himself say to Willow, who halted, looked up, and raised his arms. Startled, Ollie put his hand across his eyes, sensing a bat honing in on them. It took him a second to realize that Willow was trying to touch the stars. "Far away, you idiot," Ollie said cruelly, wounded, for the boy's simple gesture had made him realize his own smallness, and Ollie understood that wherever the boy went they would want to kill him out of jealousy for the purity of his expression and out of fear for the power of his strangeness.

He stood there with Willow on the doorstep, which consisted of a board resting on two flat stones. Ollie paused at the screen door. He could see into the kitchen, could see the cat staring at him from a basket on the dining table, could smell the smoke from the Witch's wacky tobaccky. He hated the idea of knocking on the door, of walking in. He wanted to be drawn in, to be absolved of the responsibility of acting. Finally, he heard the Witch's voice from inside: "Don't just stand there, come on in." He did as he was told.

The Witch was in the living room half-sitting, half-lying on the couch, as if in homage to the graceful "s" of ascending smoke from her pipe. "Stoned again," Ollie said.

"You got your habit for after dark. I got mine. Yours, by the way, is in the cupboard," she said.

A chill ran through him. She had been waiting for him. She had been waiting all along. She had told him once that sometimes though he might be miles away she could sense his moods and follow his movements in her mind. It was a lie, a typical tactic to keep him bound to her, and yet the idea haunted him like an unreasonable fear of poison in canned foods. She had probably heard of Willow's exploits on the radio, and then she had figured that he and Willow would come here. Not that she would admit such a thing. She'd spook up the explanation. A witch had to keep the world off balance, keep simple matters in confusion, find design where there was only blowing leaves, and keep the fear she raised in proportion to her real power, else they would burn her as in olden times.

She had thinned out some since the last time he had seen

her, aged as if from additional knowledge rather than just wear, but her hair was still boot black and her eyes writhed like snakes dropped in fire. She rose and came toward them, and Ollie caught the aroma of her and recognized the kinship between them. She shuffled past him and gave Willow a brief embrace. Ollie stiffened—with protective concern? With jealousy? He didn't know.

"I see you got electricity put in—you must be getting old," Ollie said, to fill a space.

"These days, I need good light," she said, leading them into the kitchen. Her voice had the raspiness of old women who smoke too much.

"Used to be you liked the dark," Ollie said.

"I still like the dark. Used to be you were 'fraid of the dark," she said, somehow leaving a vague threat that she could if she chose douse the lights at any moment.

"I get along," he said.

She stood there, saying nothing, imposing a moment of anxiety between them. Having made her point, she broke the spell by turning on the television.

"I got TV now. Makes the time go by for an old woman," she said.

She was very good to them, then. She washed Willow's face and brought him some milk. Later she led him to the couch and with a whisper, it seemed, put him to sleep. Ollie helped himself to the bottle of whiskey in the cupboard. He didn't dare buy hard liquor himself. He liked it too much. It would kill him some day, he knew, as it had killed or led to the murder of most men everywhere. The drink eased him down to a warm spot—at the gates of hell, he thought.

"Your whiskey?" he asked.

"I don't touch that piss anymore," she said, blowing some wacky tobaccky smoke at him. "Some old man left it here."

"And you can't remember which one, can you?" Ollie said.

"What difference does it make? You got the bottle."

"It don't make no difference to me," he said, knowing that he had left himself open.

"Course it makes a difference. It always did with you," she said.

She boiled him a potato and some carrots, mashed them with a fork, and added two tins of strained beef baby food, which he guessed she had shoplifted. She didn't have a tooth in her head, and the men loved her for it, she would brag sometimes, just to infuriate him.

She's fit as a fern in the shade, he thought, and his mind flashed back to his land and the burning sign and his old shepherd dog out there in the wild. Creatures died quick deaths from fangs, or slow deaths full of visions from starvation from lack of teeth—this was God's way, if there was a God. It was only humans that lived on without a tooth, to die of diseases unintended by God, if there was a God.

The food settled into him like a cheering, harmless lie. He was, he thought, darned near completely relaxed. They retired to the living room before the television—Willow asleep on the couch, Ollie in the easy chair with the bottle of whiskey and a glass, the Witch in a shadow, partly in the living room, partly in the cramped hall that led to the bedrooms. She was sitting in a kitchen chair she had brought in, and she lit her pipe as Ollie lit his. Soon the room was filled with the smoke of marijuana and Carter Hall tobacco. Ollie drank steadily, peacefully. From time to time he glanced at the Witch. She watched television as though trying to hypnotize it. As for himself, he did not seem to take in the programs. He would see a man rise up out of the ocean, as if born that moment, and then he would be watching some fellows in a bar drinking beer, and then some gunshots would draw his attention, and there seemed through all these fragments an unending automobile chase. Getting drunk, he thought. Wonderful. Isn't that wonderful? Occasionally, he would speak, out of character, even to himself . . . "Let us hope for a kindly summer, me lady." The Witch would say nothing, or tell him to shut up.

Soon he lost track of time. Reality was a blend of things that presented themselves, as if for introduction only, and then vanished. The television was off, and it was on, and it had been moved, or he had been moved. The Witch gave him some of her weed to smoke, and the colors from her dress burst toward him like exploding flowers. It seemed to him that certain secrets in familiar sounds were revealed to him—a volcanic rumble in Willow's snoring; something in his own jumbled speech that sounded like a chicken being strangled. He was talking to the Witch, or perhaps she was talking to him. Hard to tell the difference, he thought, vastly amused, and he laughed aloud and continued laughing until he had forgotten why. Ideas trooped in and out of his mind, like armies. For a moment it seemed to him that he was reaching into his past, into that lost mine of memory, reaching for the source of the unknown grief that had shadowed his being all these years. He was just at the door of recollection when the Witch touched his arm and jarred him into speaking. "Different facts don't change the same old shit," he said, and the door of memory slammed shut.

During part of the time they were in the kitchen, and here the Witch had sat him down for one of her little talks.

"That boy of yours is eating you up," she said. "Give him to the state. They can do more for him than you can."

"He'll die with the state," Ollie had said.

"Together, you both die. You think somehow he's your better half, but it ain't so, Ollie. He's your worser half."

He wanted to tell her of the enormous possibilities in Willow, possibilities of the kinship itself, but really he had no argument. Just a queer faith. And the conversation had dribbled away because they were both drunk and stoned.

He was back in the living room, and on the television there was a monkey dressed like a child, and Ollie was smelling the Witch's hair, a waterfall of aroma pouring over him, and the monkey seemed to reach out with desperate hands to its keeper, to ask why, oh, why, oh, why, and the Witch's arms were about his shoulders, and he wanted to say to her, "black flowers," but instead he said only, "whatever—" and she was speaking to him: "Admit it, you come to me for succor." And he was weeping, deep wracking sobs of childhood, and his face was in the cascade of her hair and he was on a boat, and he knew he was out of his senses. When they returned, the Witch was holding his head over the sink, and he was puking. She had planned this, he thought, and he had succumbed. He had succumbed totally to her and would continue to succumb, as it was meant. At the final reckoning, if there was one, the judge would say: "All parties are guilty."

"Stop crying," she said.

"I ain't crying," Ollie said in the voice of a child.

"Stop crying," said the Witch.

"Don't you have no feelings?"

"I don't feel nuthin'. It don't pay to feel. You don't feel nuthin', either. Drunk feeling don't count. Now shut up."

The Witch ran cold water over Ollie's head and cleaned him up. He was a little soberer then.

"What am I going to do, Witch?" he asked.

"You can't get by with that boy in the culture," she said, exaggerating her New Hampshire accent so that the word "culture"—"cull-cha"—had the impact of a curse word.

"I admit he's a nuisance," Ollie said.

The Witch burst into a mean laughter. "You're your own nuisance, Ollie Jordan. He's just something in your mind. Give him up. Be good for the both of you."

"As you say, something in my mind. Where he goes I go," Ollie said.

She laughed again, cackling like the old whore that she was. "You remind me of a case I heard about, an old man got elephant balls from a disease, and he carried 'em in a wheelbarrow everywhere he went."

"As you say, Witch," Ollie said, and something in his voice insulted her, and she turned on him and slapped his face. A moment later she was kindly again, and he wondered whether he had imagined that he had been slapped.

"If it has to be the three of you—you, him, and the chain—take him out in the pucker brush for a spell. He always liked it out there, and the culture don't care what goes on there. If you can't live off the culture, live out of the culture," the Witch said.

To the pucker brush: The idea took hold in him.

Having made her point, the Witch brought him to his feet and steered him into the bathroom. When he was finished, she led him to the tiny spare bedroom and shut the door. Outside, the crickets were calling in kinship. He heard himself giggle. He undressed. He felt pretty much whole—"Thank you, booze," he said. And then as if to remind him that no man is ever really one with himself, a stranger inside him said "*Plant thy seed and grow thy flower.* He lay down on the bed. Nice bed. He listened to himself make *em* sounds. He handled himself, discovering that at the moment he was not able. For the first time, he felt completely safe, and he fell into a dream that was the color green.

Later in the night he awoke, realizing at once that she had come and gone. She had bided her time, returning to the bed after the dulling powers of the whiskey had been transformed into a bile in his loins while his brain was still lulled by sleep. His thoughts took a turn: *Them ain't crickets, and these ain't bed springs a-squeaking, but oar locks a-creaking. The Witch she comes out of the sky rowing on an old flat-bottom boat.* And he was asleep again. Later still, the smell of the cesspool coming through the open window in his room shoved him like a mean brother, and he knew the Witch had visited Willow, too. He woke in the morning to the color green slowly fading into the yellow of sunshine, which diluted his memory of the night to a suspicion.

The Witch made a huge breakfast of scrambled eggs, sausage, applesauce, and coffee (Kool-Aid for Willow). The food freshened father and son. Willow began behaving like a puppy—a 180-pound puppy. At one point, he tried to embrace the Witch, who boxed his ears until he let go. Ollie was in such a good mood, he could only react with laughter.

"What are you going to do?" the Witch asked, turning the situation inside out with the tone of her voice, so that Ollie was suddenly on guard.

"Going into the woods, like you said, to live away from the culture," Ollie said.

"How do you figure your prospects?" she asked.

"I never had no prospects. I never had no luck. You know that," Ollie said.

"What if I said I had some luck for you?" the Witch asked.

She was up to something. She had softened him with a good breakfast and now she was going to eat him in her toothless mouth, like a mushy boiled egg. "I'd say, if it's luck you got for me it's bad luck."

"It don't matter, Ollie," she said. "Your luck has been so bad that any more luck either will be the same or worse."

He didn't like her using his first name. "If my luck could get worse, you'd be the one to do it," he said.

"I want to give you some luck," she said.

Ollie didn't know what to say. The Witch almost was showing affection. It curdled him inside. He found himself nodding. The Witch rose and then went to her bedroom. When she returned, she was holding a small wooden carving of flowers, roses maybe, the arrangement coming into focus now as a butterfly. The wood had dried and cracked, and the stain that had made the flowers red had gone bad and was now the color of dried blood. Still, he liked the carving, liked the way it felt in his hands.

"It's a charm. It will bring you luck," the Witch said.

"I don't need this. I need money," said Ollie.

"I've got money."

"I know you've got money, and I know how you get it."

"Take the charm."

"Looks like a butterfly, a goddamn butterfly. How did you come by it?"

"I'll say that you've seen it before, in the old days," she said, and it was as if he were trying to recall a dream bathed in orange light.

"I can't remember," he said.

"All for the best."

The Witch gave him some money, making it clear that if he took the money he was to take the charm. It was really very pretty, and it was light and could fit in a coat pocket. He didn't believe in her hocus-pocus, her astrology charts, her funny cards, and he didn't believe in this charm. There might even be some danger in it. Anything from the old days he had to suspect. But he couldn't deny that it felt good in the hand, that it seemed to belong with him.

Mrs. Clapp

The storekeeper was surprised when a black man came into his store, wiped his brow with a red handkerchief, remarked casually about the heat of the day, bought a six-pack of Coke in cans, and walked out. The storekeeper was so surprised that he followed the man outside, for what purpose he could not have told you. The man got into a svelte Oldsmobile and joined a wife and a couple of kids. The man smiled at the storekeeper, the kids smiled, the storekeeper smiled and found himself returning the good-bye waves of the kids as the car started moving down the road. The car had New Jersey plates. Tourists, he thought, and went back into his store.

It was the first time since he had arrived in New Hampshire that he had seen any black people and he found that black people now affected him in a different way from the way they used to. He was oddly at once sympathetic toward them and yet repelled, as though they were carriers of some disease. It was a while before he realized that his new attitude had been drawn unconsciously from the native world of Darby.

That afternoon, in the hour before the old-timers would start arriving to chew the fat, the storekeeper took stock of himself and his relationship to black people. It came to him that a big reason he had come to this town was that there were no black people here. Not that he would have admitted that at the time. Not that he was a bigot—then or now. There was no man, no thing, no idea that he truly hated in this world—except maybe the New York Yankees. Still, there was the feeling in him that he was a bigot. It took him about twenty minutes of stumbling about in his thoughts to find an explanation, and when he did find it, he acted it out in a passionate, glamorous, imaginary plea before the black man that had come into his store, the man, his dark skin like a judge's robes, standing there in the theater of the storekeeper's mind.

Every heart is a lonely heart, the storekeeper argued in his mind, unaware that he had cribbed the phrase from Old Man Dorne. Every heart seeks fellowship with his own kind to soften that loneliness. It's not that I'm against the black. It's that the black gets in the way of the fellowship of the white, just as the white gets in the way of the fellowship of the black.

Let me give you an example. I'm not from around here; I'm from Pee-Ay, and I was brought up, courtesy of my dad and my Uncle Chet, a Pirates fan. It was an honorable thing to be a Pirate fan, and any time I was rooting for the Pirates I was not lonely. Heck, I didn't complain when they got Clemente and guys like that. I applauded, because you see then the fellowship of the team was white. Well, there came a day when there were more starters on the team that were black than white, and that was the day that the fellowship of the team turned black. It was a lonely day for me. The hard part to understand is that there can't be a gray; the fellowship is either black or white. That's why the fellowship of, say, a neighborhood changes in a flash and catches people off guard. Overnight, they go from comfy to lonely. Then comes the hatred and the evil actions. I feel as bad about this situation as you do. There's but one way to stop the hatred and that's to reintroduce the security of the fellowships—yours and mine—and then all the hatred will pass and we can treat each other like polite strangers. The thing that tipped the scales when I was weighing reasons to come here—unconsciously, I mean—I mean, I just at this moment discovered this myself—is that the fellowship of the team they root for here, the Boston Red Sox, is white. Oh, I know they got Rice, and I root for Rice, but the fellowship of the team is white. See, it's like the Pirates got Garner, but basically the fellowship of the team is black. Come World Series time, I'll root for the Red Sox, you root for the Pirates, and we'll both be happy . . .

At that moment, the storekeeper was interrupted in his thoughts. Old Man Dorne came in the store, followed moments later by a man with a bandage on his nose.

"I see a family of coloreds down the road, stretching a bit by the lake," said Old Man Dorne. "Scare me to death every time I see those people. They've all got the shanks of chorus girls, tough hides, tough skulls, and brains untainted by all those past generations of inbred Europeans that afflicts us hearts here in Darby. Someday they'll rule the world. Mark my words."

"The world maybe, but not this backyard. They couldn't stand the cold here," said the man with the bandaged nose. He spoke with a slow, melodious drawl, accompanied by a small, secretive smile, as though minutes earlier he had bedded the wife of some prominent official. That smile elicited such a jab of concern in the storekeeper he was taken with an urge to lock his cash box.

Old Man Dorne sent the man a nasty look, but the man either did not notice or cared too little to respond. The storekeeper realized now that they had not come in together, but they knew each other.

"I expected to see Mr. Flagg here," said Bandage Smile.

"Flagg's gone—heart attack took him in the spring of the year," said Old Man Dorne.

"We all got to go," said the man, still smiling, making small talk, leading up to something.

Old Man Dorne said nothing, averting his eyes from the man.

The man, perhaps aware that he was wielding considerable influence merely by his presence, stood still silently smiling for a long moment before finally addressing the storekeeper.

"How about forking over some Carter Hall pipe tobacco," he said, and when the storekeeper took his money, he added: "You sell much of this tobacco, do you?"

"You own stock in the company?" asked the storekeeper.

"Nope. Just want to know where my kin are," the man said, and left the store. The parting comment puzzled the storekeeper and made him uneasy.

"That's Ike Jordan," said Old Man Dorne. "Kind of gives you the heebie-jeebies, don't he? He's an auctioneer by trade, but who knows what else he's mixed up in."

"Funny customer—my day for 'em. The black people first, then that one with the nose," said the storekeeper.

"School's out a week now. Americans of every ilk and heart are taking to the roads," said Old Man Dorne, as if that closed the door on the subject.

The storekeeper was about to explain his breakthrough in understanding race relations, but as he fumbled for expression, he realized that some key parts of the knowledge that he had acquired just minutes ago had slipped away. He could remember that word "fellowship," but for the life of him he couldn't gather up the ends of the argument that had given the word meaning. So he said nothing. He waited, mildly uncomfortable in a small grief, but confident that some other equally small event would occur to freshen his psyche.

Minutes later another one of the old-timers entered the store, his eyes shining with a recently found nugget of information.

"You'll never guess what I saw," he said. "Had rolled-up pants like a stork and was wading to beat the band along the roadside shore of Spofford Lake."

"I can guess," said Old Man Dorne.

Ike Jordan drove off in his mighty Cadillac and now that he knew he had been recognized, removed the bandage from his nose. He also removed his teeth—"my smile," he would call

them, immensely vain—and placed them on the dashboard.
The bandage was for the sake of strangers. It was a trick he
had learned while serving time at the county farm. An old con
man had told him, "Put a bandage on your nose, commit a
crime, and all the witnesses will remember is the bandage."
Not that Ike had any intention of committing a crime, at least
not today. He just liked the idea of deception, and so frequently he put the bandage on. It made him feel hidden. It
never occurred to him that by repeatedly wearing a bandage
on your nose, eventually some people will get to know you by
that mark, that the bandage could become an identification
card as well as a mask. Ike Jordan was known by his friends as a
smart man with a stupid streak and by his enemies as a stupid
man with a few dangerous smarts. He could read the subtle
tale on the face of a man who had more money in his pocket
than ability to manage it and who was begging you to swindle
him in order to relieve him of the burden of it; but he had no
insight into his own meager abilities as a gambler or even his
own foolish hunches, which time and again paid off even less
than the law of averages should allow. He often drove with his
teeth on the dashboard because they reminded him that he was
a successful man.

He was taking this little excursion into the town of Darby
for a couple of reasons. He had a pretty good idea that somewhere in this town he could find his half-brother Ollie. He
wasn't going to demand that Ollie return the beer he had
taken from him because that would show that he cared.
Rather, he wanted merely to engage Ollie in conversation, to
smile upon him, to humiliate him if possible, to show his own
ascendancy. Normally, Ike would not dare take on Ollie, but
he sensed now that his brother's power was on the wane. It was
time for a challenge—family battle, Jordan style.

Another reason he had come to Darby was to scout town
properties for possible burglaries. Ike Jordan was a proud
burglar. He thought it the curse of his profession that you
could get public acceptance for your talents only by getting
caught. Sometimes he imagined that he had died and in the

newspaper the next day there was a comment by a prominent public official, say the police chief in Keene, to the effect that Ike Jordan was one wing-dinger of a burglar. As it was, he was satisfied (most of the time) with the adoration of his young kin, whom he had taken on as apprentices in his craft. It was the craft that had spurred Ike Jordan into being a reader. He had realized early on that the newspaper was full of tips, and so he had taken his few years of education and enlarged upon them through study. He was not sorry. He found the obituary columns especially useful, for they provided the names of persons who would be sure to be away from their houses during funerals. He also read all the realty ads for hints on the value of items that might be in certain homes. All in all, Ike Jordan was one of the most careful, grateful readers of *The Keene Sentinel*.

Not that finding an empty place to burglarize took that much work. The skill came in finding the right place, and also in developing a system of selling one's wares. So it was that Ike got into the auction business. He fancied himself very honest in that business, although that wasn't exactly true. Occasionally he cheated a buyer on general principles. He never auctioned the goods he stole. He trucked them to an associate in Connecticut, where he was able to exchange them for goods stolen from other areas. Thanks to his profession as a burglar, he had acquired knowledge in antiques, art, architecture, history, etiquette, and even psychology, for he learned that people outside the Jordan kinship tended to judge their fellow men by appearances. Oh, he had his blind spots, but for the most part, he considered himself a pretty well-rounded guy.

He drove along the roads of Darby, sometimes concentrating, but more often just enjoying the nice day. He wasn't trying very hard to find Ollie. He only wanted to show himself that he was ready to take him on, if it came to that. He knew that Ollie might be at Howard Elman's house, but he didn't want any part of Elman. Nevertheless, he decided to take a ride past the Elman place to see what had been done since the fire there last spring. He found that the house had been removed, a new trailer was parked in its place. The change did not interest him, but the changes to the Swett house up the hill captured his attention. It was evident from the remodeling job that someone with means and flair had bought the property from Swett's heirs. He listed the house as a possible for burglary, one of a number that he filed away in his mind.

The property that intrigued him most was the widow Clapp's residence—a brick, colonial house with a granite foundation. He remembered reading the obituary of Osgood Clapp a while back. Osgood and Amy Clapp had moved into the house recently from Keene. But the item that he had filed away for future consideration was that Osgood Clapp had been a past president of the New Hampshire Antique Clock Association. The place must be jammed with clocks, he thought. Old clocks were wonderful items for burglary. They were easily moved, easily valued, easily disposed of. And they were beautiful. The idea of stealing the clocks stirred him. He took only a professional's dispassionate satisfaction in stealing purely utilitarian items, but it gave him great pleasure to take things of great beauty. Driving by, he saw that the house sat behind some maples that partly shielded it from the road. He resolved to learn more about the house and Mrs. Clapp. As he turned the Cadillac back toward the main highway, he realized he had some studying to do. He put his teeth back into his mouth, the bandage back on the nose. Now, I can think better, he thought.

The widow Clapp sat in the living room of her fine, old house, surrounded by clocks, her feet in a pan of warm water to soothe the hurt joints. She had disconnected her hearing aid and was listening to the waves crashing on the beach of her mind. Someday they will find my empty skull, she thought, and they will hold it to their ears and they will hear the ocean, as in a conch shell. More and more, she preferred the sound in her head to what she heard with her ears. What she heard was a gentle moan much like the sound at York Beach on a night sixty-five years ago when Osgood was courting her. It was a violent sound, yet restful, too, because you could depend on it and because it judged not. She used to like to listen to the chattering of her grandchildren, the ring of the telephone, the birds that woke her in the summer at five o'clock, even the damn television, which she associated with the sound of gunshots (Osgood Clapp loved westerns), inchoate music, and what she apprehended as the *er, er, erup* of David Brinkley, although the voice she heard might actually have belonged to Walter Cronkite or Harry Reasoner—any newscaster.

But things had changed for her, or the world had changed. Hard to tell which, and really she didn't care. Time, quite literally, was rushing by for her. It was as if the world were a movie and someone had speeded up the reel. Cars raced by her house; her family came to visit, scurried about like hungry mice, and was gone; television shows came on and before she could grasp the plot, the program had changed; she sat in her chair after tea, and before she knew it the sun was setting. She reminded herself now to keep an eye on the telephone. It had a light as well as a bell, and she could plug in her hearing aid to answer it when the light went on. Even with the hearing aid turned up high, the voice on the other end would be small and distorted. Every day her son Philbert—no, Raymond: Philbert was dead, must remember—called from Keene, sounding like Donald Duck, to inquire as to her health. The truth was the purpose of each call was an inquiry into her state of mind. He was getting ready to lock her up in an old folks home. "Must watch the telephone for the light," she said aloud. "Must prove . . ." She lost her train of thought. "Oh, yes, must prove competence." What did it matter to them whether she was competent or not? Crazy sense of duty, or maybe it was fear that the neighbors would talk about them, say they weren't meeting their duty. Well, that was saner. Worry the neighbors and eventually they'll bring you down: rule of life.

When Osgood was alive, she had hated to face her own old age, because his old age had been so repulsive to her. Now that he had passed away—how she liked that phrase, "pass away," like fall leaves in the wind—her attitude had changed. So what the aching joints, so what the high blood pressure, so what the dimmed senses, so what the longing to be touched? Old age had its compensations. Whereas before her mental world was cluttered with worry and imaginings in dull black and white or even just in words, now that world was as full of color and story as a wild dream. So what that trivial matters such as the name of the new grocer or the precise location of the aspirin seemed to escape the grasp of her mind? The important things, such as the time she ice-skated all day in the January of her twelfth year, came back to her time and again like a beloved movie to entertain and instruct her. If middle age was time to gather, old age was a time to dispose, so that one could see better the value of what remained. Old age was a transition period between this world and the next. They think I'm senile, she thought, but I'm already part ghost, and that's why they're scared of me. She sensed now that all the clocks in the house were striking five o'clock. That was impossible of course, since she had refused to rewind them after Osgood died. Still, she could hear them sounding, each and every one. It passed through her mind that Osgood was trying to reach her from the beyond. She considered that idea for a moment and found it good. She turned up her hearing aid. The clocks stopped. It was quiet in the house. There was only the sound of her own breathing. She noticed now that the water in the pan was tepid, her feet soft as overboiled potatoes. "My how time flies," she said, to hear her own voice.

After Ollie Jordan left the Witch, he immediately drove to Keene. He had a half-assed idea that to survive he must light out for the woods. He had a vague plan about hiding Willow from the Welfare Department by bringing him to a place he had discovered while hunting deer a few years back with Howard Elman. But at the moment survival was not a problem. He had food in his belly and money the Witch gave him in his pocket. The closer to Keene he drove the better he felt, and the better he felt the vaguer his plan became. Even when he arrived in Keene, he knew that it was wrong for him to be advertising himself in broad daylight. But jeeze, he felt so good. The charm the Witch had given him was working, the charm and money were making him carnival-crazy, he thought; and having identified the nature of his mood he set out to enjoy it. He parked his vehicle in the lot behind Miranda's Bar. He chained Willow to the steering wheel and locked the doors, although he left the windows open to keep the heat from broiling the boy. The short walk west on Roxbury Street from the parking lot to the bar was pleasant, although he knew that someone from the Welfare Department might leap upon him at any moment and take Willow away to a school for the mentally retarded. But at the moment, he was absolutely confident that he could handle such an eventuality. It was the charm, he thought. He entered Miranda's, looked dead on at the Greek behind the bar, and said, "bee-yah."

The bartender was startled. "I'm not open—too early," he said.

Ollie had seen the bartender a hundred times and knew his name to be George but nothing else about him. He saw that George recognized him, too.

"Well, whoopie-do—the door was open. I'm a paying customer, and I got money," Ollie said, and he unrolled the bills that the Witch had given him.

The bartender looked at the clock. "Ten twenty ay-crisely-em," he said. "The place opens at eleven, but I suppose that's what I get for keeping my door unlocked. Did you have a brand that you were interested in?"

"I'll take a Molson, if you got it," said Ollie, bragging about his money in the roundabout way of ordering expensive beer.

The bartender locked his front door, brought Ollie a beer, snapped on the television set, and started mopping the floor. Ollie took a swallow of beer and turned his attention to the TV. A children's program was on the air.

It seemed to him that he had seen this program before, but had never given it much thought. Now he homed in on it. His senses and reflexes were sharpened from food, from the Witch's touch, and the program was a universe for him to consider. After half an hour had passed (two and a half beers), Ollie began to shape in his own mind what the program meant. It was about all these creatures who lived in this Says-me Street. It was the strangest place he'd ever seen. The fellow he most admired on the program lived in a garbage can. He was the only one of the characters that understood that the world was a dangerous, unpleasant place. There was another creature, a giant bird, who appalled Ollie. The bird was so unnaturally huge, so ignorant of the obvious. Furthermore, it seemed unnatural that the other creatures on the program did not make fun of the bird. Not true to life, he thought. A couple of the smaller creatures, a Bert and an Ernie, reminded him of members of his own family. The Bert creature was practical-minded, but he was constantly frustrated by the Ernie creature, who had a knack of presenting foolish ideas in a sensible way. The Bert and the Ernie were like a married couple, he thought, like his Uncle Alvin and Aunt Leona. The Bert maintained a realistic grasp of circumstances, while the Ernie did not, yet in the end it was the Ernie who prevailed. True that life sometimes went like that, he thought, but it was downright immoral for television to glorify such disorder. At one point Ollie thought, Bert, don't take crap from Ernie—bat him one.

The make-believe creatures on the show, for all their defects, at least were somewhat believable. They showed certain human frailties. They even looked like people he knew. But the real people on the show were completely unreal to Ollie. They were always reasonable, and they were always smiling and dancing; they didn't argue, fight, or shout; they threw around a lot of unwarranted affection but seemed to have no sex drive. Maybe they just hide it, he thought. There were also black and white people, people of both sexes and of varying ages, all apparently getting along, and that, too, was unreal to Ollie Jordan. Throughout the story there were frequent interruptions by cartoon characters promoting the letter "v" and the number "6." It took Ollie a while to figure out that the whole purpose was educational, and this realization was accompanied by an unaccountable surge of anger.

As the show continued, it took on a vaguely menacing quality. At one point, the bird got stuck in a Volkswagen, its long neck and head protruding through the sun top. No one seemed to know what to do about the situation. The answer was clear to Ollie: cut open the goddamn car with a blow torch. It angered him that none of the creatures or people on the show could come up with that simple solution. Then his anger gave way to unease. There was something strange going on. Someone should know how to free that bird. It was as if they were all crazy, as if they were trying to make the people who were watching the show crazy as themselves. The only sane one on the show was the fellow who lived in the garbage can, and they were all trying to change him, make him one of their own, make him crazy. It struck him now that the people on the show and most of the creatures probably worked for the Welfare Department, and the show was their way of molding minds. The idea saddened him and made him fearful. He felt a great kinship for the fellow in the garbage can, but he doubted the fellow's ability to stand up to the forces around him. There were just too many people against him, too much cunning to overcome. Finally, he turned away from the television set. It was just too depressing. He finished his beer, but it did nothing for him. He felt menaced by the TV. He paid up and left. He was resentful. Says-me Street had robbed him of his good mood.

Donald's Junkyard

When Ollie got back to his truck, his nose told him that Willow had shit in his pants. He smacked the boy in the face and—as usual—immediately was sorry. "If I tie you up, how can you help it?" Ollie said, knowing that his tone would serve as an apology, knowing that Willow would understand apology no better than he understood the purpose of the blow. He cleaned the mess as best he could, rolling up Willow's trousers and underwear in a ball. Once again, he had a bareass son beside him. A sign? And, if so, of what? That he could not provide, as a good father must? Perhaps. The thought depressed him. He wondered what to do with Willow's dirtied clothes. They were evidence, he thought. If they were discovered by the Welfare Department they might be traced back to him. Ollie didn't bother to consider how such a trace might be done. The fact that the idea had occurred to him was enough to convince him that it had some merit. He tried to think about the problem, but got lost for a moment in an intrusive revery about a green place full of singing. He was jolted then by voices, two men talking on the street about land taxes. It seemed to Ollie they were conspiring against him, and he drove off in a small terror. Must get rid of the evidence, he thought.

He was frantic, and his mind was working with the fragments of thoughts, one upon the other. He believed for certain that he was being pursued, and yet he knew that he was not being pursued; he must get rid of the evidence of the dirtied clothes not so much to divert the pursuit as to rid himself of the feeling of pursuit. He drove until he found himself at Robin Hood Park in Keene. The water in the park pond was brown, with white lights tossed about on tiny waves. He took his bundle and got out of the truck, with the intention of weighing the bundle down with rocks and throwing it in the pond, but there were some kids fishing across the way. Ollie stood there, unsure now of what to do. He wondered vaguely whether the kids worked for the Welfare Department. He noticed now that Willow, although chained inside the truck, had rolled the window down and was waving to the kids. Must do something, Ollie told himself. About fifty feet away was a trash barrel, and so he decided to chuck the bundle in the barrel; but when he got to the barrel he could not do it. Ollie was a collector of trash, a dump rat, and all his instincts cried out for him to take away, not to deposit. He rummaged through the can and found a damaged kite, some brown paper bags, and a red crayon. He rescued these items and returned to the truck and drove off.

Calmer now, he pondered his goods: kite, bags, crayon, shitty pants. It seemed to him that, somehow, he had been commanded from on high to take them, that they held some meaning. He tried to think now, but fell back into his revery of the green place. It was the place up on the hill called Abare's Folly that he and Elman had found. A place as hidden and as beautiful as a great idea imprisoned in a wild mind. And the solution to the problem of the dirtied clothes came to him, as he knew it would. He wrapped the dirty pants in the brown paper bags, tied them with the string from the kite, wrote with the crayon "Welfare Department" on the package, and dropped it into the first mailbox he happened upon. The Welfare Department would find the pants anyway, let 'em get the stuff direct, he thought, and laughed to himself. "Willow," he said, "you ain't the only one with a good sense of humor." Willow did not answer. He was looking out the window. Looking perhaps for the boys who were fishing.

Ollie's good mood returned, if somewhat dimmed; his good sense exerted itself. He must have clothes for Willow, and for himself too, he realized, not just to cover Willow's bottom, but for warmth and even for style in the days to come. He headed for the Salvation Army Citadel on Roxbury Plaza.

Ollie liked the Salvation Army. He liked the spiffy uniforms of the soldiers for Christ. He liked the way the brigadiers, by maintaining a certain aloofness, allowed a man to keep his own aloofness intact even as he begged at their feet. He liked the lovely singing that came from their chapel, which he had never entered. The singing seemed to him to blend sadness and celebration, as if the singers were on the deck of a great, sinking ship giving their all before it slipped into the deep. He liked, in a harmless lecherous way that enriched his interior life, the pale ladies in blue who rang bells around Christmastime.

In the citadel there was a secondhand clothing store. Here Ollie came to buy summer outfits for himself and Willow. There were plenty of clothes to choose from. Members of the richer classes of the city discarded many of their clothes here, partly to assuage a vague guilt and partly because the citadel was in the middle of town while the dump was five miles out. It was the Witch long ago who had set certain standards of dress for the Jordan menfolk. She insisted that they wear suits in public, preferably dark wool suits. She wasn't particular about shirts, however, and as a result the summer uniform was a dark suit, felt hat, T-shirt, and shoes which ranged from boots to sneakers. In the winter, the T-shirt was replaced by a union suit, and the ensemble was covered by an overcoat and galoshes. In addition, the Witch liked men to have what she referred to as "a little ball room," and so she always bought trousers several sizes too big. Ollie normally held his up with suspenders, and Willow usually wore a rope belt. Ollie had contributed to the style that the Witch had wrought by devising a certain way of walking in public. He was young and vain then, and he walked with a slight goose step, holding the cuffs of the oversize suit jacket in his palms. He fancied he looked pretty dapper. He had long since lost the vanity of his youth, but the habit of his walk remained, and he had passed it down to his sons and to the kin who had come to live with him during the prosperous years by the Basketville sign. Ollie bought two suits each for himself and Willow, along with two huge canopylike overcoats, two pairs of pants, some under things, and a hat for himself. The total cost came to twenty-four dollars.

He returned to the truck and dressed Willow in some plaid slacks and a suit jacket. "Who says Willow Jordan ain't sharp?" Ollie asked, admiring his son, and off he drove, not headed for any place in particular.

Having discovered that his mood had improved, Ollie automatically set aside his mission to retire with Willow to the boondocks. That can wait, something in him said. It was a beautiful day, and he wanted to enjoy it. Why waste it with labor and thought? Still, he needed to start planning, he realized, and felt his spirits beginning to dampen. The clash of want and need made him irritable. He resisted an urge to cuff Willow in the face. The boy was hanging his head and both arms out the window. He seemed delirious with the joy of meeting the wind. Ollie reached for a beer. The single most impressive achievement of mankind, in Ollie Jordan's view, was the invention of beer. A man could think better with beer in his belly. Beer dulled one's aches, washed out the insides, provided nourishment, reduced the appetite during bad times, whetted it during good times. "Too good a day to waste with irritability," Ollie said aloud, knowing that Willow cared not.

They were moving down Main Street now, past the Central Square common with its great trees, statue of a Civil War hero, and park. The late morning light in the green of the grass seemed to bounce back into Ollie's face. It reminded him of how much he detested a lawn. He had nothing personal against grass, which like anything else would grow where it could. But a lawn was something else. A lawn was an example of the madness of mankind. It was crazy that anyone would want to plant a lawn, feed it to make it grow ever faster, and then cut it down routinely at great expense and labor. For a long time he thought there was something wrong with him, that he had failed to see some obvious advantage to the cultivation of short grass. After all, the richest people had the biggest lawns and the shortest grass, and rich people didn't get rich by being stupid. Thus, he had theorized that perhaps short grass was a source of nutrition or an intoxicant, but the theory didn't stand up to a test of boiled grass and beer and he had abandoned the idea. As the years passed, he realized that there was no mystery. There was no good reason for a lawn. It was merely a make-work thing for people who couldn't get out of the habit of work itself or of having work done for them. It was bad enough that the public nurtured their lawns in and around their abodes, but somehow he expected the city to know better.

Take Willow to the wild place now, a thought, which came like a voice, sounded inside him. He shook it off.

"Too fine a day to get balled up in serious thinking, eh, Willow?" he asked. Willow cut loose with rip-roaring laughter.

Ollie drove on aimlessly until he found himself at the gate of Donald's Junkyard. On impulse he decided to pay Donald a visit. He had no reason to make the visit except to pass some time.

Here was a vast pasture of derelict cars, put out amidst the startling green beauty of the New Hampshire hills, framed by stone walls built by the forefathers. Donald's Junkyard was an honored place in Jordan lore. It had begun under Donald the Elder as a pig farm. Slowly, through Donald the Elder's hobby of tinkering with machinery (in preference to caring for his animals), the place was transformed from a farm into a hospital and mortuary for machines, and finally into a business. When Donald the Elder died, the business fell to his eldest son, Donald the Younger.

Donald the Younger brought a new element to the business: a colorful personality. People from all over Cheshire County came from miles around to dicker with him—and to hear him swear. It was said that Donald Jordan could weather the paint on a church merely by speaking. He rarely used conventional curse words, preferring to brew his own in the cauldron of his mind. Ollie Jordan pretended, even to himself, to be unimpressed with Donald's swearing. There was no meaning behind it, no anger, no idea that set it forth, no goal that brought it home. "It's just show-off swearing," Ollie would say. The truth was that Ollie viewed Donald as a rival as top guide to mores for the Jordan clan.

As he pulled his truck into the yard, Ollie saw Adele's child playing in the dirt by the house and Fletch Jordan's pink and black Buick. Some of the kin who had lived with Ollie in his shacks under the Basketville sign had sought succor from Donald. Ollie understood, but it pained him to realize that he already had surrendered so much of his leadership. Someday he would find the means to regain his role.

Ollie chained Willow to himself and walked in search of Donald. He was easy to find. Ollie just followed the sound of his voice. Donald and his son, known as Donald Again, were in a shed pulling out the engine of a Ford Pinto with a rusty chain hoist.

"A man would have to have darned little pride to drive a car like that," Ollie said.

"Saint Bugger, bless my moon, if it ain't cousins Ollie and Willow come down off Fart Mountain from preaching the gospel to the good folk of I-91 to break wind with us junkyarders. Hello, Ollie. Say hello, Again, to your cousins."

" 'Lo," said Again. He had always been a quiet boy. Ollie distrusted him because he seemed contented with work.

That was the end of the greeting. The Donald Jordans continued their labors. Ollie unchained Willow, lit his pipe, and sucked on his beer. Willow sat himself among some junk parts in a corner and started stacking them in odd patterns, like a child playing with blocks. No Jordan was expected to shake hands, embrace, or greet a member of the family in any conventional way. Jordans passed a subtle eye signal among themselves as an invitation that they were willing to be tested in conversation. It was a signal that had grown out of generations of crowded living, and it was so much a part of Jordan manners that it was almost unconsciously delivered. Without the signal, Jordans ignored one another; sometimes they ignored one another for days.

"Willow was testifying as to his sense of humor," said Ollie, with deliberate dignity. You could not joke for long with Donald. Jokes were Donald's weapons. If you joked with him, he would soon gain ascendancy over you.

"Heard on the radio how Willow's bare ass humored the town of Darby. Did I laugh—thought I'd shit my pants," said Donald. He was a shade darker than most Jordans because the automobile grease had settled into his skin like a pigment. Like Ollie, he was a slim, hard man.

Ollie looked at Again for a hint of Donald's true mood. Again was almost grim. Why was he not smiling? He should be smiling. Again was his father's accomplice. Ollie probed.

"I daresay your business is booming," he said.

"I daresay my business is slow as a Frenchman trying to get a hard-on in hell," said Donald.

Again did not smile.

"I see you got a new garage—nice block building. Next I imagine you'll be advertising," said Ollie.

"I'll suck a pig's ass first," said Donald. "They tell me you was with the Witch last night. How is the old hag? Still gumming every old man in the county?"

"Still banging, I imagine," said Ollie. He mustn't let Donald take the offensive, mustn't show his sensitivity about the Witch.

After considering the matter, Ollie decided that the reason Again was not smiling was that the Donalds were fearful that

Ollie would ask for succor. After all, the Donalds were becoming wealthy; they were working regular hours; they had prestige outside the kinship; they had duties to the culture. He and Willow would be a reminder that they, the Donalds, had duties to the kinship, too. Armed with his suppositions, Ollie launched a new offensive on Donald the Younger.

"What would you say if I asked you for succor?" Ollie asked.

"I'm bound to give you succor," said Donald. There was no conviction in his voice. Ollie felt he had an advantage now, and he pressed it.

"And Willow?" he asked.

"Uh-huh," said Donald, wetting his lips with his tongue. Ollie could see that Donald wanted very much to signal an end to the conversation.

Ollie made as if to speak and then held off, deliberately holding Donald in a moment of anxiety before releasing him.

"I didn't come here for succor," he said. "Me and Willow will be on our way in a minute."

Donald's self-control snapped away from him. He realized that Ollie had been putting him to a test and that he had just barely passed.

"Damn your soul to a hell of barfing choirs—you can't go anywhere with him," Donald said, pointing at Willow.

Again nodded vigorously.

So that was it—they were afraid of Willow, Ollie thought.

"He's in the kinship same as him," said Ollie, pointing at Again. Ollie's voice had all the righteousness of a maiden aunt preaching on morals.

Donald the Younger stopped his work and put his hands together like a man praying; the hands looked like two complicated greasy-black gears about to mesh. Ollie challenged the gesture with a humorless smile of his black, jagged teeth.

"Ollie, the kinship ain't what it was," said Donald the Younger, with a tenderness so genuine and so enveloping that, in a second, Ollie felt himself plummet from the peak of his ascendancy.

"I'll say it ain't," said Ollie, righteous, cold, but the cunning gone out of him.

Donald immediately took advantage of his opponent. He pointed his finger at Willow, who by now had constructed a small castle of junk metal, and said, "Send his blasphemous ass up to Concord or Laconia. He ain't doing nothing for you, and he ain't doing nothing for this kinship—what's left of it."

Ollie realized he had been stupid and wrong to come here. Had he the means he might have apologized. As it was he pressed on, even as doing so sickened him.

"He is the kinship," said Ollie.

"Then you know what's wrong with it," said Donald.

Ollie experienced a brief moment of peculiar peace, like a man resigned to dying. The Welfare Department, he knew now, had taken his land and seduced his wife; those whom he had succored were scattered to the four winds; those who were obliged to give him succor regarded him as a menace. He and Willow were completely cut off now, from both the culture and the kinship. It was a situation that could only spell disaster, and yet there was that feeling of peace, as if—at last—he was getting what he really wanted, a chance for union with his divided self. "Come, Willow," he whispered, and the boy seemed to understand.

After Ollie and Willow had gone, the Donalds noticed for the first time the junk castle that Willow had built from the spare parts of automobiles. They found it so restful to behold that they left it alone, and each day thereafter as they entered the shed they would look at the work and take pleasure from it.

Ollie frittered away the remainder of the day. He knew that something in him had changed. He knew because he was afraid. He bought some more beer and drove around with Willow, the two of them stopping at various rest areas and parks, where great white pines loomed over them like great ideas. They would stay, Ollie sitting and drinking and Willow exulting in the nuggets of green trash barrels, until someone came or until Ollie felt pursued. During this time, it would have been logical for Ollie to be making plans, or at least to be reflecting on the nature of the changes that he knew were swirling within him. In fact, he spent most of the time wondering whether or not to buy hard liquor. Like his father before him—the father who, through some frightening alchemy, was but a shadow in his memory—Ollie had a weakness for hard liquor. He knew that if he succumbed to it, he would lose his son to the Welfare Department and himself to . . . to something horrible that once briefly he had experienced but forgotten and that remained in him as a sense of loneliness, of grief. "Still," he said, talking to himself but aloud at Willow, "the joy of straight juice might be worth the cost." The more he thought about the matter, the more beer he bought; and the more beer he drank, the more piss stops he made, until the gravity of the situation lightened and he made up his mind to buy a bottle of whiskey. It was six o'clock. The state liquor store was closed. Ollie was grateful. He was quite drunk, a condition he recognized by a dull sheen of green that seemed to him to rise up from the earth like a scent. He bought some hot dogs and potato chips, and he and Willow ate supper on a dirt road that thrust into Robin Hood Park. After the meal, Ollie and Willow lay in the back of the truck and went to sleep. In the middle of the night, Ollie woke out of a nightmare.

"Willow . . . Willow," he whispered. The boy did not stir. Ollie touched his face. It was cool. He lit a match and brought the light to Willow's face. The boy's eyes were open, and they were calm and full of wonder; they moved from the sky to the match, and instantly Ollie blew out the light. Ollie looked up into the sky. He could see a few branches sway slightly and he could feel the intense green of them, and he was cheered, almost giddy.

Niagara Falls Park

Ollie Jordan took his son Willow to a place far up on the side of a hill known on the geological survey maps as Prospect Hill but called Abare's Folly or just The Folly by the people of Darby. A logging company owned most of the hill, but had not touched the land in years. The slopes were undeveloped—and for good reason. Abare's Folly was a 1600-foot-high chunk of granite, with slopes too steep to accommodate anything but logging roads for skidders. The soil was sparse, the weather unpredictable and mean. Yet somehow dense stands of hemlocks and hardwoods took hold on the granite. The presence of trees didn't cheer up the place, but rather added gloom to inhospitality. Even hikers avoided the hill, mainly because the trees prevented views. Near the summit, where the trees grew like the wind-blown hair of women at a beach, the last logging road ended, blocked by granite outcroppings. "Willow, behind the ledges is heaven," Ollie said.

A relatively flat shelf of about five acres jutted out from the side of the hill. Here hemlocks grew with sugar maples, black birches, and white birches. Boulders of varying sizes with green mossy backs, resembling basking turtles, parked on the forest floor. There were also boulders of white and russet and ink blue, and a spring which gushed out of a crack in a ledge, flowed about twenty feet to fill a small pool, and then continued down for a date with Trout Brook far below, which continued on to the Connecticut River and the Atlantic Ocean. Here he and his son might find refuge, Ollie believed.

For the first week Ollie and Willow lolled. The weather was perfect, with warm sunny days and gentle breezes from the south in the tops of the trees. Nights were cool and there were few mosquitoes. Ollie had vague plans to build a shelter, but there seemed no need. They slept under a crude lean-to of maple saplings, which Ollie had cut with his Sears bow saw, and some clear plastic. They ate food out of cans that Ollie had brought along—hash, sardines, tuna fish, peas, soup. Once in a while Ollie boiled a potato in the one pot that he had. He had planned to ration the two cases of beer for a month; but at the rate he was drinking it, the beer would be gone soon. Ollie settled in a place that included a patch of sunlight through the trees for much of the day and that was dominated by a flat-top rock about six feet square and two feet off the ground. He named it the altar stone. There were plenty of dead branches on the lower parts of the hemlocks, and with these he built a fire on the stone. He spent nearly all his time sitting before the fire, watching and listening to the flames, drinking beer, smoking his pipe. On the fourth day, it struck him that he was happy. "This is it—no thinking, no doing," he said to Willow, who had found a comfortable place in the crook of a tree. He, too, was happy. Ollie had freed him from the chain. He figured he was taking a risk, but he believed that here Willow was free from the culture as the culture was free from him, and that furthermore, a creature should not be fettered here. Sometimes he listened to Willow babble to himself and was filled with love. It would not be so good if Willow made sense, he thought.

It was during the fourth night that the first disturbing event occurred. Ollie usually stayed up all night, watching the fire, returning to the shelter before dawn and sleeping off and on during the day. But one night he sat before the fire and something dark rose up out of the flames to encircle him. The thing was so black that the night was bright by comparison. A moment later, Ollie opened his eyes and saw that there were only a few coals on the altar stone. He had not been awake at all; he had dreamt the fire, dreamt the apparition. He walked the few feet to the plastic and sapling shelter. Willow was gone. And it was as if he were back in the dream, as if he himself, Ollie Jordan, were gone, too. This mind that reported to him the world, this bag of bones of a body that hauled him about, were not his. He lay down to make himself—itself—smaller. He wanted to cry out for the self that was out there in the forest, but he had a terrible fear that the voice that would speak would not be his own, that it would be the voice of the darkness that had come out of the fire. Finally, he said, "Willow?" There was no answer, but at least the voice that he heard was his own, and the feeling of strangeness in him began to fade. After a while, he noticed a difference in the night, not so much a lessening of the darkness as a softening. A few birds began to chatter. Dawn was coming. Weariness, the only mother that had ever brought him comfort, stroked him now, and he fell asleep in her arms. He woke in late morning. Willow lay beside him snoring. Had Willow really left? Was there something out there affecting their minds? It didn't matter. He was happy. But the questions continued to nag at him during much of the day. Finally, he concluded that the way to solve the problem, if there was a problem, was not to sleep at night until he heard the birds of dawn.

During this time Ollie often exercised his mind by asking questions that actually he felt no real need to answer. "What good is sense?" he asked Willow, who responded with a Bronx cheer. The sounds of the wind in the tops of the trees: Did these make sense? What of baby sounds? They made no sense and yet there wasn't an adult on the earth who couldn't be moved by the beauty of a baby cooing. Furthermore, as children imitated their elders, the beauty of the children's own utterances began to decline. Meanwhile, adults would imitate the sounds of their young ones—itchy-bitchy coo. Shit like that. The end result was that the children became adults, and the adults became fools. Having grappled with this idea and having finally subdued it, Ollie gave it voice.

"Willow," he said, "if I got something you want, and you take it, then I ain't got it no more. Everybody knows that. What they don't know is, you ain't got it either. Not only that, but the more you take from me, the less we both got."

Willow growled.

Ollie's most important task during the first week was to name the property. A number of possibilities came to mind, but none was satisfactory. "The Wild Place" was accurate but it had no oomph. Other names he considered included "Ollie's Secret Woods" and "Willow's Backyard," but these names made it seem as though he or Willow owned the place, and really neither had been here long enough to make such a claim. What was needed, Ollie decided, was a grand but familiar name. One day down by the spring, he looked at the water trickling from the ledge above, and the name of the wild place came to him: Niagara Falls Park. Later, for the purposes of conversation, he shortened the title to "The Park."

"Willow, The Park's got plenty of good dry firewood," he would say.

"Tow-hee, tow-hee," said Willow, as if to say, "Now here's the latest thing on your hit parade."

If the first six days on The Folly taught Ollie anything, it was that life, to be good, to be free, must be bare of duty, desire, involvement. He fancied he was becoming wise. He had vague notions of coming down off the hill to return in triumph to his clan, to preach to them the secrets of happiness. "Empty that mind," he'd say. "The trees—smell 'em. Sardines—eat 'em. Beer—drink it. The fire—watch it." And then it rained.

At first the rain was pleasant, coming as he napped in the afternoon, a pitter-patter in the trees like the sound of hamburger frying in a pan. He listened for a while with his eyes closed, and then he opened them. Willow stirred uneasily beside him. From his nest under the plastic tarp, Ollie watched the first drops kick the ashes on the altar stone. Moments later, the last of the fire went out. The rain increased. He could hear the wind building in the tops of the trees, until cold drafts worked their way under the open ends of the shelter where father and son lay. He reached for the one blanket he had, covering himself and Willow. A feeling of dread rolled over Ollie. It was worse than mere fear. It was like a realization hitting a dying man that he had lived his life all wrong.

It rained that day, that night, the next day, and the following night. Temperatures fell into the fifties. The ashes on the altar stone were washed away. The beer supply ran out. The matches got soaked and Ollie could not light his pipe. He hiked over the ledges to the truck in the hope of finding matches. He found none. But he did start the engine and warm himself by the heater. When he returned to the shelter, he discovered that Willow had gathered dozens of hemlock boughs and made a nest under the plastic. He was dry and comfortable, and Ollie was proud of him, but he had left no room for anyone but himself. So Ollie spent most of the time in the cab of the truck. The seat was not wide enough for him to stretch out on, and the floor shift jutted up into the middle of the vehicle, so that when he lay down it always seemed to be sticking into his gut or his back. He made frequent checks at the shelter and discovered that Willow was doing fine. Willow slept a great deal, and when he was awake he retreated into some private realm. He was accosted by neither cold nor hunger. He was doing what any animal does in a storm.

Ollie did not endure so well. He suffered from wet, cold, and dread. There were ways, he knew, to increase his comfort, but he felt powerless to act. Having been betrayed once by his instincts, he feared that to yield to any new idea was to leave himself open to further betrayal. In addition, he was withdrawing all at once from alcohol, tobacco, and caffeine. He found himself painfully and uselessly alert. He could not keep warm, even with the heater on in the truck. He was afraid of running the engine while he slept, because his cousins Merwin and Imelda Jordan had died of monoxide poisoning while parked at a drive-in theater. Remembering the incident reminded Ollie that these days you could see naked women in the movies. Progress, he thought. After that, he spent a lot of time thinking about naked women. In fact, that was about the only thing that made passing time in the rain bearable. But thinking about women made him terribly lonely, and he wished that Helen were here to give him succor. At dawn he went out into the rain to check on Willow. The boy slept all innocently, like a child. He reminded Ollie of the Witch herself during a moment long ago. Ollie worked his way into the nest until he was beside his son. "Room after all," he said. Willow touched his forehead and Ollie, sinking—at last—into a restful sleep, thought that perhaps it was he, Ollie Jordan, who was the son, and Willow the father. "New kinship," he whispered, and fell asleep.

When Ollie woke, the rain had stopped. Willow was already up, sitting twelve feet off the ground in a crook of a branch on a maple tree. He was eating. He had opened a can of Dinty Moore stew and was helping himself. The boy was contented. Ollie realized that Niagara Falls Park was a different place for Willow than for him. Willow could take on the mood of the weather, like any other animal. Given some time out here, some protection while he learned the ways of the forest, Willow might find The Park a good home. But he, Ollie, could not, for he was a man. There was no animal knowledge left inside of him. The week in the woods had taught him that to survive he must rely on his abilities as a man. He must scheme, build, dominate: He must think. He cupped his hands and said to Willow, as if sharing some great secret, "A man's nothing if he ain't a stinker and a thinker."

"Tow-hee," said Willow.

Ollie took inventory of his things, discovering that he could not possibly get by for another week, let alone the long haul. He was wet, cold, and hungry. Think, he shouted to himself.

And so he thought, and an idea came after about an hour. He gathered some birch bark and a couple of reasonably dry pine cones, soaked them with some gasoline that he got from the truck carburetor, put the ingredients in a hubcap, and set them on fire by crossing wires on the battery. This experiment was so successful that he nearly incinerated himself. The fire soon burned out, but still Ollie was thrilled by his own cleverness. Eventually, he figured that he could transport the fire in some sticks lashed together. He got a big blaze going on the altar stone, set his clothes up on branches to dry them, and started a smaller fire to boil water. Soon he was drinking hot coffee—the best that he'd ever had in his life. He lunched on tuna fish from the can and a couple of biscuits about to go bad. After the meal, he drank more coffee and smoked his pipe. Well, he thought, I'm happier than a pig in shit—if a little lonely. He was tempted to put aside the unpleasant memory of the storm. But he was wiser now, realizing that he must take only a morsel of contentment and get on with the business of survival. He studied Willow during the afternoon and concluded that he could leave the boy for a day or two and he would stay at The Park because that was where he wanted to be.

That afternoon he left for Keene, backing the truck a mile down the hill because there was no room to turn around. Even with four-wheel drive, the truck would not move on the logging roads once the snows fell in late fall. Keep thinking, Ollie said to himself. He stopped at the first store he saw and bought some beer.

Grant Us Peace

The City of Keene loomed strange and beautiful to Ollie Jordan. He saw the clock on the steeple of the First Congregational Church for the first time in a week. Ten minutes past three. Wonderful invention, the clock. He must salvage one for The Park, one with little arrows instead of numbers. He watched pretty women walking down the street. He liked the ones with the high-heeled shoes. He liked the way their calves bunched in the back. He crossed the street to Central Square and sat on a bench to rest. Here was an island surrounded by traffic. He watched the cars go by. What he enjoyed about them were the pretty colors. They were like big metal, rolling flowers.

Soon a small blind man, carrying a fiddle almost taller than himself, crossed the street to the square. He was accompanied by a pregnant woman with mischief in her green eyes. She was carrying a guitar. They sat upon the grass, and Ollie heard the woman sing, all at once sweet and strong so that he wanted to weep for something lost.

The TV speaks to Emily in her rocking chair.
The Secret Storm rages and then subsides.
A woman confesses how she rid the chafe
From her hands.
> *Roses for Emily.*
Emily's waiting for Love of Life to come on the screen.
The sun has wilted her plants,
And the leaves are in mourning.
The wind tips the rocker first forward then back
And blows through her thin, gray hair.
Outside, the cat yowls for the back door
To open itself.
> *Roses for Emily.*
She's waiting for Love of Life to come on the screen.
She always liked this room—the smell of the sofa
And sounds of the shade cord tapping on the window.
On the floor, years ago, played the Lieutenant boy
She lost in the war. On the lawn today, Mr. Robin bobs
For a worm, like a fine gentleman
Tipping his cap.
> *Roses for Emily.*
Emily's waiting for Love of Life to come on the screen.
The wind carries the fragrance of flowers inside,
To linger by her rocker, like an oarsman pausing
To watch the sea. The neighborhood is napping;
Children lie softly as fur. The rower dipping
His oar first in the water and then the sun,
The insistent cat, the flowers teasing the wind,
The robin and his great dignity; the children,
Even the woman with the chafed heart
Have what Emily had until 3 o'clock. The Secret Storm
Has ended and Love of Life comes on the screen.
> *Roses for Emily, Roses for Emily, Roses.*

The woman's voice left Ollie Jordan hungry for succor. He shut his eyes so that he could see better the women that he had loved. He drifted briefly. And then he was hearing an argument between two men. Ollie opened his eyes. One man had soft brown eyes and soft brown skin and lips the texture of fish flesh. He spoke fervently.

"The radiation from nuclear fallout has lowered the average IQ throughout the world. The more nuclear power plants are built, the greater the radiation in the atmosphere. It's sapping our brains, I tell you. I can feel it in myself sometimes, and I can see it in others . . ."

The other man, standing casually but stiff inside, a body at odds, smiled mirthlessly.

"You want us all to get leukemia to prove your point," he said. "If there's IQs going down here they belong to those that turned their backs on good food like meat, the flag, the good Lord. You can take your antinukes and . . ."

Ollie was annoyed. He didn't like an argument that was going no place, that, in truth, had much in common with the lovemaking of those who like to hurt and be hurt. He wanted them to go away. He wanted peace to think about the pregnant woman and her rose-petal voice. Pregnant women drew him. They brimmed at once with sex and sweetness. He thought about Helen, how serene she was during pregnancy, how ready—and how bitchy after the baby was born. He turned to catch sight of the woman with the guitar. She was gone; the blind man, too, was gone. He shut his eyes again.

He had met Helen Abrahms at the Cheshire Fair thirteen or fourteen years ago—he couldn't remember exactly. He was a young man then, but already the father of two children by two different women. His wife Iola (he called her Cousin Owl) had left him, running off with her baby—it was a healthy one, a good one—to a place of dreams called Reno, never to be seen again. Ollie had found temporary succor for himself and Willow with the Witch. Ollie was working at the tannery then, pulling skins, earning some money to get away. He went to the fair looking for adventure, as young men will. He had seen Helen standing at the wheel of fortune. She was lean, bony, but with flair to her hips. He breathed in the smell of her long brown hair—wood smoke, fried foods, the piss from babies, farm animals—and he knew she was of his own kind.

"You want to play the wheel?" he asked. "I'll pay."

"No," she said. "I've been too long without luck to think I can get it now. I just like to watch it go round and round. It don't matter to me where it stops."

"I never had no luck either," he had said. "Anyway, it don't matter at all: it's fixed." He had the confidence of a young man who believes everything he has overheard.

"That's better than what I got," she said. "Nothing I got is fixed. It's all broken."

For a moment he had thought that she was making fun of him, but then he had figured she had just misunderstood him. Now he realized that she had understood him all along and had used his idea to suit her own purpose, as women will with men. They had talked on. She knew his Uncle Jester, who was the half-brother of her Cousin Homer's Aunt Carlotta. He knew her half-sister Harriet Thatcher through her ex-husband Boynton Bigelow, who had served time in the state penitentiary with Ollie's Uncle Mortimer.

Ollie and Helen strolled about the fairgrounds until they happened onto a commotion. An enormous fat man wearing overalls and red suspenders had gotten into an enclosure of prize 4-H pigs, and with apparently amorous intent he was chasing a sow. He had the look of a man who has drunk himself into a state beyond stupor into a hot glaze of awareness. Moments later three policemen were in the pigpen, splashing about in the mud amidst the sounds of scared pigs.

"Man's got a mighty unusual sense of humor," said Ollie in admiration.

"Man's crazy and mean," said Helen, her voice low. She was shaking with fear and Ollie did not understand. Then it dawned on him that this was the man she had come with to the fair, her man.

He hustled her away from the area, buying two tickets for the evening's main attraction, an automobile demolition derby. Sitting high up in the grandstand, Ollie and Helen munched on shell peanuts, watched the cars collide below, listened to the wild music of revving engines and steel hitting steel, and talked. She had two children of her own, one still on the breast—sort of—even though it was two. Also she cared for a third one belonging to "him," which was how she identified her man. Ollie found out later the man's name was Pork Barrel Beecher. They exchanged more family information and then came to an unspoken but mutually understood agreement that Helen was to leave Pork Barrel and live with Ollie. Having accomplished that business, they relaxed, turning their attention to the demolition derby.

"It don't make no sense to me," she had said.

Ollie explained the winning techniques of the game. "You've got to keep moving, the more often backwards the better, so's they don't smash your front end and put your vehicle out of commission. If you're smart you don't get in the fray until the end when your neighbors are all bummed up. Him that still moves when all others is still is declared the winner and gets a case of oil."

"If the way to win is to lay back until the cows come home, why don't they all lay back?" she asked.

"Then there wouldn't be no demolition," he had said.

As the evening wore on, he saw that she had gained ascendancy over him. What surprised him was that he was glad.

The next day he had driven out to the Beecher place, a shack surrounded by some poplar trees that had overtaken a field. He could smell the cesspool kicking. Pork Barrel lay unconscious in the driveway. Helen had bailed him out of jail, brought him home, put more booze to him in the hope of knocking him out, and when that tactic had not worked entirely, had assisted him into the peaceful realm with the aid of an iron frying pan laid on top of his head. Ollie feared that Pork Barrel was dead, but the body was warm and perspiring and out of the mouth came occasional gurgles and squeaks. The mosquitoes were gorging themselves on the blood-alcohol mixture. "I'm for leaving him as is," Helen had said. But Ollie had pitied the body and sought at least to get it away from the mosquitoes. So, with the help of Helen and the kids, he was able to put Pork Barrel in a wheelbarrow, lay a two-inch plank along the front steps, and wheel the body into the shack. He remembered he had heard a soft noise that had made him think of dirt being thrown in a coffin hole. For just a second he had been gripped with a feeling of unaccountable terror, similar to what he later experienced that night of the dream at The Park. But the noise had only been the sound of Pork Barrel pissing in his sleep. Apparently, the motion of being transported had reminded the body that it was alive and had duties to perform. Ollie left Pork Barrel in the wheelbarrow, and took Helen and the kids away with him. That first night with Helen had been the most passionate of his life. What had heightened the sex for him was a fantasy of Pork Barrel dead. Even now the thought stirred him. Pork Barrel had not died. He had been arrested and jailed for almost killing his cousin Emile with a broken bottle. He had only served six months (because his victim was his cousin and not a stranger) and Ollie saw him now and again on the streets of Keene. The man did not seem to recognize him.

His life with Helen had been pretty good, Ollie thought. She was older than he was, and in the early years she treated him like a child, insisting he hold down a job and keep his drinking under control. They got on rather well. He realized now that it was only after he had taken command of his own destiny that their life together had begun to come apart.

Ollie began to walk the streets. Soon he heard himself humming the tune to "The Tennessee Waltz." He didn't know why the song came to mind, but there it was: a sadness. He figured if he walked enough he would bump into the woman with the guitar and the blind man. Perhaps he would follow them until they sang again.

In their years together, Helen had asked for little, had given little, had offered no explanations for her actions, and had required none concerning his own. In conjugal matters, she let him have his way as long as he was not drunk. In this manner, she modified his drinking habits so that instead of getting drunk from seven to midnight, he nipped from noon to bed-time, staying mildly inebriated for most of his waking hours, but rarely getting outright drunk. He was happy for the change in himself. Too much drink all at once made him feel strange, out of control. Yet, except in the morning when coffee would do, he required small amounts of drink in his system to feel stable. Without drink he was sick and dizzy, as if on a boat rocking in the sea.

Helen didn't seem to mind when he hit the kids, including those that were hers alone, but she was absolutely unreasonable about being struck herself. It seemed to him that her position was peculiar. Everyone he knew hit everyone else he knew. Occasionally, a tooth would pop loose, or there might be a serious accident, such as the time Mortimer Jordan had knocked his wife Amy Lou down the stairs and killed her, but that's what you got for living in second-floor apartments in the city. Usually little damage resulted from domestic battles. They certainly were less dangerous than automobile accidents. If you had a problem with people you lived with, and you hit them or they hit you, the hitting would solve the problem. Without hitting, the problem would remain and everybody concerned would feel bad. He had tried to argue this matter with Helen, explaining that he never hit to hurt her but just to relieve himself: "It ain't personal. It ain't to ruin you. Chickens peck each other. Cats fight. So do raccoons, dogs, and pigs. Every manner of critter hits his own kind. Act of love, I tell you." But she wouldn't listen. She merely repeated her longtime policy with him. If he so much as slapped her, she would murder him in his sleep. "You ain't natural—you're downright vicious," he had said. "Don't you hit me," she had responded.

There was no doubt that hitting loved ones was a family tradition within the kinship. As brother Ike was fond of repeating: "Women and children need to be beaten, women to keep them from becoming confused as to their position in life, children to teach them right from wrong." Right or wrong, it always had been done that way, Ollie thought. Any other way, right or wrong, meant a weakening of the kinship itself. Murder him in his sleep—the very idea. Who does she think she is? She was just being selfish. He shouldn't have let her set policy. He should have beat her anyway. If he had, chances are they'd still be together as a family. There was something in him—something in every man—that wanted to strike at women, children, anything helpless. There is no doubt about it, he thought, I was right and she was wrong.

Ollie reveled in a sense of justifiable outrage, but only briefly. Soon his loneliness got in the way. He found himself again thinking kindly of his woman. After all, what were a man and a woman but two sides of an argument? Divide the pair, and each was left shouting his position to the sky. "And the sky don't care," he heard himself say aloud, and the sound of his own voice brought him out of his thoughts.

He was standing in front of St. Bernard's Catholic Church in Keene. It was Saturday afternoon about four. People were entering the church. He couldn't understand it. He thought Catholics only went to church on Sunday. It offended him that most of them were so casually dressed. He was proud that he was wearing a suit, and he was glad that he had put on a fresh T-shirt before coming to Keene. He stood before the church steps, standing rigidly at attention, his hands holding the cuffs of his suit jacket. He figured he was showing them up. A young man in black came into view. He wore glasses and he had a frank stare that seemed to catch people, hold them, touch them, and release them. Now he was shaking his hands with people. "Good afternoon, Father," said a woman. The use of the word "father" cut into Ollie and opened him. He wanted to weep for all the terrible things he had done and that had been done by men everywhere. The man—the "father"—was coming toward him. He was extending his hand. Ollie was shaking it. It was all Ollie could do to keep from breaking into tears. "How are you today?" asked the father. "I'm new here," Ollie heard himself mumble. "Welcome to our church," said the father, and was gone, shaking other hands.

Ollie calmed down. The man's a priest, he said to himself. He knew a little bit about these things. He was not totally unfamiliar with religion, although the idea of God seemed strange to him. He was tired from walking. He decided to rest in the church. If somebody called the cops, he could produce the "father" who had said he was welcome.

It was the first time he could remember having been in a church. The air was different here. It magnified the importance of the simplest sounds—a whisper, a step, the rustle of ladies moving inside their clothes. Not a place to cut farts. The ceiling was extremely high—maybe three stories. There was no dividing line between wall and ceiling. The walls, decorated with colored glass windows of big fellows wearing long dresses, curved at the top until they were one with the ceiling. He felt as though he were standing under the belly of a great, protective bear on all fours. The people sat on heavy wooden benches with curved backs. It was as if they were at a ball game. He took a seat toward the rear because he did not want to draw attention to himself. He was comfortable with the place, despite the vague fear that the people might call the cops on him.

He wasn't exactly sure what was going to happen here. Some kind of ceremony. On the front wall was a figure of a man on a cross. This was Jesus Christ, Ollie knew. Christ was one of the guys from way back when, who shot off his mouth about the culture and got his comeuppance for it. Served him right, Ollie said to himself. What he didn't understand was how Christ had become a religion. He didn't seem to offer anything. Life's a bitch, religion said. But everybody knew that. What was strange to Ollie was that religion, having decided that life was a bitch, had come up with a reason for it: God done it. But instead of being angry at this God and seeking to bring him down, religion had said that God was good. It didn't make sense. Still, Ollie told himself not to draw too many conclusions. After all, he had not given much thought to religion, and now that he was in a church it was only fair that he kept an open mind. There might even be something for him here.

The ceremony began with the father that he had seen before coming out dressed up in a bright green costume with two boys with long black dresses and white tops. Everybody in the audience stood up, and Ollie was quick to follow. The father walked around arranging things and reading from a big book, while the boys fussed about with other duties. It was kind of hard to catch the meaning of the words of the father, but Ollie realized they were prayers. Mainly, the prayers told God what a great fellow he was and what cruds people were and would he please straighten them out. Maybe them, but not me, Ollie said, silently addressing this God, and he offered his own prayer: If you are what they say you are, then you done it, and don't put it on me.

Throughout the ceremony, the people were up and down. Now kneeling, now sitting, now standing. He figured they tried all these different positions to keep from getting bored, but he couldn't understand how they all knew when to get in the next position. He kept looking for a signal from the front, but he never caught on to it. After a short time, the father stopped fiddling around the table and gave a short speech into a microphone. Something about people overseas who didn't have enough to eat, and about how lucky we all were here in the USA. After he stepped down, some fellows came by with baskets and people put money in. Ollie wasn't sure what the admission fee was, but he put a nickel in the basket. Then the ceremony got serious. Some little bells rang, everybody knelt, and a hush fell over the audience. He marveled that the hush had been transmitted to him as though it were a thing that could be felt. The high ceiling in the church had something to do with the effect, he figured. The father was busy with something at the table. Ollie could see a container that looked like a metal beer mug and a tray holding a big white cookie. After praying over the cookie, the father raised it up in the air, and the bells rang some more. One of the boys was ringing the bells. The people in the audience bowed their heads. Ollie knew this was important stuff, but in what way was beyond him. Just when matters seemed about to peak, everybody took a break. The audience stood up, the father gave them all a big grin and said, "Peace and Christ be with you." And then a most remarkable thing happened. People started shaking hands with one another. A woman to the right of him offered her hand, and Ollie took it. "Peace and Christ be with you," she said. He returned the greeting: "Peace and Christ be with you," he said. Ollie got into the spirit of the thing, shaking hands with as many people as were within reach and exchanging that message: "Peace and Christ be with you." After the hubbub, everybody knelt and the ceremony became serious again. Finally, the father raised the cookie over his head and, with an emotion in his voice that Ollie couldn't quite identify, said, "Lamb of God, you take away the sins of the world, grant us peace." Moments later the father ate the cookie and drank the contents of the metal mug. Then most of the people walked to the front of the church, where the father gave them all a bite to eat from a metal mug—not the same one that he had drunk from. Presumably what they were eating were little cookies, but for what purpose was a mystery.

Ollie now had an idea of one of the charms of religion—the mystery. He tried now to make sense of one of those mysteries: Why the little white cookies? Something to do with food. He groped about in his knowledge of Christianity. A big picture came to mind. The Last Supper. It had been painted by an Italian. Christ and his buddies getting together for the last time. Having a meal and couple of beers probably. Could it be that the ceremony he was witnessing at the moment was a re-enactment of that meal long ago? His sense of logic told him that the answer to these questions had to be yes. The issue tumbled about in his mind until the church service ended when the father said to the audience, "May Christ's peace be with you." Christ or no Christ, there ain't no such thing as peace, Ollie thought.

He left the church skeptical of the purposes of Christianity, but—undeniably—soothed, too. There was something to religion. No doubt about it. He'd have to look into it when he had the time.

It was now almost five o'clock. He must start thinking, solving his problems at The Park—shelter and food. As he walked along, he tried to concentrate. Nothing came to mind. Why was it, he asked himself, that he could think just fine when he wasn't trying to think, but that when he had a problem to work on, he could not think at all? No matter. It was a pleasant day. Something would pop up. He bought a prepared sandwich at Romy's Market on Marlboro Street and he saw his cousin Tug Jordan sitting on the steps of the apartment house near the market. From the tone of his voice, Tug appeared to be having a heated discussion with someone concerning the Boston Red Sox. However, there was no one else in view. Tug would talk to anybody, including himself. Ollie drove off. He didn't mind being seen by his kin in Keene, but he didn't want any conversation. Oh, he would have liked to get some information as to the whereabouts of Helen and the kids, but in return he would be expected to provide some information about himself and Willow. He didn't want to do that. Once he told one relative where he and Willow had gone, the word would get around to all the kin. The Jordans enriched their lives with talk about each other. In fact, Ollie dearly missed the daily chit-chat that revealed who had the latest case of sugar diabetes, who had food stamps to trade, who had won twenty-five dollars in the state lottery, who was pregnant by whom. But he restrained himself from mixing with his kin because he still thought of himself as a man on the run from the Welfare Department. Indeed, the idea had become entwined with his sense of self-worth. He was convinced more than ever that his role in life was to keep Willow out of the hands of the Welfare Department. Already he could see signs of progress in Willow in his ability to adapt to the woods in a way that he had never been able to adapt to the culture. He was doing right by his son, he believed. The only question for Ollie was, Could he himself bear to continue this life—especially once winter came? He had no answer. He doubted his ability to sustain his own physical needs in The Park, let alone his son's, too. He told himself to think but the moment he gave himself that command, he rebelled against it.

He filled the truck with gas and bought some groceries and more beer. He knew he was running low on the money that the Witch had given him, but he didn't bother to count what he had left because he knew it would depress him. He remembered that Helen had a savings account with a couple hundred dollars in it, but he didn't know how to get at it. Besides, the banks were closed now. For the moment, it was best to drink a beer or two, drive around town a little bit, check things out.

All in all he liked Keene, he decided. He liked the way the big trees stood on a street corner like tall men standing in line at the liquor store, straight and untroubled. Forest trees grew one upon the other, twisted and battling, like drudges laboring on piece work at a tannery or a textile mill. City trees had health and dignity.

It was clouding up. The day was going to end in a shower. He drove to the Robin Hood Park pond. Here he had come as a boy to murder frogs. The kids called the pond "The Rez" for reasons that were mysterious to him, until somebody told him the place had been a reservoir years back. Now he sat in the cab of his truck, smoking his pipe, sipping his beer, watching the storm gather in the western sky over the city of Keene. It was one of those thunder storms that move with incredible swiftness across New Hampshire on a summer evening. For a minute or two the air was heavy and still. Then came the wind and rain. The temperature dropped thirty degrees. The dull rumblings of the thunder became sharp crackles. The lightning reminded him of his attempts at handwriting years ago in a school, and he was amused. For five minutes, there was a chaos about him that diminished to insignificance his own chaos, and he was at peace. God had said, "Get a load of this," and Ollie had responded, "That ain't bad." The sun came out. It was still raining lightly, but the air was clean. A rainbow formed. He thought immediately of the arch he had seen in the church. If only they could put the color in the church they'd have something, he thought. Why he might even start believing in God. "Grant us peace," he said aloud. Almost at the same time, a picture came into his mind that told him in just about every detail how he would build his home in Niagara Falls Park.

A Deal

Ollie Jordan did not return to Niagara Falls Park that night. The stores were closed and therefore he could not shop for supplies, he told himself, although he knew that Grossman's was open. The truth was he wanted to celebrate his vision of the home he would build. It was a wondrous thing. He was proud of himself, and he was proud of the kinship. He decided to risk going to Miranda's. He might see someone there from the kinship, who almost certainly would learn from him where he and Willow had gone. But that possibility now did not seem so threatening. Indeed, it occurred to him that matters in general did not seem so threatening. His mood was lighter, freer. Why? he asked himself. And with the question posed, the answer took shape. He felt no sense of pursuit, either by the Welfare Department or by other darker forces. Why he was being left alone he did not know. Their own reasons, he thought; they'll be back by and by. In the meantime, he could take advantage. Have a beer in a public place. Enjoy the smells of the public. Breathe their breath.

He did not see one of his kin at Miranda's. Instead, he saw Howard Elman, who was the only man he was close to outside the kinship, who was indeed his only friend. He was a big man, with a pocked face and a nasty way of looking at people. He was the human equivalent of a bulldozer. He was the kind of man that shrewd men automatically measured and found dangerous because in a confrontation he would be the type to move ever forward. Elman was sitting at the bar when Ollie came into Miranda's. He did not offer his hand in greeting. He did not even rise. In the ten years they had been friends, the two men had never embraced. And yet there was an intimacy between them that each felt, although they would not think to speak of such a thing. They moved to a booth, sitting across from each other with a pitcher of draught beer and some potato chips. Ollie would put one in his mouth, soften it with a swig of beer, and chew it with his black teeth. Delicious. He felt larger, as if he were partaking of Elman's bulk. Elman loaded his glass with beer and then took a long drink from the pitcher itself. Ollie followed suit.

"Heavenly, ain't it?" said Elman.

"Just so," said Ollie. "I imagine that in heaven the beer is free, and the bartender is an angel that will tell you all the secrets."

"It doesn't matter, because you ain't going to heaven," Elman said.

"Just so," said Ollie, and he raised his glass to his lips, almost in the manner of a toast. Elman drank the rest of the pitcher and ordered another.

Ollie settled in. The business of catching up on each other's news was at hand. Ollie and Howard had a ritual for dispensing such news, as they had rituals for nearly every act in their relationship. The news would come in great gabby salvos. One man would start, talking in grave tones but off the top of his head, the truth being up to the other to interpret from the evidence presented. The idea was to exaggerate and talk on so that the other could not get a word in edgewise. However, each valued his drink more than the game, and thus the listener marked time until the speaker paused for a drink and then he would interrupt and launch his own salvo. Elman permitted Ollie to fire the first round by asking him a question.

"I heard you took off for the pucker brush. Is that so?" he asked.

"It's so all right," said Ollie. "That boy of mine and his sense of humor has got me into more crimey trouble. After we was evicted from the estate, most of my kin took off for parts unknown. Helen hauled the kids to Keene, and won't you know, moved in with the Welfare Department. Me and Willow knocked on Ike Jordan's door. 'Ike,' I says, 'hole me up, hole me up.' Well, you know what a horse's ass he is. Likes to do a man a favor so he can lord it over him. I couldn't stand it no more. 'Let's go, Willow,' I says. I figured I take the boy up to Canada, though I know deep down that ain't worth nothing, what with the spruce trees and the people there, as well as here, being black in the heart. Thinking about that turns me around, and, Howie, damned if I don't find myself driving up to the estate that I built, and they evicted me from and started me down this long, dark road. As my Uncle Remo used to say before he drowned in black waters, 'Don't love no whore, don't steal a shoe from a one-footed man, and don't go back to no old home.' Worst mistake of my life was going up there. Dozer wiped the Jordan mark clean off the face of the earth. Could of cried. Fact is I did. The tears just poured. But I never really had a chance to get properly aggrieved. I looks up and what do I see but Willow sitting on top the sign stark naked. 'What's this?' I says. 'Get your ass down.' Naturally, he ignores me. He just waves at the people on the highway. Next thing I know there's fifteen cops up there and a squad of little ladies from the Welfare Department promising Willow a blow job if only he'll come down—of his own free will, you know. Then they get to talking to me, saying how they're going to teach Willow to wipe his ass and how to say, 'Beg your pardon, ladies and gents, I just cut a fart.' Well, I wasn't going to put up with that, so I kind of wandered off. With the help of Ike's siphon hose (thank you, Lord, for making Ike a practical-minded thief), I load up a can with gas—high test, from one of the cop cars—and snake back by the sign on the steep side by the highway. Right under their noses, Howie! Willow's got 'em all entertained, so they're looking up. I douses the sign, touches a match and *foosh!*—up she goes. I wish I could of sat there and enjoyed the sight of all those state troopers with blackened faces, screaming, 'I'm blind, I'm blind,' and all those welfare ladies speechless for the first time in their lives. But you know how it is when you got work to do. I was watching Willow. He's no fool, and he scrambles down the sign before he gets hurt. I'm waiting at the bottom. 'Time to saddle up,' I say, and I hop on his shoulders. Off we go like the Lone Ranger and Silver. I can feel the wind in my face and I can hear the blind cops firing their Smith an' Wessons—*ksh, ksh, ksh*. I ride Willow maybe five miles through the pucker brush until we get to that big rock near the Boyle place where you can see Ascutney Mountain. 'Whoa, Willow, whoa,' I says. So we sit there on the rock, Willow catching his breath, and me smoking my pipe and watching the smoke from the sign burning up. We've been on the run ever since, staying in the woods up on The Folly. Terrible nice up there, though it's hard to make the few dollars a man needs to live on, what with the lords of that place being the bears and not caring about the minimum wage. Willow likes it just fine; but me, well, you know I need to shoot off my mouth from time to time, so I come into town to buy some smokes and see what's what . . ."

At this point, Ollie paused to take a drink, and Elman, seeing his chance to speak, began his own monologue.

"I know sure as God made hell on earth that you can live like an Indian with that crazy boy of yours as long as the weather stays kindly," Elman said, "but when the falling of the leaves comes, you're going to need shelter and foodstuffs, just like I did when I was unemployed back in the winter and I was forced to sell the better part of my land to that she-wolf neighbor of mine. You've got to stand up straight to the likes of her, I'll tell you. Turn your back, bend over to pull a weed, and she's delighted to tuck the hoe to you. Ollie, it's ones like

her that's taken over these parts. You know their way: They
tuck it to you, you tuck it to them, everybody tucks it to
everybody else, until we all get along like farts at a bean
supper. I'm not complaining, mind you. Mrs. Zoe Cutter
made me see the light. It's not enough to be mean. You've got
to be sly. This ain't a world for the pure heart, Ollie. I'm
grateful to the she-wolf. She made a fox out of a bear. After we
was burnt out—terrible thing, a fire—I kind of took stock, what
with being kissed off by the lords of my shop, and my missus
sick, my boy gone over the other side, and my little girl
Heather sent off for schooling by the she-wolf. I went to work
for myself. Howard Elman—businessman. Seems crazy, even
to me. But it's so. Every day first thing in the Christly morning, me and old Cooty Patterson collect rubbish. You'd be
surprised how much swill and old ju-ju beans people throw
away every week. I got a dump truck, which I fixed into a
honeywagon. Based on my good looks, they're going to give
me credit at the bank for a new truck with a compactor body.
Well, it ain't new, but I'll make it new. May have to take on
some help pretty quick, too. Hard to find a good man who'll
work for low pay twenty hours a week for a prick like me. I
like to air out the back of the honeywagon now and again, and
I like to imagine that Mrs. Cutter up on the hill gets a whiff,
but I don't know. Course, I don't know nothing. Never did.
Ask my smart boy, Freddy. He'll be glad to swear on the
frigging Bible what an asshole his old man is . . ."

At that point, Howard Elman paused and took a long drink
from the pitcher of beer. Ollie took over the conversation.
They blabbed on for two more hours, getting ever more
incoherent. Their conversation might have seemed like the
pointless ramblings of drunks, but the fact is that Ollie Jordan
and Howard Elman were making a deal. The two men con-
versed in a peculiar code, developed over the years without
either ever admitting that that was what they were doing. It
was as if they believed they were living under a totalitarian
state, with agents and recording devices everywhere, and the
only private conversation was through code; as if God's plea-

sure was like a dictator's, gathering the expressed aims of simple men as evidence for damnation. The code also preserved Ollie's and Howard's reluctance to ask a favor from a friend directly, and it added luster to their friendship, each feeling a sense of adventure in the presence of the other.

The two men had been making deals for years. They loaned each other machines, money, labor, but they never spoke of loans. What's more they both leaned toward complicated deals, meticulously negotiated but never acknowledged. Neither could have explained that the process included a recognition, in the small, nasty part of his brain, that really he had bested the other in the deal and, simultaneously, in the better part of his brain, that in truth a fair bargain indeed had been struck. The deal must meet each criterion, and furthermore the code was constantly being updated so that it took an hour of sideways conversation just to discover mutually what the rules were that day. In the end, Ollie Jordan agreed to work for Howard Elman three days a week until the first snow, when they would renegotiate the deal. Howard Elman agreed to pay Ollie Jordan what he could afford, day by day in cash.

Their deal consummated, Elman announced that he had to get a haircut, which of course was impossible at nine p.m. in Keene, N. H., and left. Ollie eased out of the door of Miranda's and flowed effortlessly down the steps onto the sidewalk. He felt like a canoe on a quietly moving river. It was getting dark, but there was something left of the sunset in the western sky over Keene, a small halo of golden-red light. It reminded Ollie of the church he had been in earlier and of the house he would build deep in the woods. It reminded him that the color green of the forest was a lonely color. "That's why they cut the trees down," he said, in a flash of insight, and his loneliness came upon him, all sweet and sad, the hardness taken out of it by the booze.

St. Pete's

Ollie slept that night in his truck. The next morning, as soon as the stores were open, he bought some rolls of heavy-duty clear plastic and returned to Niagara Falls Park. He recognized it as home by the smell of empty sardine cans "going ripe," as he would say, and by the rest of his litter on the forest floor. Willow was waiting for him.

He fetched his groceries, gave Willow half a dozen Sunbeam sugar doughnuts he had bought, and set to work making a fire on the altar stone to heat some water for coffee. Willow ate all the doughnuts, lay down in his nest, and fell asleep. He looked husky and healthy, if ragged, as he lay there, and Ollie thought, My God, he's actually gained weight out here. It struck Ollie that Willow must be going out into the night hunting down creatures to eat. The idea disgusted him, and he pushed the problem of Willow out of his mind. After all, he had work to do, a vision of home to be brought forth.

In his vision, Ollie saw a home of clear plastic held up by whippy maple saplings lashed together to make arches. The vision told Ollie that his home would resemble the church he had been in earlier, but if his mind had been clearer he would have seen that the structure would more closely resemble a Quonset hut. The vision itself was pretty, and it danced and changed and entertained him; but it wasn't until afternoon that he actually set to work to bring it forth. Nothing happened. The moment he started to think about the details—such as selecting the proper sized saplings to cut—the vision grew blurry. If he sat down and emptied his mind of thought, the clarity of the vision returned. He became very confused. He had to release the vision in order to make room in his mind to figure out how to bring it forth, but once he released it, there was nothing to bring forth.

The problem, he decided, was that the vision didn't like company. He tried to trick it. He strolled about, whistling, holding the vision on the front porch of his mind, and then he would casually pick up his bow saw and meander over to the grove of young hardwoods. But by the time he grasped the sapling in his hand to get the thickness of it, he would be wondering just what he was going to do with this young tree. Was the tree the right size? How would he join it with a brother to form an arch? How would he bend the arches? How would he put them up? Where? He didn't even have a site for his building. Come to think of it, he needed to clear a space, cut down big trees, take into account drainage. What would he do for a door? The details filled his mind, like mooching relatives filling a house. The vision went out the back door. He sat down again, leaned his back against a tree, lit his pipe, invited the vision to be his guest. In came the vision, out went the details, and he was right back where he started from. He did no work that day, or the next. By the third day, the vision had become vaguely menacing. Where before he had imagined himself inside his new home, the sunlight pouring through the plastic like a warm, shining rain, now the light in his mind grew hot and threatened to scorch him. *Silently burning, silently burning*, choirs sang in his mind. He realized he must bring forth the vision or be consumed by it.

Finally, on the fourth day, he contrived a fury and plunged into the saplings with his bow saw. He cut down dozens of trees, each about an inch and a half in diameter. He lopped branches and peeled off the bark. He laid out his work on the forest floor under the pines near the altar stone. He had no idea at this point just how he would use the poles. He knew only that they were necessary. After he had more than enough, he paused to take them in. They were lean and whippy and beautiful—cream-colored, like a woman's skin. He inhaled their fragrance, caressed them, and slept. When he woke, the vision was gone, but in its place was a modest, sensible idea of how he must build his house. He was sad. The vision had been so much better.

He paced in the land for an afternoon until he found a building site, not far from the altar stone, where the land was humped slightly; the rainwater would drain off. The place was dense with black birches, red maples, and red oaks, all between three and ten inches in diameter, and there was also a boulder about three feet high.

The next morning Ollie worked for Elman and negotiated to borrow a chainsaw and some other tools. He returned to Niagara Falls Park with the chainsaw and two dozen doughnuts. With the doughnuts he bribed Willow into clearing the trees from the house site and cutting the lengths into firewood. Willow stacked the wood in odd shapes, often changing the shapes until they met his purpose—whatever that was. Meanwhile, Ollie worked with an ax and pick to remove the stumps. The stumps could be removed easily by drilling holes in them and pouring kerosene in the holes every day for a week to soak and then setting them on fire, but that surely would get the attention of the Darby Fire Department. Chief Bell and his crew would come clanking up Abare's Folly in the four-wheel-drive Land-Rover Bell had convinced the town to buy. Right behind, curious, as if he were visiting a whorehouse, would be Constable Godfrey Perkins. Ollie could not risk a fire, and for once he overcame the urge to do things the easy way. He dug in with ax and pick, working all the daylight hours, getting so exhausted that he actually slept well at night. Willow finished his work in a day and a half, but it took Ollie three days to finish his. Ollie tried to get Willow to help him, but the boy refused to be bribed or bullied. Ollie was proud of him in a way. He's getting to be his own man, he thought. Well, maybe not a man. His own somebody, anyway. Willow did help Ollie push aside the stumps. Even after they had been moved off the house site, Willow tugged and pulled them and arranged them to suit his mysterious purposes. The stumps were often five feet across, brown, and dusty, with a thick headlike center, from which arms and legs twisted out. No doubt about it, thought Ollie: Below the earth under each tree is a creature with an idea.

After he had finished clearing his house site, Ollie basked in the feeling of a job well done. He decided he needed to reward himself, so he drank beer steadily for two days, taking time from sitting by the fire at the altar only to piss in the woods and to snack on sardines and crackers. Then he slept, waking uncharacteristically with a hangover, and so he did not work the next day. Gradually, he returned to his former, slovenly habits, staying up all night, sleeping during the day, finding excuses not to work on the house: He needed supplies and must drive to town; he owed Elman labor; he must tidy up the site some more; Willow's bottom needed cleaning; and so on. Then in the middle of a sultry night, while he was dozing as he sat cross-legged by his fire, the vision returned to him, more vivid and vague than ever. It seemed to him that his mind temporarily had grown sharper. He could see how men with visions could be driven to serve great causes, or evil causes, or causes that didn't matter. "A vision has got no sense of right and wrong," he said to Willow, who was not there.

Late that night came a violent thunderstorm, with lightning that lit up the sky. Out of his past, out of the lost time, he got a glimmer of a dark world suddenly made bright by a slap in the face and then gone dark again. Just as the rain broke, he ran for the shelter and scurried under. Moments later, Willow came out of the trees like some ape and joined him. He was shivering with fear. Ollie held him in his arms, noticing that his son's smell had changed, becoming sweeter yet more alien somehow. Ollie wondered whether he should wash him. He used to think that the smell of the kinship was in the blood and came through the pores of the skin, that it was as permanent as a curse. But now he was thinking that he might be wrong, that a man's smell might just come from the air of the place that he inhabited. The idea struck him as important, and he decided to ponder it. But the rain and the comfort of lying in someone's arms put him to sleep. He dreamed of naked men freezing in the arms of women made of ice.

He woke cold. The rain had wet his right side. Willow was gone. The vision was gone, too. In its place was a vague command to lash together two maple saplings with some nylon cord. He set to work. He braced the end of the pole in the crotch of a big tree, and bent the pole until he could brace the other end against another tree. He had created an arch under tension. He fastened another pole to the two sides of the arch about halfway up. He knew now exactly how he would build the house. He also knew that the vision would never return. He made sixteen arches, stood them sixteen inches on center, and lashed them together with poles placed perpendicular to them. He covered this framework with clear plastic, and he laid plastic on the earth. He now had a structure thirty feet long, open at the ends, with a high-arched ceiling. It was a great house, none like it anywhere, and it deserved a name. Looks like a church, he thought, and decided then and there to call his house St. Pete's.

"Hello, St. Pete," he said. The sound of his voice gave him a longing. He wished he could show off the place to Helen, or Elman—somebody. He took the good luck charm the Witch had given him and hung it from a string inside St. Pete's. Then he went down to the pool where he kept his beer. Summer was getting on, but the water was still cold. He brought three beers to the house site and sat away from it where he could take in its magnificence. It was, he thought, the greatest achievement of his life.

The Scarecrow

The Fourth of July started wrong for the storekeeper. First there was the fight with Gloria, and then there was the trouble with that Jordan character that kept him from seeing the parade.

That morning Gloria had taken his arm (she rarely touched him outside of relations), and she had said with concern: "The birds are eating the strawberries in the garden."

"Get nets," he had said.

"What do you mean—get nets?"

"Put nets over the strawberries and the birds won't get 'em," he had said.

"Where am I going to get nets on the Fourth of July?"

"Worry about it tomorrow, huh?"

"Thank you for your cooperation. Thank you very, very much."

He was stung by that uncalled-for second "very," and it provoked him into saying something he shouldn't have. "I'll pave it. That'll solve your problem."

"It would take Einstein to solve you," she had said.

They continued to argue until each knew it was time to back off and let the coldness come over the heat.

Back in Hazleton, Gloria had always wanted a garden, but they'd not had the room. The Flaggs' growing space, between the house-store and barn, had been a big selling point in getting Gloria to migrate here. But as things turned out, the garden became a strain on their relationship. In the Darby circles that Gloria moved in, skill in working the soil was a rung on the social ladder. Gloria felt that she was expected to maintain a garden up to standards. She resented him for not caring. He resented her for involving him. Once, just to kid her, he had suggested they pave the growing space for a store parking lot. Now all he had to do was mention that word "pave" and Gloria would get infuriated.

The storekeeper did not enjoy this battle with his wife. He wanted peace, but her preoccupation with the garden had jabbed a vague fear inside him. He wished he could explain it to her. He wanted to tell her that he loved the store and the house and the TV, with its great antenna sticking up from the roof, and he loved the indoor plants she moved from window to window, as though keeping them from getting bored, but that the outside here, the air, the sunlight, the brooding hills in the background disturbed him, made him homesick, not for Hazleton, but for a region in his mind that he had left. The plain fact was he did not feel completely settled in Darby. He dared not confess his unease to Gloria because he was afraid he would unleash certain doubts in her that would start them back on the road to Hazleton. So he stayed in the store as much as possible, and when Gloria hinted that she wanted him outside for some reason, such as working in the garden, he responded meanly, in the crazy hope that somehow she would apprehend his fear.

After the argument, the storekeeper experienced a rare attack of nerves. He watched as Gloria and the kids prepared for the Darby Independence Day parade. The kids played in the school band and Gloria would ride in Gregory Croteau's Cadillac as a member of the Darby Garden Club. The marchers were going to start at the fire station and proceed a short way to the town common, right past the store, and then to the school grounds for the beginning of the annual Darby Independence Day clambake. Just as his family was about to leave, the storekeeper announced that he intended to keep the store open during the parade because he expected a surge of business. Gloria knew immediately that this was a lie; he thought she would burst into tears. Back in Hazleton, where he had been the meat manager at a Weis supermarket, he had vowed he would never work on a holiday when he had his own store. He could see that Gloria believed that he was trying to make her feel bad by keeping the store open. How could he explain he only meant to relax for a while in the comfort of his store?

Later, he stood alone behind the counter trying to think of a way to make things right with Gloria, until he was distracted by events outside his window. Fire Chief Bell and other volunteer firemen were laying out parade markers on the road, as if no one knew the way. Constable Perkins was hanging around, but not doing any work, of course. The Bingham boy zoomed down the street on his bicycle, somehow balancing his drum on the handlebars. The storekeeper heard himself chuckle. All at once, he found himself keenly looking forward to watching the parade, even if it was only going to last about ninety seconds. A parade in a dinky little town—how strange and wonderful. They were going to march right by his store, his own kids included. He felt proud and patriotic. This is what makes America great, he thought, all aglow with insight. He left the counter and picked up one of the tiny American flags he'd been selling. He'd close the store, stand on the steps, and wave the flag at his kids. When Gloria approached in the Cadillac, he'd do something really dramatic. He'd blow her a kiss.

The storekeeper was holding the flag when Professor Hadly Blue entered the store. "Am I glad you're open. Can't live without the *Times,*" he said, and put a *New York Times* newspaper under his arm.

"Parade started?" asked the storekeeper.

"They were lining up when I walked by. A great scene. Diane Arbus would have loved it," said the professor, who put his money on the counter and left.

Arbus—the name didn't ring a bell with the storekeeper. But then again, he didn't know everybody in town. Not yet, anyway.

The sounds of the Darby Drum and Bugle Corps seeped into the store and excited the storekeeper. But before he could get to the door to turn his sign around to say "closed," another customer had come in.

"I'm about ready to close for the parade," said the storekeeper, but the man didn't seem to hear.

He had a stubble beard and greasy skin, and when he opened his mouth to speak, he revealed a mouth of black, decayed teeth. The storekeeper recognized the man as Ollie Jordan.

"Need some Black Label, a case, and a pack of Carter Hall tobacco," Jordan said.

The gossip in Darby was that Jordan and his idiot son were living in the hills, but nobody seemed to know exactly where, and no one cared enough to pursue the matter. The storekeeper had seen Jordan drive by the store in his funny looking truck, but he'd never stopped before. Apparently he'd been doing his shopping out of town and for this the storekeeper resented him.

"I don't have a whole case of Black Label in the cooler," said the storekeeper. "I'll have to go out back to get it."

"I can wait," said Jordan, "but I want the tobacco now. I run out."

The storekeeper could hear the parade getting closer. Godfrey Perkins was running the siren in his cop car. The thing to do was tell this Jordan fellow he'd get his beer after the parade and he'd darn well have to wait. But there was something about having the man in the store that dirtied up the storekeeper's vision of the parade. He wanted Jordan out of his store, pronto. Maybe he could discourage the man from buying. God, I must be soft in the head to turn away business, he thought and gave Jordan his tobacco.

"Beer in the back is warm—piss warm," the storekeeper said. "You come back after the parade, it'll be nice and cold."

"I can pay, I got money," Jordan said.

Oh, no, thought the storekeeper, I hit the guy where his pride lives. He thinks I think he wants credit.

"Parade's coming. I can hear the band—dee-dum," said the storekeeper, trying to plead with the tone of his voice.

"I got money. See, right here," Jordan said, laying a twenty-dollar bill on the counter.

The storekeeper took the bill and returned change for the beer and tobacco, laid his little flag to rest on the counter, and then jogged toward the rear of the store. If he got a move on, he could get back with the case just in time to watch the parade go by. He blundered into the back room without putting on the light, and the quick plunge into darkness made him believe he was going to lose his balance. He remembered now that in high school he was called "bird head" because his head was small, his neck long, his shoulders broad. "Those bastards," he whispered. He backed out of the room, snapped on the light, and went in again. He breathed hard. Harold Flagg, the previous storekeeper, had died of a heart attack—probably because of the demands of this damn store. The storekeeper grabbed the beer case and broke into a run, slowing to a quick walk once he got into the store. He didn't want Jordan to see him rush, although why in the world he should care was beyond him. Jordan was sitting on one of the straight-back chairs near the counter. He had lit his pipe and he looked content— the S.O.B. The storekeeper laid the beer at his feet, picked his flag off the counter, and quick-stepped to the front door. He stood on the steps as he had planned, flag in hand, and he could see the dregs of the parade in the distance—a couple of kids on bicycles, somebody's green Pinto automobile. The storekeeper waved his flag once and went back into the store. Ollie Jordan was just leaving.

"Parade passed me by," said the storekeeper.

"Why these people would want to walk on a hot road, when they could be drinking beer in the shade, I don't know," Jordan said.

"Ah-ba," was all the storekeeper could say. Not that it mattered. Jordan was walking away from him.

The storekeeper had just closed the store when Old Man Dorne drove by in his Buick, stopped, backed up, and said from the window in a voice that didn't sound quite right to the storekeeper, "Going to the clambake?"

"I guess so."

"Want a ride?"

"I guess so," said the storekeeper.

In the Buick, the storekeeper got a whiff of booze breath. That was odd. He didn't think Dorne was the type to drink in the daylight.

The storekeeper was comforted by this car. It had air-conditioning and therefore the windows were rolled up and the only sound was the reassuring doze of well-muffled machinery at work. Dorne didn't pull into the school parking lot, but stopped the car alongside the road. The storekeeper watched parade marchers mingling about. He didn't see Gloria and imagined that she was in the school preparing potato salad or something. He looked at his watch. It would be another hour before the feed started.

"Why am I always early for things I don't want to go to in the first place?" he said.

"Hard morning, eh?" Dorne said.

"It shows?"

"Little bit. Come on, let's go for a ride." And the old man drove off without waiting for an answer. Moments later, he reached under the seat and produced a paper bag. Inside was a bottle of Seagrams 7 whiskey. He handed the bottle to the storekeeper, who took a drink. The booze quickly settled him down. He felt like a high school boy again, driving around, seeing what's what.

The old man stayed on back roads, some of which the storekeeper had never been on before. There were roads that climbed into the gloom of deep forests, roads that followed streams through valleys, roads that came suddenly into open spaces with a big, blue sky hovering over green fields being mowed by black and white cows.

"Guernseys?" said the storekeeper.

"Holsteins," said Dorne.

The storekeeper saw pleasant but run-down wood-frame houses where machines and sheds and barns and garden plants and weeds and wild flowers and various grasses grew every which-a-way in harmony with the messy, disreputable forests that surrounded the homesteads; and he saw shacks and trailers where the messes had got out of hand; and he saw new houses, fancy and expensive, amidst brand-new lawns and huge septic-tank leaching fields that had been imposed bulldozerwise on the landscape. The scene left him wondering, Who do these people think they are? Country folk were either too rich or too poor.

The storekeeper got more and more relaxed. He found himself talking a mile a minute about what had happened that morning. Dorne laughed loud, a big roaring but sad laugh. There was no meanness in the laugh, and it made the storekeeper feel a kinship with the actors in the human comedy. Soon he, too, was brimming with mirth. "Don't life shake up the bladder?" the old man said and pulled the car off the road to a stop. The two men went tottering in the woods to take a piss. The storekeepr could smell pine needles.

When they came back, Dorne looked suddenly weary. He asked the storekeeper to drive.

"Tired?" asked the storekeeper.

"Sick," said Dorne.

They were traveling the road that skirted the steep ledgy hill known as Abare's Folly when Dorne pointed to dirt ruts disappearing into the trees. "I bet if you went there, you'd find your friend Ollie Jordan," he said. Impulsively, the storekeeper peeled off the blacktop and onto the dirt road. The car did bumps and grinds for about one hundred yards before the storekeeper realized he couldn't go any farther. Dorne was laughing again as the storekeeper backed up. "If you'd treated my Buick like this a month ago, I would've had you shot. But today I don't give a damn," Dorne said.

A shimmer of fear gripped the consciousness of the storekeeper. He darned near had had an accident. It was time to head back to Darby village.

"Don't think too bad about Ollie Jordan," Dorne said. "His kind are not like you and me."

"You know him well, do you?"

"I know him better than he knows me," Dorne said. "I knew his mumma way back when. Fact is, and I wouldn't have admitted this until recently—I got no shame left, you see; I'm free of it—fact is, I'm related distantly to the Jordan clan."

With that, the old man told a story about a relative of his who had made a living burning piles of wood for charcoal production, and how somebody had been incinerated in the pile. The storekeeper never did get the relationship between Dorne and the Jordans. But he was only half-listening; he was rerunning mentally a scene from a movie on television the other night called "The Birds."

They were almost in the village, coming up on Dorne's white colonial, when the storekeeper blurted out: "Where can I get nets?"

"You can't get nets on the Fourth of July," Dorne said.

"That's what I told Gloria. But, see, the birds don't know it's a holiday. Even if they did, they wouldn't be going to the barbecue when the strawberries are so cheap in Gloria's garden."

"You want to do something for your missus?" Dorne asked.

"I want her to take hold here, like in the garden," and the storekeeper wondered why the idea he wanted to express was so clear in his mind, yet so muddled in the speaking of it. But Dorne understood.

"You don't need nets. You need a scarecrow, and by golly if I can't make a scarecrow, seventy-eight years of sweet life come to this heart undeserving," Dorne said. He ordered the storekeeper to pull the Buick into his driveway.

The old man zig-zagged into the house, while the storekeeper waited in the car. He was getting edgy. He didn't like how the day was taking on a booze-yellow glow. He glanced at his watch. Dorne soon returned, carrying an armful of clothes, on top of which was a wide-brimmed, oddly shaped purple hat with a feather, like something out of a pirate movie. The storekeeper did not like this hat.

"You're not going to make a scarecrow from that suit?" he asked.

"I haven't worn it in the last twenty years, and I ain't going to wear it in the next twenty. This is not a burying suit, you see?" Dorne said, and chuckled. "Now let's go to your place."

Dorne found tools and lumber in the shed behind the store as if he'd been there before—and probably he had. Even though he was still under the influence, he was graceful and sure in his labors. He made a cross from 2-by-4s, cutting a wide groove in two pieces and joining them with a couple of nails. He had the storekeeper dig a hole in the garden, and then the two men planted the cross. The suit jacket hung pretty well on it, but the pants had to be fussied on with the help of another piece of wood and some coat hangers. Dorne made a head by stuffing a pillowcase with wood shavings from the shed, then tying it around the throat of the cross. The storekeeper was visited by intimations of strangulation. Dorne topped the scarecrow with the hat.

"Quite the hat," said the storekeeper, liking it less and less.

"I got that hat at the Tunbridge World's Fair back in—I won't say what year. I was a young feller and I thought the hoochie-coochie dancers would like me with that hat. I haven't put it on since. Better it graces the noggin of our friend here, Mr. Strawberry Savior."

"He doesn't have a face," said the storekeeper.

"The birds don't think you or I got any more face than him," Dorne said. "Besides, the hat will hide his face, I mean his lack of face."

Old Man Dorne was quite proud of himself. Much as the storekeeper disliked the hat, he realized that he had to accept it, that it was not proper for him to criticize it now. He experienced a surge of resentment at this perception. He made a mental note to replace the hat at some future date.

"This fellow will work for you twenty-four hours a day," Dorne said. "And he won't complain, not even about the weather, and he won't demand minimum wage."

It wasn't until the next morning at breakfast, while they were eating cereal with strawberries and maple syrup, and Gloria was in good humor as a result of the gift of the scarecrow, that the mystery of Dorne's behavior came clear to the storekeeper: The old-timer was dying.

A Night

August passed, September passed. It was disturbing to Ollie that he could not remember clearly certain incidents in the last two months, but he told himself that, on the whole, it had been a successful time. He had worked mornings three or four days a week with Elman on the trash route, and that had been all right. He was able to scrounge enough materials to furnish St. Pete's rather nicely and to board in the ends to include windows and a door (painted red). It was amazing the things people threw away—clothes, appliances, furniture, knick-knacks, not to mention glass containers, metal cans, and plastic holders of a thousand shapes and colors. And food! A man could live like a King of Arabia, just on the food his neighbors threw away. But what bothered him most was the tremendous amount of paper that people used—especially reading matter. People read too much. They read about everything. All over the world. It would come to no good. People would fill their minds with strange ugly things until they couldn't help being strange and ugly themselves. It could happen: a world gone mean and mad at once, as if all the eyes of mankind saw monsters everywhere in weather, in plants, in mirrors, in the faces of those most loved.

"Willow," he said, and the birds went silent as Ollie's voice carried through the night. Willow did not answer. Willow had gone somewhere, on his own personal errand. Ollie was getting cold. He shouldn't be out here. He should be inside getting warmed by his new wood stove, but he liked it by the altar stone. He liked the open fire and the solemn dignity of the stone itself. If God ever had something to say to him, it would be here. He rose, put two more sticks on the fire, and opened another beer. Somebody's got a plan, he thought. Even Elman was reading lately. He was taking a course, or some goddamn thing, and he would wear these little glasses, and he would sniff, as he held up a magazine: "Ollie, I want you to get a load of this," he would say, and he would read aloud some stupid-ass thing. Once he went on and on about somebody inventing a thing that would hold a million conversations.

"You don't believe that shit?" Ollie had asked.

"Course, I do," Elman had said.

"Just because they print it don't make it the truth," Ollie had said.

"Yah, yah, I know they lie, but that's only to screw somebody they want to screw," Elman said. "Those microwaves don't screw anybody. There's no reason to lie about a microwave. The difference between these educated people and the ignorant people is the educated ones don't lie unless they want to screw somebody. Now your ignoramus will lie to protect his pride or for sport . . ."

And on Elman would go. It was appalling. Somebody taught Elman book reading, and every time he got on the subject he became a horse's ass. But, really, he had no complaints against Elman. He was a good boss, as well as a good friend. He was good company, too, and that's what Ollie needed after spending all those hours alone or with Willow, who had grown oddly powerful, not like a man but like a storm, or something godlike anyway.

"Willow?" he said. "Willow." Ollie hoped he'd return soon. Willow left every day at noon, sometimes not returning until late at night, sometimes not returning at all.

Ollie now was visited by a mental image of great pulsating hulks of metal and of plump, overturned chairs that were feminine somehow, suddenly bursting with their stuffing as though slashed by big knives, and of a dark-hatted slouching man, with pitted skin that resembled corroded aluminum. The man milled about menacingly like a whore killer on a whore street on a Saturday night, and Ollie could hear crows spreading evil tales in the fiery sky of the image. He knew that the picture in his mind was the distorted shape of a lost memory. He strained to identify it, failed, and then the image was forgotten, and he was thinking that he didn't like the way towns got rid of their trash these days.

It used to be that the fires in dumps simmered twenty-four hours a day and you could sneak in and pick it over for fascinating items. But now they buried the trash in layers, like a giant cake. Sanitary landfill. He didn't like it. Nothing to pick. Just layer upon layer.

"Umm," he said aloud. "Willow! Willow! Get your ass home."

The boy had done well. All right, he was getting mysterious and peculiar. But so what? All great men were mysterious and peculiar. The point was that Willow had developed, on his own, ways of survival. Thanks to Willow they had had a bountiful late summer. Ollie figured that the boy was raiding gardens at night, taking vegetables and returning with them to the park. He picked only the best and apparently he was very clever, for Ollie quizzed Elman closely about rumors around town of someone stealing from gardens. There were no such rumors. The boy had learned to move about without being seen. He never took more than he needed. Either the gardeners never missed portions of their harvest, or they put the blame on raccoons.

Willow never ate the food he brought home. In fact, unless Ollie brought home doughnuts or pies, he never ate at all in Ollie's presence. The idea that Willow was taking game somehow and feeding upon it both revolted Ollie and made him proud, but it wasn't the kind of thing he liked to think about so he pushed it around in his mind trying to hide it. The vegetables that Willow brought were beautiful things, and sometimes before he ate them Ollie would look at them through the sunlight fragmented by the trees and he would marvel at the work of God, God being another idea he was working on these days. He especially liked the ripe red tomatoes, some of which were big as grapefruit. Sometimes he ate them like apples, breaking into them with the black, jagged teeth, tasting the innards as they ran down his cheeks. They looked and felt like burst hearts. But most of the vegetables he cooked, boiling them into a gooey stew so that their individual identities vanished. In the stew he mixed sardines or Spam or hamburger or whatever he had that day. Sometimes he foraged for crayfish and frogs, for their legs. These meals brought him strength. He felt better now physically than he had in years.

Frosts had put an end to most of the garden vegetables, and lately all Willow brought were squash and pumpkins and occasional store-bought vegetables and fruit. Ollie couldn't imagine where he was stealing these from. He wished Willow would bring him meat, and he broached the subject, but Willow pretended not to understand. Ollie imagined that meat was sacred to Willow because it came from animals, which to Willow were his kin. If you thought about it, you'd have to come to the conclusion that all creatures were kin. The evidence was there: All creatures had flesh and blood; all creatures suffered and died. He figured that Willow had developed some religious ideas about the business of killing and eating animals, and that was why he refused to bring his father his game. It's easier for me, Ollie thought, I eat my meat from the can. It was hard to get religious about a can of sardines or Spam. But with that thought, he began to consider for the first time the idea of canned meat. How did they catch all those tiny sardines and how did they get them in the can? He imagined men with sailor hats and pea coats dragging the oceans with huge nets made of screened-door material, women with sweat

on their brows and great sagging breasts working in a stupor
with sharp knives cleaning the fish, and other women, more
dainty and careful, packing the fish in cans and sealing them
through some process beyond his imagination. The idea made
sense, to a point—but what of Spam? It was meat, no doubt
about that. Was there such an animal as Spam? If so, why had
he not seen one on television? Of course, it could be they were
small—can-sized creatures. Spam, ham, he thought. Hell, if a
ham was a pig, maybe a Spam was a small pig, say the size of a
football. You wouldn't need cowboys to herd them. They
could live in rabbit pens or something. He found this explanation unsatisfactory and filed away the problem for future consideration.

"Willow! Willow Jordan come home."

He should put on a coat, but the coat was in St. Pete's and he
didn't want to leave the fire. It would break his train of
thought. He built up the fire instead. It was beautiful and ever-
changing, it threw heat in his face, like a passion, and it
warmed his spirit, but it had no arms to wrap around his
shoulders. He was shivering. He wished now that he had a
woman, not for sex, for a man could handle that chore himself,
but for arms. "Oh, Witch," he whispered, and he hunkered
down closer to the fire, turning his back upon it to warm the
place that shivered between his shoulder blades. The cool of
the evening fell upon his flushed face, and for a moment he had
the sensation that he was feeling the touch of the night itself.

There was something out there that had interest in himself
and in Willow. He didn't know what it was, but this much he
knew: It had something to do with the darkness. He didn't feel
threatened by it, not just yet. Only an idea, he cautioned
himself. Mustn't go too far with it. Ideas of dark strangers
were always dangerous: You don't believe in them and you
don't believe them, and then you invite them in the house, and
then you do believe in them, and they strip you for your things
and kill you. Still, undeniably, this was an interesting idea to
think about. He issued a mental challenge to the stranger that
he did not believe in: Show your face to me some midnight.

For a moment he felt awesome, powerful, as though the weight of the altar stone had been transformed into energy for his own being. He felt as though he could lift that stone and hurl it into the stars. The feeling of power would pass quickly, he knew, so he gathered what he could of it for his mind, and expended it in a probe into the darkness, and he could see a shape squatting behind the trees, watching, and then the power was gone, and the shape was gone, and he was merely thinking now.

There might be, out there, he thought, a fellow from the Welfare Department spying. But if so, why hadn't this fellow called the cops and had him and Willow arrested? The answer was obvious: It was all in his imagination. Unless . . . unless. It was possible that the Welfare Department had plans for Willow that had something to do with his staying out here. Thus, they might station someone here to watch the place. But why just at night? Umm. Willow slept all morning, sometimes in trees, sometimes in his nest, sometimes in St. Pete's. But there was no reason to observe him then, nothing to be gained from him. Therefore, the fellow from the Welfare Department could take the days off. Have a few beers. The more Ollie thought about this explanation, the less satisfactory it became. After all, if the Welfare Department were on to him, they certainly could afford to have shifts of fellows watching him. He looked at the fire and then at the altar stone, attempting to draw from them their power, and he was seeing the dark shape. It was Willow huddled over another darker shape, as though plotting with his own shadow. Was it possible that Willow himself was in league with the Welfare Department, that he was meeting with them secretly at night?

"Oh, God," he said. "Willow, come home to Daddy."

He stood up. His back was burning from the fire, and his face was cold. He started to dance around in circles, trying to find the happy medium between heat and cold—warmth—because warmth was akin to arms. What he really wanted was arms. He tried to hug himself, but these arms—his own arms—seemed alien to him, alien even to flesh, as though they were wires, and he released himself. He wished he had some strong drink instead of just beer. He reached for the six-pack that he kept cloistered in a brown bag by his side, in a kind of absurd caution as though he were getting around a law against drinking in the woods. (It did not occur to him that if he were to get arrested it would be for littering, for the land here was covered with his empty beer bottles, cans of all kinds, but especially sardine cans, empty foam containers, and paper, paper everywhere—thrown by him to the ground, blown by the wind into trees, carried into small earthen caverns by curious rodents. Ollie noticed none of this work that he had done, although he was struck by the sense that Niagara Falls Park had become more comfy of late.) The brown bag was empty. Now he'd have to go into St. Pete's to get some more beer. He could put up with a little cold, but life in the night without beer was not worth living. Reluctantly, he went inside.

It was not that he disliked the place. In fact, he was altogether too comfortable in St. Pete's. That was the problem. Here with a small fire going in the stove he had salvaged, with his fanny settled into the easy chair he had salvaged, with his feet on the chopping block (Ollie split the firewood inside), with his drink and pipe in reach on the end table he had salvaged, with the portable radio (that he had salvaged) blaring, with the shelves he had made bursting with the knickknacks he had salvaged that testified to his enormous competence, with thoughts of danger and evil seemingly unable to get rolling in the pleasantness of this place—here, he could fall asleep in the night.

But sleep in the night is what he did not want to do. It was not so much the nightmares that bothered him, because he remembered so little of their content even as he woke, but rather the feeling itself of waking out of the nightmare. It was a feeling that there was someone else in his mind. According to Ollie Jordan's law of personal survival, sleep must be fought off until the dawn's first light. He would sit there all night by his fire, drinking beer and thinking, and when the first few birds began to chirp moments before the darkness could be perceived as lifting, only then would Ollie return to St. Pete's, slide into the bed (salvaged), lay his head upon the pillow (salvaged), cover himself with blankets (salvaged), and sleep the gentle rest. He feared the coming of winter, not so much for the cold as for the longer nights, more chance for nightmares.

Sometimes he napped in the afternoon. He cautioned himself to waken before dark, but often he slept over and woke in a nightmare, which was bearable as long as it came in early evening, for Ollie Jordan had categorized the different darknesses of the night. Dusk, the first darkness, was not a dangerous darkness, but it was uncomfortable. During this time, the eyes of hunters opened. Sometimes, coming out of a dream, Ollie could see in his mind countless tiny lights that were the eyes of hunting creatures of all kinds. He would lie there terrified, not so much by the lights, for he knew they were only in his mind, but by the thought that when he opened his eyes the lights would still be there. He would open his eyes, and there would be no lights, just the dusk which was like the smell all around you of the breath of a man whom you cannot see who wants to injure you. This was a time for a quick drink, to ease the nerves. Much as Ollie was opposed to work, he had to admit that around dusk it was good to keep busy—split firewood, patch the roof, lay in leaves for insulation around the perimeter of St. Pete's, haul water. Once total darkness had replaced dusk, he would relax, sit and smoke his pipe, settle down to serious drinking, that is, measured drinking. This was a good darkness, this time between dusk and midnight, and his impulse was to drink hard in celebration of a good thing (the only way Ollie Jordan could imagine to celebrate a good thing was to drink), but generally he was cautious, because he knew that if he drank too much too soon, he might fall asleep and wake during the dangerous darkness, the time between midnight and dawn. Ollie had become convinced, through his recent experiences, that the true danger of the late darkness was that during those hours the barriers of time itself were weakened. Then spirits could move back and forth into past and future. The dead, or whatever was the name of the evil out there, had errands to do, errands that required living bodies to motor around their vaporous forms in this, a world of substance. He further speculated that certain bodies, through the porthole of the sleeping mind, could be influenced to do the work of the spirits, but only late at night when time could be bridged. A man could be haunted, even by his own ghost.

Still, he had mastered the knack of staying awake, he said to himself now, and it wouldn't hurt, really, to sit for a moment in the soft easy chair. The warmth of St. Pete's was settling into him. Watch out, he had said to himself. Don't get too warm. The warm man falls asleep. Well, he'd sit down just for a moment. Nice, nice, nice, nice—this chair. Ollie had salvaged it on one of his trips in the honeywagon with Elman. A dog had shit upon it and a certain Mrs. McGuirk had thrown it out. Ollie had brought the chair to St. Pete's and covered the offending stain with sheepskin (salvaged). The next day Mr. McGuirk asked Elman what the hell he had done with his chair, and Elman had said merely that he didn't have it. That was the end of it, for no man would want to challenge Elman's eyes, even one outraged at the loss of his easy chair. Ollie fetched beer now, which he kept in a cool spot in St. Pete's, and he lit his pipe and sat upon his chair. He smelled, or imagined he smelled—he wasn't sure which—the pooch that most certainly must have gotten his ass kicked after messing on this chair.

He missed his own dogs. He wished he had a dog. That would be his next project, he decided: Get a dog. Dogs were like men—such fools. Such sex lives. A bitch in heat will stand in one spot, as if ordered by a general. As for the males that came to her, it was the smell that brought them. The evidence had hit home once, years ago. He had owned a bitch hound, a wonderful animal on a rabbit track, useless at other times. He wanted to breed her with a weimaraner owned by his Uncle Cleo. Meanwhile, he had to keep her away from Rotten Ralph, an all-breed-no-breed mutt Helen had from her days with Pork Barrel and which she had refused to destroy. Rotten Ralph was a flop-eared, short-legged canine sex maniac. He had a good nose, the right disposition, and the courage to be a first-rate hunting dog, but he lacked the interest. All he wanted to do was chase bitches. In order to protect his prize hound—her name was Lillian—Ollie imprisoned her in an old pigpen. This was one of the best enclosures he had ever made, so good that it had kept a great pig, whose name was Everett P. Wilkes, from routing his way out through the earth beneath. If it could keep Everett from getting out, it could keep Rotten Ralph from getting in. Lillian spent her considerable free time lying on a wool blanket that Helen had gotten away from the Salvation Army. (These were the days before she had begun to come under the spell of the Welfare Department: good days, as Ollie remebered them.) Rotten Ralph dug, sniffed, and threw his body against the enclosure, but he could not get in. One day Cleo brought his weimaraner. He was long-legged, sinewy, and gray as a storm cloud. Ollie introduced him to Lillian. The two hit it off immediately, and Ollie and Cleo drank beer and watched the dogs mate. It was especially gratifying to Ollie to see a frustrated Rotten Ralph on the outside, pacing and whining and throwing himself at the enclosure. Several days later, Lillian stopped quivering and the stock-car whine of her voice changed pitch, and Ollie knew she was out of heat. He released her, and off she went on a run. Rotten Ralph showed no interest in her. Rotten Ralph entered the pigpen and attempted relations with Lillian's blanket. All this time, driven by a smell. It made a good story. Rotten Ralph getting what he deserved—nothing. Except that when the puppies were born, they were all flop-eared and short-legged.

Let's see, what was it he was thinking about? Dogs. Oh, yes, he must get a dog. A man needed a companion. A son wouldn't do. Even a good son, a normal son. The normal son sasses you back and breaks your heart. He knew the hurt that Elman carried over the desertion by education of his son Freddy. Not that the crazy son was any better than the normal son. The crazy son drew the blood out of you, drop by drop, like a mosquito with a limitless appetite. ("Willow," he said, but he only whispered the name.) As a boy Willow had been normal. Well—admit it—not normal. Crazy even then, and private. But affectionate in his own way. He would walk up to the women of the household—any woman for that matter, sometimes strangers—and stroke their heads. The trouble was he kept up the habit after he had passed his childhood. It was hopeless talking to him then, as now, but Ollie used to pretend that he understood. Patting the ladies is fine when you're a boy, he would say. Not so good after your manhood firms up. Scares the ladies. Got to learn to be sneaky with a woman. Steal a pat and steal a heart. Take a pat when the moment's right. Never beg a pat, or a woman will hate you. His advice was useless. No matter what he said, Willow could not, or would not, respond. Ollie didn't know what would be worse: to find out that Willow truly was an idiot and had never understood him and that everything he had said to him had been thrown down an empty well, or to find out that he had been right all along, that Willow was wise to him and to the world and had been mocking both. If that were to happen, Ollie knew he would fill with rage and he would beat his son for the pain he had brought him. *But then again, you beat him anyway*, a voice said inside him; *as to hurt, you and he are even.* Well, then, Ollie thought, maybe I won't beat him anymore. I'll save up all he owes me in hide, and when the moment's right I'll take it all off him at once.

He was getting angry, which was a good thing, for you could not fall asleep when you were angry. The trouble with anger was that it stole away from you in the middle of the battle it instigated and left you fearful. He could nurture the anger, or he could let it go early while he was still in command of it. Let it go, he said to himself. The fact was he wasn't really angry at Willow, or anyone, not even himself. He was angry because his mind chose to be angry, and he was hunting around for something to be angry at. Why, he thought, when a man gets in such a mood does he take it out on his loved ones? Beat the kids, beat his wife—if she let him. Umm. The answer that came to him was that a man would not risk the high cost of fighting an enemy unless there was profit in it. The cost that he expended beating a loved one was small by comparison to challenging another man and it achieved the purpose of relieving his anger. The fact was, he realized, that he—or any man—wanted a dog to pat it or to kick its ass, depending on his mood. God should have given men dogs instead of wives and kids. The world would be a better place under such an arrangement. His anger was slipping away now. He wished he could keep just enough of it to use as a barrier against . . . certain forces. Gone, the anger was gone, and in a second he felt hunted. Anger went out the door and terror came in. He rose from his chair and calmed at the moment of his standing. There was nothing here or out there to be terrified of. There was nothing for miles that wanted to devour or embrace him—unless a man's loneliness had shape and plan. He opened the door of St. Pete's and shouted, "Willow!"

Ollie could feel the deep weariness settle into him now. He mustn't return to his chair, or this time he would fall asleep. He put on his coat and went outside. It was quite cool, forty or forty-five degrees. The nights would come when he couldn't go outside, when it would be difficult enough to keep St. Pete's warm. He had enough food—well, almost enough. Firewood wasn't a problem, really. Willow had cut and stacked more than they could use. Ollie had split the green wood and left it in the sun to dry. It wasn't seasoned yet, but it would burn well enough when mixed with dry dead branches that were free for the taking from the thousands of trees that were his companions here in Niagara Falls Park. In fact, a green fire would last longer in the stove. Then again, a green fire was a smoky fire, and smoke from his chimney might draw attention. The Welfare Department might come to investigate. He didn't like that thought one bit. It disturbed a man's coziness. Still, he must face facts. They would see his smoke. They would come. He supposed he could burn a fire only during the dark hours, of which there were many more in the winter than during the rest of the year. That was the answer, but it was not a satisfactory one. Long hours in the cold, even daytime hours spent

sleeping, were not good for a man's health. He was reminded
of his half-sister Luella who, with her ridiculous husband, fell
sick when nobody would sell them any oil to heat their apartment in Keene. Mr. Ridiculous wasn't working at the time,
and anyway they didn't pay their bills when he was working.
Luella died. Mr. Ridiculous went south.

What was it he was thinking about? Something about a dog.
Oh, yes, he wanted one. Elman would know somebody with
puppies. People who live in the town always know someone
with puppies. Kittens were even more common. But he didn't
want a goddamn cat. The only thing a cat was good for was
finding out the most comfortable place in a room. You put a
man in a room and he would sit in the chair that was provided
even if it was in a draft, even if the chair was uncomfortable.
Men, like dogs, endured. A cat would never put up with
discomfort. A cat searched the premises for the softest place
with the best air, and then laid claim to it. The best a man
could do with a cat was to take a portion of its territory for his
own comfort. He didn't want to bother Elman about getting a
dog because Elman didn't like dogs. He didn't know why. It
was puzzling. It used to be that Elman was quite the dog
fancier, but he had changed. It was nothing he said or did, yet
Ollie could tell from a word, an expression on his face, that
Elman had developed a hatred of dogs. Maybe Cooty Patterson could find him a dog, but he didn't trust Cooty's judgment.
The old man, out of instinct, would recommend the runt of a
litter.

Ollie paced about the plastic confines of St. Pete's, ponder-
ing the problem of how to get a dog, not because he actually
wanted a dog, but because it busied his mind. He was afraid to
sit down because he knew he would fall asleep he was so tired.
He didn't like pacing, but it was better than standing still. The
trouble with being on your feet was that the beer didn't taste
so good. You couldn't concentrate on the drink, and it sloshed
around in your gut, which wasn't good for your health. Maybe
he'd sit down just for a moment. He'd light a cigarette and hold
it in the crook between his ring and middle finger, and if he

dozed off the cigarette would burn his finger and wake him up. Somewhere in this house he had a pack of cigarettes (salvaged). He rummaged about, his purpose as much to admire his own taste and effort in the art of salvaging as to search for a cigarette.

Here were some child's toy blocks, a pile of girlie magazines ("One hand turns the pages,/The other drives the car,/Going down the highway of love/Hand in hand with my best friend . . ." Where had he heard that song?); here was a saltshaker (empty), some fish line, a flower pot full of bottle caps; here was an alarm clock, a bouquet of plastic flowers, a broken canoe paddle, assorted lamps and shades, a deflated football, a short knife crudely sharpened (it made him think of the betrayed sound pigs made when you stuck them in the throat). Let's see, what was he looking for? Oh, yes, a dog. But Ollie, he said to himself, you won't find a dog on your shelf. So it couldn't have been a dog. He wasn't so crazy or so drunk that he would search for a dog where he knew there would be no dog. Or was he? What difference did it make? There was no dog here. He could find no dog here. Whatever he had been looking for could keep. He sat down in his chair, stuffed his pipe with Carter Hall tobacco, and lit it, but a peculiarity in the familiar feeling of smoking made him realize that the pipe had something to do with the reason that he had been pacing about just minutes ago.

Was it possible that the Welfare Department had spiked his tobacco? It was a terrible thought for him. Even if such a suspicion could be proven, he would find it impossible to quit his pipe. When it came right down to it, his only two pleasures were drinking and smoking. They were enough, too. He wished for no others, could imagine no others that would satisfy him. He knew that some men could please themselves by watching television, or (like Elman these days) reading books and magazines, or playing cards, or dancing, or even generating certain useless types of motion, such as flying model airplanes or pushing tiny trains round and round a track. But none of these pastimes appealed to him. Ollie Jordan's idea of heaven was an unlimited supply of beer in a pleasant spot (the altar stone would do) and a corncob pipe that would never wear through, and angels that brought him tobacco.

Maybe the angels could help with sex now and again. Of course the wings could be a problem. He wondered briefly whether there really was a heaven, but that was too big an idea to consider, and he immediately let it go. Still, the idea of copulating with angels remained, and that was nice. Past copulations did not seem to register well in the memory. Perhaps that was because copulations at their moments did not seem to register in time. It was only the thought of future copulations that fired the imagination, stirred the loins. Time itself insisted on placing the quest for copulation on the horizon, to drive a man—or moose, any critter—to mate and pass on himself. Time was a strange thing.

He thought about the time in his life now missing in memory. Was it possible that one night long ago, a ghost had come into his dream and jerked him out of time, so that he hadn't forgotten that time at all but it had never happened? If time could be so traversed, then was it possible that someday the spirit would return him to the time he had missed? The idea of being jerked about in time seemed reasonable to Ollie, but why this was so was beyond him. He flirted with the notion, until it occurred to him that perhaps he was part of some important mission that someday would become clear. He thought of Willow. Someone had put him and Willow here and kept them together. Had to, else there was no sense to his life at all. It even was possible that whoever it was had recognized the dangers of the Welfare Department, as Ollie himself had, and that they were all fighting in the same army. Ollie thrilled to this idea. But a moment later, it struck him that the reverse was possible. The entire mess of his life and his son's had been established by the Welfare Department, or the evil force that guided that group, for a purpose that had nothing to do with them at all. It was possible that as men controlled the lives of certain rats in laboratories, so did creatures far superior to men control men's lives. This seemed more likely to Ollie than the previous idea, and he was depressed by it. The trouble with staying up all night was that you had too many thoughts, and it was difficult to know which were the good ones. Every man and every generation had different ideas on just about everything. How was one to know the truth? Even the simple pleasures, say the joy of watching a child make a funny face, or the warmth of alcohol coming into one's system, escaped a man's mind because as he felt them, he could not think about them, but could only recognize them after the fact through the distortion of his memory. All a man can know that is certain is his own hurt. But then again hurt was more likely than joy to be twisted by the memory into, say, a presumed lesson of life. He took a drink on the beer. It was like iron in his mouth. He drew pipe smoke deep into his lungs. The pleasure of these things emptied his mind of thoughts, and for a moment he was at peace. At the next moment he was on his feet. He had almost dozed.

"Thought you had me," he said aloud, and the voice was not his. He had dozed. Not long, but just enough for something to steal into his mind, if only for a second, for he was still whole, still himself. So they had spoken for him. So what? They hadn't taken over. He walked to the door and went outside.

"Willow," he shouted, and the voice was his own. "Willow, come home. This is your daddy speaking." There was a vague, indistinct answer, and he recognized his own, mournful echo. A close call. A few more minutes of sleep, and they might have had him.

A star was visible through a hole in the trees, but the moon had long since hidden its face. His fire on the altar stone had died, but there was still a mound of coals, like a bruise. He refreshed the fire, adding some dry pine sticks. He watched the smoke gather about the coals, and then the sticks burst into flames. It was crucial now that he not fall asleep. He fetched his portable radio (Ollie had salvaged it, and Elman had fixed it for him), and placed it on the altar stone to listen. He imagined that the reception was better on the rock. The late-night talk shows were in full swing. People complained about taxes, politicians, ideas of right and wrong; they harped about Puerto Ricans (whatever they were); they harped about Negroes (Ollie knew what Negroes were: men from jungles who were not found in New Hampshire because they couldn't stand the cold); Negroes harped about whites; everybody harped about everybody else; people told stories about being taken up into space ships, about miraculous healings, about strange and wonderful occurrences. One woman said she saw God. She was thinking about leaving her husband, who was hitting the bottle and her, too. God showed up one night while she was searching for her sleeping pills. He (the husband) used to hide them. He (God) appeared in the bathroom mirror and said, "Only believe in me and the wounds of your soul will be healed." He advised her to stick to her husband. The next day the husband quit drinking, and the man and the wife had been living happily ever since.

The story made Ollie sweetly sad and prompted him to make a solemn vow to quit drinking. He wished now he could weep, for purposes of cleansing, but of course he rarely wept—had no facility for it. In his mind's eye, he could see himself and Helen walking somewhere—where? Ah, the fairgrounds—and she was thanking him for rescuing her from the Welfare Department. Her voice was like mountain water—well no, not like water; more like ice-cold beer on a hot day. There was no sense in quitting drinking entirely, he was telling her, but rather a program of moderation was called for. He would sip beer to quench his thirst. She was nodding yes yes yes . . . And the sound on the radio suddenly had gone harsh, and his wonderful thought was fading, and he was angry. He wanted to hurt. He was glad Willow was not here, for if he were he would want to hurt him. He would hit and hit and hit. But this was good: You could not be sleepy and angry at the same time. He heard himself laugh. No, it wasn't himself. Crazy ghost inside. He got up and paced. He wanted to smash something. Step out, ghost, and take your medicine, he thought, but he dared not voice the thought for fear the voice would not be his own. Damn that Helen, he thought. Damn you, Witch. Damn all women. They were, at root, the problem. They nurtured the ghost that haunted a man. The woman's opening was the crack in time through which the ghosts entered our lives.

It was dark, and he wandered in his anger. He could not see his fire. The anger vanished and was replaced with panic. He must run away. Be still, he said to himself. Be still, else they'll find you. He stood absolutely still, and he could feel the sweat form on his brow from the strain. He wanted to wipe it away, but something told him to be still. He stood there for a long time, until he could hear his radio like a thing with a sick, raspy voice. He thought he could hear the voice say, *Save us, save us, save us,* and this calmed him even though he knew the words were from his own mind. He moved sideways a foot, and discovered that his view of the dying fire had been blocked by a large pine tree. He returned to the altar stone. He shut off the radio. He stood, relaxed now, while his fire went dark. He stood until he could feel, more than see, the first faint gray of dawn.

Then he said, "Willow, please come home," and he went inside and fell into a deep sleep on the bed that he had salvaged.

A Day

Ollie Jordan got up at his usual time, about noon. It was a work day, one of the three that he helped Elman with his trash collection route from 1:00 to 5:30 p.m. Elman and Cooty Patterson worked the morning round, but old Cooty was too frail to put in a full day. Ollie worked Monday, Wednesday, and Friday afternoons, and sometimes on Saturday mornings. Elman worked fifty hours a week hauling trash. At night, he struggled with his bookkeeping and with the home lessons that he told Ollie were going to lead him to a high school diploma. On weekends Elman could be found repairing his vehicles, which at the moment consisted of the honeywagon (the money-maker), a pickup truck (his fun vehicle), a ten-year-old Chrysler (to show the world he was Mr. Somebody, Ollie deduced), and a Pinto sedan (Elman said it was a girl friend for the Chrysler).

Ollie tried hard not to hold it against Elman that he was addicted to work. After all, work was only one of two flaws that Elman had, the other being clock-watching. Elman even worked when he was drinking. On Sundays, he could be found sitting on the floor of his shed, a beer at his side, a cigarette burning in the hubcap he used for an ashtray, and on the floor the parts of a machine that Ollie could not immediately identify. Ollie would be appalled by this sight. A man should drink quietly and with dignity. God had invented booze to help a man gather his thoughts. Ollie wanted to say to his friend, "Good God, man! How can you concentrate on your drinking while you are trying to fix an engine?" But Ollie reined himself in. He would not criticize Elman's ways, any more than Elman would criticize his ways: This was in the code of their friendship. Still, the realization of Elman's need to keep working, even as he drank his beer, left just a spot of tarnish on the enormous respect that Ollie felt for him.

Ollie viewed Elman's clock-watching as a less serious but more bothersome flaw. Elman was constantly concerned about getting to a certain place by such and such an hour. He didn't seem to understand that the place would be there no matter when you arrived, and if it wasn't there, why then it didn't make any difference at all. The worst of it was that Elman showed actual annoyance when Ollie was a little bit late for work, say half an hour. This flaw on Elman's part was the kind of thing that eventually could try their friendship, Ollie realized. On occasion he broached the subject with Elman in the hopes of making him see how unreasonable he was. When Elman had made some comment about having to get to the dump before it closed, Ollie had said, "The dump will be there by-and-by."

"How in the name of sweet Jesus am I supposed to do my route tomorrow if my truck is full up?" Elman had asked.

"Dump it in Mrs. McGuirk's woods," Ollie had said.

"Ain't you smart? I suppose I'd have to," Elman had said, but there was not the usual gruff friendliness in his voice. Ollie figured that Elman knew he had been out-reasoned and couldn't take the defeat. This would be understandable, but Ollie wasn't satisfied with his deduction. There was something else, some major difference between himself and Elman that had appeared during the summer. For a second he wondered about whether Elman had been tricked somehow into working for the Welfare Department, but he quickly dismissed that idea. It was just too hard to live with. Rather, he told himself that Elman was touchy in regards to matters having to do with time.

The situation bothered Ollie now, as he walked down to the stream to wash. He didn't like thinking about having to get some place "on time." He didn't like the idea of time being something you had to be on. You could be on a truck or a boat; you could get on somebody's back or his ass. He had even overheard one of Elman's trash customers, the professor feller at the college, mumble something about having troubles with "on we," and although Ollie didn't understand exactly what was intended, the professor's message of weariness was clear. But time just wasn't something you could get on. Who had invented that combination of words, "on time," and for what purpose? Ollie bet there was some evil intent somewhere. Maybe he could ask the professor. "Professor," he'd say, "you got your 'on we' and you got your 'on time,' so what I want to know is . . ." What did he want to know? He wouldn't think of approaching the professor for the answer to a question he didn't have. Maybe he could get the question from Elman, and then he could fork it over to the professor for the answer.

The water was cold in the tiny pool below the tiny falls that flowed from the stream that bubbled out of the granite about one hundred feet through the woods downhill from St. Pete's. It was so cold that on the first day he attempted to bathe in the pool, Ollie had been shocked as if bitten by millions of teeth, and it passed through his mind that the water was really liquid mica formed in the torture chambers of the granite that made up the body of Abare's Folly. He had jumped out, though he knew that the snarling beasts of one's imagination were no reason to be frightened. Since then he only dabbed a little water on his face upon rising. Once every couple of weeks he did build a fire by the pool and boil water for a sponge bath. He hadn't had a real bath since leaving Ike's place and he felt no poorer for the lack.

For a while during the summer, he would drag Willow

down to the pool, and once even risked taking him to the Connecticut River for a bath, but all the excitement sexually aroused Willow, and it made Ollie feel strange to see him in that state. As a result, he had decided to let the boy take care of himself. That decision made him sad and puzzled him, too, until he realized that he wanted very much to bathe Willow. Sometimes, in unguarded moments, he allowed himself the pleasure of the mental image of Willow stripped naked and swimming in the water. Later, the thought of such thoughts horrified him, and he worked at burying them in the caverns of the mind where things were forgotten. Willow thereafter took care of himself, and did a surprisingly good job. He was frequently scruffy from cavorting in the woods, but there was no old dirt caked in the creases of his skin, no faint glisten of smudged body oil, no earth texture to his face, no matted hair, no sign of those who wash not at all. In fact, on occasion Ollie could swear he smelled Ivory soap on the boy, but of course that was impossible. He fancied that Willow was clean, as the wild aninals were clean, that is, in spirit from the blessing of the forest itself and therefore—magically—clean in body, too. He imagined that even he himself was being cleansed by the forest. He continued the sponge baths out of a vague obligation to an old habit, but once winter came it would be too much trouble to bathe and he would quit the routine without regret. After all, bathing served no purpose other than to keep Mrs. McGuirk from talking about you, and since he didn't have any neighbors of her sort—no neighbors at all unless you counted the critters, the trees, the boulders—there was no reason to continue bathing. Still, he enjoyed the walk down to the pool after rising. He could swear he smelled the sun high up in the trees, and by taking the same route every morning, he got familiar with certain objects—a knot dripping jelly out of a wild cherry tree, the glitter of a boulder as the light hit it, some ferns that reminded him of pretty ladies at a square dance. These softened the hard ache of his loneliness.

He sat by the stream for a moment, listening to it as another man might listen to the news on the radio, and then he dipped his hand into the cold water, marveling at it for a moment before he splashed some on his face. Liquid mica. The water ran down his neck and he shivered once. He sat by the side of the pool for a moment and watched tiny sticks and leaves flow downstream. He had everything a man could ask for, except for peace of mind, and now he had even that. It was the morning itself that delivered peace, he thought. (Actually, it was past noon.) War battles, murders, horrible acts against the self, vicious acts against one's fellows—these might occur in the morning, but he bet they were never planned during the morning. The minds of creatures are naturally at peace in the morning, he thought. He should have some coffee and a bite to eat—he must remember to eat more—and be on his way to his job, but it was such a nice day. Maybe he'd just sit here for a while, thinking about how good the coffee would taste. Maybe he'd take a little nap afterward. Maybe he'd take one now. So pleasant here. The sun had touched a patch of pine needles and, just moments ago, had moved on. They were still warm, and he lay among them and shut his eyes. He lay between sleep and wakefulness for two of the most peaceful minutes of his life.

A moment later something told him to open his eyes. Willow was looking at him, his expression full of wonder and leashed strength.

"Damn your ass," Ollie said. "Where have you been? Can't you stay home, like a normal boy?"

It was his usual speech. It meant nothing. He expected Willow to grunt and go off. Instead, Willow smiled at him, like a baby who has just discovered a secret of nature, such as locomotion or the playfulness of light. He sat beside Ollie and put his head on his shoulder. Ollie put his arm around the boy and held him. It was one of those moments that Willow gave, always unexpected, and mysterious in their origin, and very precious to Ollie. The moments always came when he was in a good mood, as if Willow could sense it in him.

"Aren't you glad you came to Niagara Falls Park with your daddy? He's taking good care of you, you know. Look at St.

Pete's. You ever see a house so pretty for the money? You watch, it's all going to be nice here. You watch."

Willow purred. Ollie stroked his head. It was cool. Soon the cold weather would come, he thought, and Willow would need something to cover his head. At that moment, he decided upon a project for the day. He would salvage a hat for Willow. A moment later Willow was gone, and Ollie was opening his eyes again, wondering whether Willow actually had been there or whether he had dreamt him. Anyway it didn't matter. What mattered was the hat. He would get a hat. The thought made him chuckle. The very idea of a hat made him chuckle.

He returned to St. Pete's and heated water on the Coleman stove. He preferred to start the morning with a beer, but that interfered with his coffee need. Someday he'd have to quit coffee. It wasn't good for a man. He knew he should hunt up some food, but that seemed like a lot of trouble. Luckily, he stumbled upon a half-full can of tuna fish that had been opened yesterday and forgotten. He ate the contents, satisfied in his own mind that he had done the right thing for his health, and then he opened the front door to St. Pete's and absently tossed away the can. He checked the fire in the wood stove, not because it needed checking but because he liked the chore. The coals were still plenty hot and he tossed in a few dry sticks. He would let the fire go out during the day, because the sun would warm St. Pete's, and he'd rebuild the fire tonight.

The stove was a simple affair, made from a fifty-five-gallon oil drum. Elman had a welding torch, and one Sunday afternoon he converted the drum into a wood-burning heater. The door was from an oven in an electric stove that had stood in Elman's yard for years. Elman had even installed a baffle inside the stove. Ollie put the stove in because, for reasons vague even to himself, he didn't want anyone other than himself and Willow to step foot on the grounds of Niagara Falls Park. The stove pipe went up at a slight angle through a metal slot Ollie built, with great difficulty, in the roof of St. Pete's. The stove worked very well. It only required Ollie's care to keep St. Pete's warm. Of course it was possible that sparks could escape through the pipe, fall upon the curved plastic roof of St. Pete's, and burn the place down; but, well, he had other more important things to worry about. After all he had built St. Pete's once, and if it was destroyed he could build it again. The stove nestled in a cradle of rocks piled about three feet off the earth floor of St. Pete's. That was Elman's idea. He said that in the winter, a hot fire would heat the rocks in the evening and the rocks would continue to give off heat all night, keeping Ollie and Willow warm even though the fire might burn low in the stove. Although Ollie Jordan had been heating with wood for years, such ideas never occurred to him. Ollie went along with the idea because it was easy, but later he realized that keeping warmth in around the stove for long periods meant he could leave for a day and his beer wouldn't freeze. It was only then that he appreciated the idea of warm rocks.

After he finished his breakfast and coffee, he lit his pipe and took a short walk in his woods, looking for a good place for a toilet. He had considered installing an outhouse, but such places were stinky and unsanitary, and besides they were a lot of work to build. It was better to do such business Willow's way—the animals' way—that is, pick a new place every day, a scenic and private place that also possessed a certain—what should he call it?—a certain feeling of safety, that here for the moment one could not be attacked. After he finished his business, he headed back to St. Pete's, finding Willow dozing in the crook of one of his favorite trees. Another month and the weather would be much colder. Willow would need a hat then—no doubt. Must get a hat for the boy, Ollie said to himself. It was a big task. He'd have to inspect the trash he and Elman collected very carefully. After all, a hat was not a large object, and not commonly found in refuse. Of course, it was the kind of thing that people, out of habit, were apt to leave at the head of the heap. Still . . . still . . . hard work.

"God, you made this world a royal pain in the ass," he said, almost believing that he really was addressing a supreme being that was listening. Well, he'd go to work. God or no God, you gotta have money to buy your beer, he thought to himself. He felt good about making the decision. He felt as though he had made a sacrifice on behalf of world order, or something. As a result, it was only reasonable that he give himself a treat: He'd drink a beer on his way to Elman's. It was necessary for Ollie to justify the beer, because someone had told him, long ago, that the sign of an alcoholic was a man who drank before going to work, but of course a rule could be broken if a man did something to justify a treat. Around three p.m., when they reached Keene on the honeywagon route, Elman would want to stop for coffee, but Ollie knew it would be easy to get Elman to buy a six-pack instead. If Elman did not stop for beer, Ollie would start to get nervous. He didn't like going more than a couple of hours without a beer. To do so was to cheat himself, and the worst crime a man could commit was against his own self. It was best to drink steadily, as God intended. He didn't respect these guys who deliberately built a beer thirst and then drank their day's quota all at once. They were pigs—guys like Pork Barrel Beecher; they were ignorant. You had to drink with some responsibility. After he got out of work, he'd drive to Spofford, gather in the beauty of Spofford Lake with his eyes, and replenish his own stock of beer at Mort's Grocery. He didn't like to stop at the general store in Darby because he didn't want people in town to know that he was still around. The Welfare Department had informers everywhere. On the drive home, he'd drink a beer and eat a bag of potato chips. He liked the feeling of a chip softening in his mouth until he was ready to chew. When he got home, he'd play with Willow—provided Willow was home—and then maybe he'd do a little work. During the summer, when the days were long, he could risk a nap. But these days he dared only doze in a chair to get some rest before the coming of the night.

He left for work, noticing that some clouds were moving in from the west. Fall rain coming. Long rain. He was disturbed. The road that wound up The Folly to Niagara Falls Park was getting worse. During a couple of showers in the summer, water widened the gullies made by his truck's wheels and even washed out in a few places, so that he had to spend a whole day filling in the ruts. He could only patch this road so much. Every rain made the job harder. Once winter came, the road would be impassable. He'd have to park the truck at the bottom of the hill and walk down from the park. Kids might discover the truck and vandalize it, or worse, somebody might report seeing it to the Welfare Department. Even if he got away with leaving the truck parked at the bottom of the hill, there was the problem of hiking up the hill to Niagara Falls Park burdened with groceries and beer. How would he haul all that beer up the hill, through snow and ice and fierce, burning, blue wind? He'd have to get some kind of rucksack; maybe risk taking Willow with him to share the load. He couldn't imagine Elman tolerating Willow on the trash route.

The hopelessness of the situation crashed in upon him and he struggled with the problem in his mind. He could drink hard liquor. Booze accomplished the same purpose as beer, using less liquid. The idea suddenly thrilled him. He loved booze, but had avoided it because of the dangers it posed. Now there seemed to be an excuse to buy it. He could justify booze! His heart beat with anticipation. Slowly, as the truck bounced and slid down the dirt road, the thrill wore off. The booze could destroy him. He knew that. There was no doubt in his mind. In addition, there would be other problems besides lugging booze. He needed winter clothes for himself and Willow, especially boots. He should store some food for those days when the weather would be too bad to leave St. Pete's. How the hell was he going to store food? He remembered that in the old days the Witch kept her vegetables in a root cellar, but digging one of those was a lot of work. He was too busy for such a project. There were other chores that had to be done. The truck needed antifreeze, St. Pete's should be insulated somehow. These were important matters. They must be dealt with. But not now. Not now. Today's chore was to find a hat for Willow. He mustn't let himself get sidetracked. It was best to see a thing through before you took on another thing.

Ollie finished his beer in front of the Cutter place just up the road from Elman's. Using the hook shot he had perfected over the years, he tossed the empty bottle over the cab of the truck into the ditch to the right. He disapproved of throwing bottles on the road because they could cause flat tires. He pulled into Elman's yard and parked the truck on the grass behind the shed so it couldn't be seen from the road. There was only one sign of the fire that had destroyed Elman's house and barn—a huge pile of blackened rubble that had been arranged by a bulldozer, driven by Elman. To Ollie it looked like a church designed by the Devil, and it baffled him that Elman should build such an edifice. But of course it would have violated the code of their friendship for him to raise the subject, so he said nothing, waiting for Elman to explain it on his own. He never did, and to Ollie the result was one of those small, nagging mysteries that plagued a man in odd moments.

Ollie arrived only a few minutes late. He found Howard Elman in the kitchen of the trailer sipping on a coffee, his nose in the news magazine that he treated like a Bible. He was wearing his new spectacles, and he looked menacing to Ollie, like one of those fellows who come to your house and want you to repent. Elenore Elman as usual was not around. The question of where she was never came to Ollie Jordan's mind. The fact was Elenore was hiding in the bedroom, as she always did when Ollie showed up. He made her feel uneasy, as though by totally ignoring her he somehow reduced her essence. Besides, she found him ugly and sickly looking. She figured her life would be better if she just never laid eyes on him.

Elman slapped the magazine, like a man affectionately patting a horse on the rear. "Ollie, the way the world's going, I imagine somebody's going to blow it to smithereens in about thirty minutes," he said in the highfalutin tone he used only when he was going to talk about something he had been reading.

"I don't care," said Ollie.

"Nor I," said Elman, still highfalutin, peering over the glasses now at Ollie. "Before my studies, I never gave current events much thought. I see now I was better off in my ignorance. The more a man knows, the more he's got to worry about. Not that I've been worrying, mind you. It's just that if I was one to worry, I'd be worrying today about what was going to happen in the next thirty minutes. As it is, I know what's going to happen. Either nothing's going to happen, or they're going to blow us up."

"If they blow us up, might be a nice ride sailing along in the sky," said Ollie.

"Except you and I are both going to land right into the hottest spot in hell," said Elman.

Ollie nodded. Elman had a preoccupation with hell. He was always talking about dying and going to hell.

They left a minute later, Elman disappearing into the interior of the trailer. He could hear him shouting (Elman shouted sometimes, even when he was wearing his hearing aid), telling his missus that he and Ollie Jordan were going on the route. They'd make a run later at the Keene sanitary landfill, and he'd be back about quarter to six. For all the world, Ollie couldn't understand why Elman went into there every day to see her. After all, she knew where he was going, knew when he was coming back. What was the point of explaining it all? Oh well, it wasn't his business to criticize.

They left on the route, Elman behind the wheel, Ollie on the passenger side. Elman placed the glasses in a case (he claimed with pride that it was unbreakable), unbuttoned a pocket of his shirt, inserted the case, and rebuttoned the button; all the while he was starting the truck, shifting it into reverse, and backing it out of the yard.

Ollie blew his nose on his fingers and then daintily wiped them on his shirttail. The nose hurt him: It was beginning to act up again. From time to time during all of his adult life, Ollie's nose swelled, reddened, pulsated, and seemed to throw off heat. He had always had this problem, and he accepted it as one accepts any permanent burden.

He resisted the urge to tell Elman he was looking for a hat for Willow. Somehow, he thought he might jinx the search if he said anything. But the quest excited him, took away some of the dreariness of the work. He was very attentive to everything around him. You never could tell when you'd find what you wanted, or even something better. He lapsed into a fantasy of finding a hundred-dollar bill, but in the main stayed alert. They made several stops at houses, working their way toward Keene, but Ollie saw no hats or even cast-off materials that might be made into a hat. But he was patient. The scrounger must be watchful. He could not force events, but only recognize in them the elements that were important to him, like a crow circling above the world, waiting to eat leftovers from, say, a rabbit killed by a fisher cat.

They pulled into a place known to Ollie only as The Club. It had been built in the 1920s by rich people, who later had lost their money, Elman explained. The Cutter woman, Elmer's neighbor who had given him all the trouble, had bought it and turned it into a vacation spot for people from down-country. Beyond that, Ollie knew little about The Club, but he was grateful to its members for contributing a rich lode of refuse. Indeed, he had furnished parts of St. Pete's with some of The Club's castoffs, including a wicker chair with a ripped seat, a small rug that somebody had vomited on, and a supply of plastic cups and glasses, plastic utensils, and foam plates that was so steady that Ollie couldn't help being lulled into a belief that never again would he have to wash a dish. On the grounds was a big house that looked like something out of a movie about the Romans: dozens of shrubs with Marine haircuts, a lawn that went on and on for no apparent reason, some garages and fancy-painted sheds. Still, The Club was in the shadow of a big hill thick with forest, and Ollie felt that the trees were biding their time and one day would take over the place. When the weather had been warmer he watched women in short dresses playing tennis. He couldn't understand why anyone would want to get all tired out hitting a ball. He never did determine whether the idea was to hit the ball back and forth as many times as possible or to hit it so it couldn't be returned. Either way it made no sense. Sometimes after the play stopped temporarily, one of the players would shout the word "love" and a number. That was mysterious. The whole game was mysterious and therefore menacing. He asked Elman why he thought the game was played, and Elman said, "Exercise." But that didn't explain the short white dresses, the elaborate ceremony of it all. Ollie was finally able to dispatch this little problem from his mind by coming up with the conclusion that the game was part of a religious service, such as he had seen that day at the church in Keene.

He found the people at The Club interesting. A lot of them wore bathing suits, yet few of them spent much time in the pool. He had raised this issue also with Elman, who had said, "Sun-worshippers." Ollie had nodded, taking to heart that word "worship." The more he thought about it, the more sense it made: The entire place was devoted to religion. Now many of the minor puzzles about the place were cleared up. The young fellows and gals who waited on the tables on the patio were new in the religion. They had to wear little suits signifying their low status, and they had to wait on the others until . . . well, he didn't know what. Maybe until they did something holy. It seemed logical to him that hats would play a role in the observances of any religious group.

The more he thought about the matter, the more convinced he became that here somewhere at The Club there would be a hat. He imagined that in the past, probably, he had overlooked a number of hats in The Club's trash. After all, when you're not looking for something, you don't find it. He tried to call forth mental images from his memory of The Club in hopes of spotting a hat among them. This effort failed. The images were awash with the green of the lawn of the place, with the strutting behinds of a few of the women he had seen there, with a waiter walking like a duck, with two short white dresses filled with sun-burnt flesh playing at tennis amidst a blue sky that seemed about to fall. Still, he had worked himself up into a state whereby he was convinced that The Club's trash would be littered with discarded hats. Of course, he was wrong. The trash contained all the usual items—the foam plates and cups, slopped food as if drooled from the mouth of a great beast, various paper containers, cans, bottles, newspapers, and a few of what Ollie called "one-time onlys"—a broken plaster cast of a boat that apparently had served as a base for a lamp, a pair of sneakers that weren't at all in bad shape, leftover fish the maggots had got to already, and a box containing dozens of worn tennis balls. But no hats. Was someone playing a trick on him? No hats! Forget it, he told himself. Don't get upset. Concentrate on the business at hand—the trash. He forced himself to consider salvaging what he could. He inspected the items: the sneakers (too small), the boat (too ugly), the usuals (he had plenty in store). Finally, he left with a single tennis ball in his pocket, blurting out, "No hats!" Luckily Elman, who was always fiddling with his hearing aid, had it switched off when Ollie spoke.

Ollie felt betrayed. There was every reason in the world for him to believe that here he would find a hat. No hats! Disturbing. Was it possible that the Welfare Department was toying with him? He didn't like that idea one single bit. Face up to it, he said to himself. Got to be careful. If they knew he was looking for a hat, they most certainly knew a great deal more. They would know where he was living. But how? He hadn't even told Elman the specific location of St. Pete's. Willow! Somehow, they had got to Willow. Had to. No other way they could know enough about his movements to dog his footsteps like this. But how could they have gotten here so soon and removed the hats without disturbing the trash so he would notice? After all, he had just gotten the idea a little while ago. Jesus—dear, sweet Jesus—they were clever. It struck him that if there were a force that cunning, that evil, there must be some counterbalancing force with equal powers on the other hand, else They would have taken over long ago. Maybe They have taken over, he said to himself. Maybe he, Ollie Jordan, was the last one. But no. If They were that powerful, They could have taken him long ago. Therefore, there must be a force for good out there, aiding him. There is a God, he thought. Ollie Jordan's brain boiled with such thoughts for a while and then cooled. He didn't admit to himself that he was wrong, but he did admit it was possible that he had exaggerated the situation. It was getting on toward three o'clock, and he hadn't had beer in a while. Clearly, that was the problem. His mind had gotten away from him a little bit because he hadn't had any beer. But where were the hats?

When they were back in the truck, Elman turned his hearing aid back on, and Ollie said, "Howie, you didn't find no hats in that batch?"

"Nope. Looking for a hat?" he said.

"Maybe."

"What kind of a hat?"

Ollie looked at Elman very carefully. Elman was watching the road. He didn't seem to have an evil intent about him. Yet you had to be cautious.

"A hat for dancing," Ollie said, the words jumping out of his mouth unsummoned.

"A hat for dancing—goddamn," said Elman, giggling. "You want something for the boy, don't you? Something to make him say, 'Gee, wow!' Well, I know where there's such a hat."

"You don't say," said Ollie. He felt a dangerous surge of elation. He must rein it in, lest it gallop off with his good sense.

"The professor's got a hat like that for his prize student," said Elman and burst into laughter.

He explained that Dr. Hadly Blue of Southeast Vermont State College had a prize student who was a scarecrow in his backyard, upon whose head was a hat.

"You ought to know where the hat is," Elman said. "You've been there a million times. It's on the trash route."

Elman described the Blue place, a big, half-torn-apart Cape Cod house with an old about-to-die orchard, bordered by stone walls.

Ollie remembered the house but not the scarecrow. The idea that it had been there all along and that he never had noticed it bothered him. It was as if someone—something—had clouded his mind, deliberately kept the knowledge of the scarecrow from him.

As it turned out, there was good reason why he hadn't seen

the scarecrow. It was shadowed by an apple tree and could just be seen from the road. The only reason Elman must have noticed it was that he was soft for fruit trees and looked over every such tree with all the appreciation—and criticism—of a sportsman sizing up a shotgun.

The scarecrow hung on a cross of 2-by-4s. It wasn't too near the garden, and Ollie couldn't understand how it could scare birds from this spot, but he figured anybody who was a professor must know what he was doing. Ollie studied the scarecrow for a moment, seeing now something familiar about it. It resembled his Uncle Jake, known as Jake the snake, who had walked into the woods many years ago and hadn't been seen since. Maybe the professor had found Jake and hung him up to scare away the birds. The idea amused Ollie, and it occurred to him that being a scarecrow was pretty good work, if you could get it, the kind of work that Jake, who was lazy even by Jordan standards, had longed for all his life. Dr. Blue's scarecrow wore paint-stained blue jeans, a T-shirt, a gray tweed sports jacket with patches on the elbows, and red mittens. His head was made of a pillowcase stuffed with newspapers. Rain, wind, sunlight, and—for all Ollie knew—the moon had shaped his head and given it character, lumpy cheeks, and sagging jowls, but the same elements also had wiped away any remnant of eyes, nose, and mouth. That was Jake, all right. The head was in the shadow of a hat with a huge purple brim and yellow band out of which protruded white feathers. He had wanted something practical, something interesting, but warm for the winter, too. This was a summer hat. The winter wind might blow it off and the brim was so wide a snow storm would weigh down on a man's head. This was not a practical hat. This was a magnificent hat. This was a hat for dancing. Willow would rejoice in it, and it was better to rejoice than to be warm. Accordingly, Ollie decided that this was the hat he had to have for his son. The problem was how to obtain it. He supposed he'd have to sneak up in the night and snitch it. He didn't like such work. That was more up Ike's alley. He didn't much appreciate Ike Jordan as a man or as a relative, but he had to admit he was a good burglar. Ollie had little time to consider the problem, because after he dumped the professor's trash, Elman walked over to the scarecrow to look it over.

"Howie, you ain't going to take that hat in broad daylight, are you?" Ollie asked.

"Ollie, you've been hiding out too long," said Howard Elman. "I ain't going to take nothing. I'm going to ask the professor for it, and if he don't want to give it away, I'm going to try to dicker with him for it."

As they approached the house, they were arrested by a voice. A window was open in the house and Ollie could hear someone speaking in a peculiar kind of conversation. First it seemed as if the speaker were talking to someone else, and then he answered as if he were that someone else. The problem was compounded further by a quality of the voice, as if he were reciting words to a song. Very strange, thought Ollie, and he put himself on guard. Even though whoever was speaking had not heard them come to the door, there was something in his voice that said, "Do not interrupt," and so they stood there at the door for a moment and listened.

"We have Father Balthazar in his room, pacing, wondering why his God has gone," the voice said. "Finally, after an hour at his kneeler, he rises and scribbles in a fury in his secret journal:

> *Father, accept my sacrifice*
> *of these two pears.*
> *I will tie them in a loose bag*
> *to hang from this branch.*
> *They will turn soft and sweet*
> *changing gender as does a season.*

"Huh. Not bad. But do I really need the 'does'? Would Balthazar have brooded over the 'does'? Would you, Balthazar, you randy old curate, you?"

The question that Hadly Blue put to his fictional Balthazar struck home to Ollie Jordan. He didn't know who this Balthazar fellow was, or just what this bossy professor wanted of him, but he sided right away with Balthazar. Ollie was anxious to meet Balthazar. He imagined they'd get along. Maybe Balthazar hunted woodchucks or fixed radios or whittled charms—did something to pass the time while he was the professor's prisoner. Somehow Ollie knew that there was some kinship between himself and this Balthazar; in fact, he thought he could sense the presence of this being.

Howard Elman broke the spell between Ollie Jordan and Hadly Blue's fictional character by rapping loudly on the door.

Moments later they were ushered in by a slim, slouching man with helter-skelter brown hair. He was about thirty-five, and he was wearing blue jeans and sneakers, as if these might preserve an affinity he had with his youth.

"Yes?" he asked.

"Elman," said Elman.

There was a pause, and then the professor said, "Oh, of course, the trash man. Do I need to pay you or something? I'm a little busy. Composing, er, working."

Neither Elman nor Ollie caught the hint, and they walked into the house as if invited.

It was clear now to Ollie why the windows were open. Someone had cranked up the wood stove during the cool of the morning, and now the place was too hot. Ollie glanced into the front room, hoping to get a look at Balthazar. But there was no one in the room. He saw a wood stove and a desk piled with suspicious-looking papers. "Let's go in the kitchen," said Professor Blue. "I'm afraid the living room and my study are overly warm. I had this new stove installed, and I didn't realize how much heat it throws."

It seemed to Ollie that there was more to the situation than the professor's explanation. How was it that a professor, obviously an intelligent person, had overheated his house? He had also made it sound as though someone else had installed the stove, as if he didn't have the savvy—an obvious lie. Most important, what had happened to Balthazar? Was he here against his will? Had the professor hustled him upstairs, away from prying eyes? The answers to these questions were not forthcoming. There was something suspicious going on here.

They sat at the kitchen table. Ollie wished that he could go upstairs. He was quite certain that this fellow Bathazar was being held against his will. Meanwhile, Ollie could see that Elman was about ready to start dickering for the hat. He wished he'd hold off until they could find an excuse to go upstairs.

"What's upstairs?" Ollie asked.

The professor laughed, abrupt and squeaky, like one of those damn birds high up in the trees that Ollie often heard but never saw.

"Right now what's upstairs is a mess," the professor said. "All the plaster is down, swept into a rather impressive Monadnock in the front room. I've put insulation batts and plastic between the joists and rafters, and we're debating, battling might be a better word, over whether to put in Sheetrock or shiplap pine boards. I want the boards. She wants white walls. You know how these domestic arguments go."

Ollie figured Balthazar would be the subject of strife perhaps, the captive of one or the other. He thought of Helen and of the Witch, and of his own Willow.

Elman piped into the conversation. "My idea of hell is working with Sheetrock," he said. "Personally, I'd suggest paneling. Stuff's pretty, it's cheap, and it ain't much trouble to put up, provided you get a jig for your Skil saw. Hell, if you don't like the way it looks, you can always paint it."

Ollie realized that he didn't really want to rescue Balthazar. He had his own Balthazar in Willow. One Balthazar was enough. Maybe the professor worked for the Welfare Department and was using his Balthazar for mysterious and evil purposes. Maybe not. Either way, there was nothing he, Ollie Jordan, could do about the situation. In fact, if he admitted the truth, there was nothing he could do about anything; there was nothing anybody could do about anything. The best a man could do was find himself a hideout, furnish it, and live on.

Elman shifted in his chair. He was getting edgy, ready to

open discussion on the purpose of their visit. He spoke. "Ah, professor . . ."

"Hadly. Please call me Hadly," said the professor.

Howard Elman nearly blushed, like a child brought up to respect his elders suddenly called upon to act familiar. Except of course it hadn't always been so. Elman had been raised in foster homes. He was just now, in middle age, cultivating reverence for those he considered his betters, as if in a way they were kin he owed. This his friend Ollie Jordan could see, and he was struck with a peculiar grief. Soon he would lose Elman, too.

"Well, ah," continued Elman, struggling to manipulate his words so that he would not have to say either "professor" or "Hadly." "We, ah, have come here to, ah, negotiate the, ah, acquisition of your scarecrow's chapeau."

Where in the name of the crazy God who had invented this crazy world did Elman get all those words from? From the things he had been reading, the answer came to Ollie.

"I want the chapeau for my boy," said Ollie, and Elman grinned and nodded, and then both Ollie and Elman were nodding.

The professor seemed confused. "What?" he asked.

"The chapeau," repeated Ollie.

"The chapeau," repeated Elman.

After a pause, the professor said, "I have to admit that I really don't know what you're talking about."

Elman arose from his chair, and Ollie could see that Elman was back to his old self. He walked to the kitchen window, pointed outside, and said, "Professor, we're talking about the hat atop the head of that scarecrow. He don't need to scare no birds, because there ain't nothing left for them to steal that you can use. But we can use his hat, and we come to dicker for it."

The professor burst into laughter.

He had been laughing at them all along, thought Ollie.

"Doncha know," said the professor, breaking into an approximation of the local accent, "that I'd forgotten about it. I mean the garden was never mine. It was hers, my friend Kay's. I'm a January gardener. When the seed catalogues arrive in the winter, I make all the plans for the garden. I even read the *Mother Earth News* at that time of year. But with spring, I find the cold earth and the warm sun irreconcilable anomalies. To put it bluntly: I don't like outside work. I'd rather pull down plaster. Which, as you can see, is what I've been doing. As to the scarecrow, Kay put it up herself back in the early summer to buffalo the birds; whoops, there's a mixed metaphor. She got the hat from the storekeeper—you know, Joe Andarsky? His idea. Just gave it to her. No charge."

Both Ollie Jordan and Howard Elman were looking at the professor with concern, as though they expected him at any moment to have a fit.

"We considered the scarecrow and his, ah, chapeau, the ideal warrior. Keeps the barbarians at bay, kills no one," the professor said, pacing about the kitchen, giggling.

What bothered Ollie about the professor was that he had deep, mysterious ideas. As Willow was an idiot compared to himself, so he was an idiot compared to the professor. So it went, up through the chain of life to . . . where? God? Was it part of some master plan that he should get—or not get—that hat? He pondered the question for a moment, coming up with a pleasing answer to himself. If God—or whatever it was— wanted him to have the hat, he would have the hat. If God did not want him to have the hat, he would not get the hat. If God didn't care, if there was no God, it wouldn't matter whether he got the hat or not. None of the possibilities required a decision on his part. What would be would be, whether it be the hat or Balthazar or anything. His own role was to await events. The issue settled in his mind, Ollie now felt easier about the professor. The important thing now was either to get the hat or not to get the hat, but at any rate to act swiftly, for there was another important element cropping up in this situation: Ollie was feeling thirst for a beer.

As it turned out, there was little need to press the issue, for the professor gave them the hat, laughing all the while.

They were almost on the cutoff road to Keene when the mysterious Balthazar crept back into Ollie's mind.

"You think he's on the up-and-up, the professor?" Ollie asked.

"Eh?" said Elman, turning up his hearing aid. Ollie repeated the question.

"Don't know. Don't know's I give a damn, as long as he pays me first of the month," said Elman.

They drove on toward Keene. The clouds had backed off; it wasn't going to rain. The wild hallucination that is the turning of the fall leaves had passed, and now the leaves were falling. They were, Ollie thought, like ideas that were fine until tried, each one a grief. He could feel the harsh edge of his own intelligence slashing away somewhere in the tenderer parts of his mind, a signal that he needed a beer—and soon.

"Good to have a cold drink on a hot day," he said, realizing as he spoke that actually it was a cool day.

Back in the truck, even before Ollie took the first drink of beer, he felt calm. Ollie drank four beers; Elman drank two. It seemed to Ollie, as he reviewed his day's work and got ready to leave, that Elman gave him a funny look, as one might give a favored dog that had been hit by a car and would have to be put away; but the look vanished in a second, and Ollie forgot it. He had something else on his mind: the hat. It had become a major issue that needed to be mulled over. Exciting. Now he would have something to keep his mind busy during the long night to come at Niagara Falls Park. On the drive home, he deliberately did not look in the hat, smell it, inspect it with his fingers, or even think about it. He didn't want to spend his mental currency on it during the prosperity of day.

He arrived at St. Pete's and Willow had gone, although something of his smell lingered. He had been there only minutes earlier—or so Ollie imagined. Ollie bundled up in his overcoat and built a fire on the altar stone. He drank another beer while he heated a can of beans and a hot dog inside on the Coleman stove. He played the radio for a minute, hoping the talk on it would lift some of the loneliness from him, but the sounds seemed ugly and harsh to him, and he shut it off. The hat lay beside him on some pine needles. He set aside in his mind the idea of beer and took in the idea of a cup of coffee. Instant Nescafe. He heated water inside, made a cup of coffee in a foam cup—wonderful invention; he was grateful—and returned to his place by the altar stone. It was time to consider the matter of the hat. He glanced at it on the ground. It had seemed so purple, so rich on the head of the scarecrow. Now, even in the waning light of a fall day, he could see that it was faded, the band ready to fall off, the feather scraggly. Where had it really come from? Had the hat belonged to Balthazar? Umm. Was it possible that Balthazar had arranged to place the hat on the scarecrow as a sort of signal? Maybe. What signal, then? Think, Ollie said to himself. The hat was Mexican. No doubt about that. What did Mexican mean? Ollie searched his memory for his knowledge of Mexico. "Si senoir," he said aloud. The fire on the altar stone crackled, as if in approval. Ollie laughed. "The Cisco Kid," he said. "Hey, Pancho . . . hey, Cisco." Impulsively, Ollie snatched up the hat and plopped it on his head. It fit. He wished he had a mirror to see himself. He bet he looked pretty fancy. If Helen could see him now. This hat might even impress the Witch. Oh, don't fool yourself entirely, he said to himself. Maybe he ought to keep this hat for his own use. "Willow, you ungrateful bastard," he said aloud, and laughed royally. When he stopped, there was a sudden emptiness, and then he was hearing the fire sputter and gurgle, like a baby.

"Willow! Willow!" he shouted. There was no answer.

Ollie removed the hat and placed it on his lap. He took a swallow of coffee. His mind went blank for a moment, and then he was remembering the scarecrow. It reminded him, he realized now, of Christ hanging on the cross in the church in Keene. He imagined acres and acres of crops, dotted here and there with crosses with men hanging from them. Was that Christ's job as God and man: to scare away the devils so men might grow? He tried to make something of this puzzling image, but could not. Just a thing in his mind, he thought.

Ideas, pictures, memories, emotions popped up in your brain, and you tried to make sense of them, even when there was none to be made. You tried because you tried. The purpose was the trying. That lucky bastard, Willow, Ollie thought. Thinking don't mean nothing to him. All there is of him is want and do.

"Willow!"

Getting real dark out, he thought. I'll be crazy pretty soon. Got to stay awake. Drink the beer in the proper amounts. Keep the fire going.

Ollie now turned his attention to the hat. He felt it, rubbing his fingers into the cloth. With little effort, he punched a hole through it. Another. Oh, hat, all those summer days on the head of the scarecrow, bearing up under the sun and rain, has done you in. Oh, hat, there's nothing to you but the look of a hat. Methodically, Ollie ripped the hat up into little pieces, and then he threw them in the fire, with the band and feathers. The stuff burning had a bad smell. He wished he could cry, but of course he could not, and even if he could, it wouldn't have mattered.

"Willow!" he shouted. "Willow!"

Hadly and Kay

Hadly Blue knew it was going to be a bad day when his superego reminded him of the appalling condition of his desk at the college. On top of the heap was his notebook, full of Freudian trails of personae not worth tracking. Pick up the notebook and read, said his conscience. Hadly did as he was told, coming across some lines written by Balthazar, the main character in the novel he had been working on for ten years. He read aloud:

OCEAN BLUES IN PLENTY

Fears of scarcity seem like an ancient superstition.
Crowds shop instead of breaking windows.
Great rolls of time unravel. Only Darwin complains
that there is vengeance in a stool.
Philosophers favor memorial services for ideas over ideas.
A man named Edgar photographs poisoned fruit.
Darwin writhes. He has not found truth; truth has found him,

and he is awash in his own flogged flesh. Monarch butterflies
begin their journey south on I-91. Bits of flotsam
from a million human wrecks litter the seas. "The earth
has little use for our troubles," Darwin says, and drowns.
Finally, it happens—no more toilet paper.
Mankind up shit creek.

He tossed the notebook onto the cluttered desk and started for class. Outside, two students were playing frisbee. Here was a useful pastime; here one could achieve grace without imploring a god for it. He had no idea what he was going to talk about in class. He had invented the course, "The Murmurs and the Paupers: Symbols in American Culture," as a jest at a committee meeting and the dean had taken him seriously. "The kiddos will love it," he had said. And they had, registering in droves.

Without a smile, without a greeting, without a glance at any of his students, he began to speak.

"The subject today is the secret sharers of Saturday morning. Let us begin with the Roadrunner and Wiley Coyote. I presume that I do not have to explain that the Roadrunner is a bird that lives somewhere in the American Southwest. The Roadrunner looks like the offspring of an ostrich and a Reno go-go dancer. The Roadrunner does not fly. Nor does the Roadrunner walk. The Roadrunner runs. The Roadrunner's vocabulary is limited to a single expletive, *"beep-beep."* The Roadrunner does not feed, does not drink, does not speak, does not feel, does not think, does not breed. The Roadrunner runs. The Roadrunner is free. The gods have decided that the Roadrunner should continue to be, solely on the basis of her being . . ."

Hadly stumbled on until he lost his train of thought. There was a long silence that made him want to flee, and then he continued.

"Let us now look at Wiley Coyote, the adversary of the Roadrunner. Wiley is intelligent—if not wise—emotionally complex, and physically repulsive. He is the ugly American.

Wiley is fixated on pursuing the Roadrunner, that is, in pursuing the American Dream. Being American in temperament, Wiley tries to catch the Roadrunner using mechanical contrivances. In fact, Wiley is a mechanical wizard of the Rube Goldberg variety. His machines are elaborate and interesting, but they don't work the way they are supposed to. Indeed, they seem to have minds of their own.

"What happens if Wiley catches the Roadrunner? The cartoon leads us to believe that Wiley will have the Roadrunner for a meal. But there are also vague sexual innuendoes. Wiley in his single-mindedness and the Roadrunner in her teasing often resemble courting creatures. One way or the other, if Wiley catches his prey he must consume her and die in a last communion. But of course he will not catch her. The myth will not allow him to. Ultimately, the purpose of the American Dream is to perpetuate the American Dream."

The sound of a doorknob turning distracted Blue and the class. Late student, he thought. It was bad form to chew out a student for something so trivial as being late, but today Hadly felt mean. When the door was half open, Hadly wheeled toward it and shouted, "As T.S. Eliot said, 'Time—time is the enzyme."

But it was not a late student who came in. It was the dean.

"Don't let me interrupt—I'll only stay a second," he said and sat down.

Dean Aimsley Jacobs had been at Southeast Vermont State College for a year, and during that time Hadly had the feeling that he resembled someone he knew. Now he realized who that someone was, the cartoon character Elmer Fudd.

"We will now turn our attention to one of the great arch-villains of our culture—Elmer Fudd," said Hadly, thinking as he spoke: My God, how am I going to back that up? "As most of you know, Elmer Fudd is to Bugs Bunny what Wiley Coyote is to the Roadrunner. But there are differences. There is a kind of existential suffering in the coyote's life of frustration. It is as if he knows that the Roadrunner is an illusion that passes through tunnels painted on rock walls, knows that she is better than he is—his better half—but he goes on anyway in pursuit. There is no such redeeming quality in Elmer Fudd. Elmer is rich enough to afford to buy his food, and thus he does not need rabbit stew. Nor is Elmer driven, as is our coyote, by psychological forces in his pursuit of his game. Shooting rabbits is merely a hobby with Elmer.

"And, too, there are profound differences between Bugs and the Roadrunner. Bugs survives because he has keen wits. Bugs is a realistic ideal of what every American male aspires to. He's smart, without being intellectual; he's a master of one-upmanship; he is mentally stable and carefree; he has a good sense of humor; he has no guilt. In short, Bugs is Wiley Coyote after twelve years of classical psychoanalysis."

Hadly's mind went blank. He put his hands behind his back and paced, trying to gather his thoughts, any thoughts. Finally, unable to utter a single word, he went to the blackboard and started to draw. As if his hand were directed by some alien force, Hadly found himself completing a fair likeness of the head of the dean.

"There's our enemy, yours and mine," Hadly said. "Now is there anyone here who can tell me who or what Elmer Fudd symbolizes?"

"Is it the AMA, or Boeing?" guessed a student.

"Don't we wish," said Hadly.

The horror went on for Hadly. The class erupted into what he considered to be the lowest form of human interaction—the classroom discussion. When it was finally over, Hadly was spent. He had nothing more to say. But miraculously, the allotted hour had passed, and he only had to gesture toward the door to get the students to file out. Then the dean had his hand on his shoulder and he was saying, "Come to my office at once."

Well, thought Hadly, the ax is going to fall. His chance for tenure was effectively reduced to zero by his performance today. He felt almost relieved. Really, he didn't belong in teaching. What wounded him was that his students did not share his love for literature. He therefore felt tender, vulnera-

ble to their indifference and armed himself in the usual way—
by constructing defenses of cynicism, of parody, of seeming
unconcern. He betrayed his beliefs to save his sensibilities. He
wanted more than anything for someone to stop him from this
burlesque of his own knowledge. Now, finally, the dean was
going to do the job. "At last—" he said aloud, as he headed for
the dean's office. By the time he reached the door he was calm,
at peace with himself for the first time in weeks.

"Great stuff, Blue—congratulations," said the dean, as he
grasped Hadly's hand and shook it like a war hero's.

"What? It was nothing. It was air." said Hadly, stunned.

"Brilliance and modesty, too," said the dean. "Admirable.
But watch out. This is not an age for the modest. The modest
get devoured. But no, don't listen to me. You're doing fine
without old Aim. You just keep firing culture shots. They'll be
heard 'round the world. Seriously," said the dean, taking a seat
behind his walnut-top desk, folding his hands, "we're in a new
era in the colleges, and you seem to have grasped the bull by
the horns in midstream. The old Liberal Arts curriculum
is out—defunct—dead—kaput—kung-fued by television and
multi-media. These kids today, they don't care about Spenser
and his fairy queens. Who does, really? Unless it's 40 percent
of the population of Frisco, if you know what I mean."

The dean winked. Hadly found himself smiling.

"They need something that's relevant," the dean went on.
"Between you and I, they need something that they think is
relevant, else they'll register at somebody else's Podunk U,
the bills won't get paid, and we'll all be teaching Am-Lit at
Jefferson High some place in Indiana.

"The thing these professors don't understand is packaging.
But, boy, you do. You're the best facilitator I've ever seen.
You had those people eating culture out of the palm of your
hand. What we need is more courses like yours. What say you
package me a proposal for a curriculum based on Contempo-
rary Culture? I'll write the grant.

"I'm sure—you sly, ambitious dog, you—that you know
we're shopping around for a dean of curriculum development.

Why you've waited this long to apply, I don't know, but now's the time. Frankly, Blue, just between you and I, I want somebody in that job that I can get along with, somebody who thinks like me, somebody with vision, somebody, ultimately, who gets to the lunch bucket on the same wave length as me. Comprendy? Course you do . . ."

The rest of what the dean said was lost upon Hadly. It had struck him that if he were named a dean he wouldn't have to teach.

"I was thinking about applying, but I'd hate to leave the classroom." Hadly lied.

"Admirable. I know how you feel. How can you crank out the feedback if you don't get any input? I think we can arrange to let you keep a hand in the academic pie. You'll want to teach, maybe one course?"

Hadly arrived at the farmhouse about three o'clock. Kay was not home yet. It seemed to him, suddenly resentful, that she conspired not to be home when he had troubling things to say. She saved her sympathy for her work, which was terribly taxing, he had to admit. He struggled to hang on to his resentment, knowing that it was a shield for some anxiety waiting to sift down upon him. She was calculatingly sensitive, a classic liberal, pulling up mankind to proper philosophical heights by the hairs of the screaming poor, her capacity to love tied to altering genetic defects through social and psychological engineering. But he began to lose his grip on his resentment when he saw her jeans thrown over a chair. The moment she got home, she would tear off her skirt and put them on. On the hip pocket, she had sewn in red thread the word "Walrus." Sometimes she would whisper to him in the morning when she knew he was half asleep: "Walrus loves Hadly." He would find scraps of paper throughout the house that appeared to be messages to her muse: "Walrus will water her plants today!" "Walrus must buy toilet paper and Tab." Ultimately, his resentment of her was resentment of himself. The problem was he believed her to be superior to him. She had brain power; she had health; she had manageable emotions; she had big ideas for the species; she had beauty to match even wild creatures. If he resented her in any true sense, it was because she knew so much without reading. "When I get an urge to read I know it's time to do something," she would say, hardly realizing that as she spoke the words she was wounding his manhood, for his genitals were wired to his cerebral cortex. How could you explain something like that to a woman?

The solitude of the house was suddenly upon him. He wished she'd get home. He was not a man who knew how to fill free time. All he really liked to do in life was read, screw, drink, and chit-chat. But he had to prepare himself for these activities, and currently he had prepared himself for talk with Kay—and she was not here. What to do? At least in the old days he could smoke, but he had scared himself out of that habit. If Kay were here she would sew something, or sweep the floor, or make a long distance call—her only vice. Hadly looked out the window. Fall was declining into winter, as grimly dignified as a politician convicted for bribery. He turned on the radio, but reception on the public stations was not good. He settled for one of the Keene AM stations. "Dee-dum, dee-doo, dee-dum," he started humming, roughly in tune with that famous rock song, "Bamboo Eating Our Yard." In an age in which music appreciation had replaced godliness, Hadly could take music or leave it. But he played to the hilt the role of the music hater, because he noticed that it disturbed his friends. From their concern, their unease, somehow he extracted a feeling of power, a whisper's worth of influence to the ear of the mover of the universe.

He was considering, with loathing, putting up Sheetrock in the back room when he got the brilliant idea to take a tub bath, knowing it would trigger in him a desire to read. He sat reading in the tub, keeping the water hot with his big toe on the faucet, sipping claret from a wine glass that he had taken in a fit of familial kleptomania from his mother's dining room in Syracuse. For an hour and a half, he was at peace with his world.

Kay arrived home at five o'clock with the good-natured

outburst of a spring day. She opened the door to the bathroom, kissed her index finger, and flicked the kiss at him.

The serpent of a draft slithered in and wrapped its coils around Hadly's shoulders.

"Close the door," he said, annoyed with her, annoyed with himself for getting annoyed, annoyed on a secondary level at her for breaking into his easeful mood like the Gong Show coming on the air as you open a letter from a friend visiting Florence, Italy.

Predictably, she fanned the air with the door several times. He threw some water at her, and she shut the door and broke into giggles. Soon she changed into her jeans, she was barefoot, she had unbuttoned the top two buttons of her blouse, she had shaken out the tight, social-worker bun of her hair so that now it fell like water the color of pine boards turning gold. Instantly, his annoyance vanished. Meanwhile, hers came forth.

"Why don't you put the toilet seat down?" she asked, lowering both the seats and sitting.

"Why should I? What difference does it make?"

"It's just good household order, that's all."

"I can see it now," Hadly said, assuming the flip tone that made him master of his classroom. "Sir Thomas Crapper dating Emily Post: 'What you think, Miss Emily, of my new invention, the crapper?' says he. 'As the French say, wee or non keep it flushed; in good society, both seats down, sill voo pleh,' says she. 'Sill voo pleh, me arse,' says he."

"I wasn't talking about etiquette," Kay said. "I was talking about order."

"I'll keep the seat down, if you keep the door closed," he said.

They both laughed at the absurdity of this bargain that, because of their particular natures, could not be.

"How did it go today?" she asked.

"Pulled through," he said, indicating that he didn't want to talk about it, not now anyway.

She tweaked the hairs on his chest, took his glass, and returned with a refill. She had poured a Genesee ale for herself. He climbed out of the tub, allowed her to towel him dry, and they both knew what that would lead to.

Afterwards, Hadly sipped the wine, Kay pulled on the ale. They lay in bed together, each hungry, each lazy, each waiting for the other to cook dinner. Finally, it was time for one of them to make a move.

"How many hours did you work today?" asked Kay.

He wasn't going to fall into that trap. "Every single one of them so far. The day is never done for a teacher," he said with an exaggerated sigh. "There is always something to find out and someone ignorant to pass it along to. The only time I can really relax is when I hear the pot boiling on the stove, the cook whistling serenely."

"Real work?" she asked coldly.

"Four hours, but I had lots of angst," said Hadly.

"You thrive on angst," she said drily.

He felt a surge of rage. How dare she not take him seriously.

There followed a moment of silence in the room. Hadly was aware now of the sounds of wind outside, mindless in its music as debaters in their rhetoric. It couldn't last between Kay and himself, he thought. The invisible third person that the two of them created was too strong, too strange; it was like mercury—beautiful, rare, and you wanted to touch it, but if you tried to touch it, you could not touch it, for it would spatter. Someday they would do something ugly to each other. He tried to imagine something ugly, to prepare himself for that day.

"What would you do if I hit you?" he asked.

"I'd murder you in your sleep."

"Of course, you wouldn't. You'd bring me to court, squeeze my balls with the help of a feminist lawyer from Cambridge. Still, that's pretty good—murder me in my sleep—I like that."

"I got it from one of my clients. Helen Jordan?"

"Her former man, Ollie Jordan, was here, you know, with the trashman. Strange pair," Hadly said.

"Yes, so you told me. You gave them my scarecrow's hat," Kay said, making it clear with her tone that she hadn't forgiven Hadly for that transgression.

"Ollie Jordan—he used to beat Helen?" Hadly asked.

"Not with regularity," Kay said. "It seems she had another common-law husband before Ollie, and he used to beat her. When she took up with the Jordan creature she promised herself—and laid it right on the line to him—that if he ever hit her she would . . ."

"Murder him in his sleep."

"Why do you always interrupt me?" she asked.

"Because I love you."

"Well, I don't love you."

"Why are you always trying to wound me?" he asked.

"Because you won't answer my questions."

"I meant it—because I love you. You can always tell a couple when they've gone beyond the courting stage because they interrupt each other. It's a sign of stability in the relationship . . ."

"You mean 'he' interrupts 'her.' "

Hadly smiled at Kay, intending to indicate his triumph over her in the conversation, since she had just interrupted him, but he discovered that she was not looking at him, that she was lost in her anger. Here, too, he was dangerously close to failure, he thought.

He twisted and turned in the bed, keeping his back to her, hoping to capture her concern. He was successful.

"You had a bad day, didn't you?" she asked.

"Pretty crummy."

"What are you going to do now?"

"Get out of teaching."

"No, I mean right at this moment?" she asked.

"You don't care if I get out of teaching?"

"Maybe I'll care after I have something to eat."

She had won, maneuvered the situation so that he must cook supper. He went downstairs, put a pot of water on to boil, crumpled up some hamburg and onion, and started to brown them. He also opened one of Kay's ales. He liked to drink when he was cooking. It took the edge off his boredom. When the water was boiling, he added spaghetti to the pot. He used to add salt to the pot, used to add salt to everything, but not these days. Salt had replaced sugar "as the thing you like that can kill you that you can do without." So they had cut down on salt—for the while anyway. Modest denial with a health purpose: such was an acceptable middle-class form of low-grade suffering roughly equivalent as a glistening for the soul to kneeling on hard benches by the women of Spain. When the meat was browned, he added the Prima Salza, and lowered the heat to simmer. Now he could relax a bit before the meal was cooked. Oh, he should make a salad, but he could easily con Kay into that job. He would tell her that he didn't want any, and she would gather some greens from the refrigerator on the vague philosophical premise that a meal needed balance. In the universe, only the inner ear cries for balance, he would say. In the end, he would eat most of the greens. He stirred the spaghetti with a fork to separate the strands and then sat down in the living room with his briefcase to correct a few quizzes before dinner. But he didn't have the heart for the job. He sat there, abstracted for a moment, and then he was seeing in his mind's eye Ollie Jordan and his terrible mouth of black teeth, the man holding his prize, the hat that Kay had gotten from the storekeeper, a hat that apparently wandered from scarecrow's head to scarecrow's head. The image inspired him to write some lines on behalf of his fictional Balthazar:

> *The sea, in her gift for composition,*
> *Has made a place, if not a self,*
> *For that rock, that kelp.*
> *Thus I am unconcerned*
> *That my hat has blown away,*
> *That the gulls are laughing:*
> *"There is less of him than usual."*

He closed the notebook gently, like a priest his missal. "Oh, Kay, I love you," he said.

"What did you say?" she shouted from upstairs.

"I said, dinner is ready."

Winter

One December night, a cold, raw rain snuffed out Ollie's fire on the altar stone. Shivering, Ollie retired to St. Pete's. Willow arrived about midnight, smelling of soap, it seemed. Ollie slapped him, only once but very hard. "Where have you been?" he asked. Willow burst into tears. Not like him, Ollie thought. The animals do not cry over pain. The animals cry only over loss. The boy went to sleep in his nest near the stove, and Ollie sneaked over to his side and kissed him on the cheek. Willow did not wake. Not like the animals to sleep so soundly, Ollie thought.

Ollie Jordan was weary. Suspicion was dragging him down. He built up the fire in the wood stove and sat down in the easy chair. He lit his pipe and sipped a beer. Soon, the warmth from the stove came over him like a caress, and he dozed off. He dreamt that he had died. Sitting on a boulder was Howard Elman. "Here we are in white hell," Elman said.

At that moment, he woke. The gray light washed over him like an ocean wave and he heard himself cry out. In the next moment, he realized that it was morning and snowing out, that the plastic roof of St. Pete's had nearly collapsed with the weight of snow, that Willow was gone. Ollie bundled up in his winter clothes, but he could not find his mittens. It was all he could do to clean the snow from the roof, and at one point the plastic broke and the snow came into St. Pete's. His hands were numb by the time he had repaired the damage. He cast his eyes about for familiar objects and found them transformed. All the marks that he had left in the forest, the hundreds of bottles and cans and paper plates and foam cups and decayed food that had fed a horde of forest rodents were now covered with snow. Where before the altar stone seemed like a table around which men might chat and drink, now it resembled a jagged white anvil. He felt like a stranger here. He found the soft cups of Willow's footsteps. They went off on one of his regular trails and vanished. In the afternoon the snow stopped falling and the wind started blowing. Willow came home early that night wearing gloves and galoshes. The boy was a resourceful thief all right, but one day he was going to get caught. Ollie worried about him. He also worried about his beer. He had only a three-day supply. He stoked up the stove and moved the beer closer to it. That night the temperature dropped well below zero.

When dawn came, the air was still, and Ollie could hear the snow falling out of the trees, like dead men dropping from gallows out of a dream. He had it in his head that he could drive to town and get some supplies (beer and mittens). One look at the truck in the snow told him that was impossible. Even if the truck could battle its way down the hill through the drifts and the ice, it would never get back up again. It was stuck here until next June, after mud season. Still, he tried. The engine would not start. "Battery's pooped out, Willow," he said, even though Willow was gone. He lifted the hood and discovered that a dead battery was the least of the vehicle's problems. The engine block had split. He had never gotten around to adding antifreeze. He returned to St. Pete's dragging his feet through the snow. He was breathing hard and he was shaking. He warmed his hands by the wood stove, while cold drafts crept along the sweat on his back. It was blazing hot as he faced the stove and cold as loneliness when he turned away. He opened a beer, lit his pipe, and sat in the easy chair. As the alcohol took hold in his system, he began to feel curiously offended and yet grand, too. It was as if winter were a conspiracy against him alone.

He sat in the chair a long time, his mind searching about for the solution to a problem as yet undefined. It was not until he had finished three beers that he realized that something else besides the seasons had changed. His charm was gone. He knew in an instant that Willow had taken it for some secret purpose

"Willow," he said, addressing the woodstove, "you took my luck away," and he opened another beer.

Ollie Jordan dropped a nickel in the kettle. The Salvation Army bell ringer said thank you but never looked at him. He liked her cool professional air. He liked the writhing light of her eyes behind the thick glasses, and he liked the way the deep blue uniform made her pale skin resemble a bottle of booze. He wanted to warm himself by her. Now he heard the carolers singing at the bandstand on Central Square. He wondered whether God spoke to them. What did it matter? God speaks to all of us, at his bidding, of course. He laughed aloud for the street to hear. He was mocking them. He knew the joke. They'd find out. When they did, they'd remember that man in Keene. Not that he was fooling himself into believing they would remember *him*. But they would remember a man like him, a man laughing out of pain at what he knew, and they would not be laughing. Poor fools. They think God loves them. They'll find out. God doesn't love; God requires love. If you don't give God love, he turns into the Devil. God and the Devil are two minds of the same One.

The carolers stopped. Now he heard the traffic sounds, at once oddly menacing and reassuring, like the breathing of some sleeping enemy. He walked on. The cold of the city street was a nasty thing, he thought. The cold of the deep woods was softer. Just yesterday, he had heard God say, "Lie down in my cold and sleep." Or maybe that had been the Devil speaking. No matter. Same difference. The trouble with cities was they didn't know what to do with snow. They pushed it off the streets, carted it away as though it were something to be ashamed of, or let it lie there in long chunky rows to get dirtied up by farting motor vehicles. God did not mean snow to be moved except by his own forces of wind, rain, and sunshine. Ollie was singing now, "Hail, hail, the gang's all here, what the hell do we care? Do dum, dee dum. Hail, hail" . . . the song drifted away.

These moments of pursuit were not so bad anymore, he thought. They weren't good exactly, but tolerable. More than tolerable, actually. They were . . . fun. So much of his life these days was spent sitting, waiting. God did not speak to the man on the move. God spoke to him who stayed put. This was the lesson that Ollie had learned, isolated for days on end on Abare's Folly. The problem was God spoke so rarely. Ollie got lonely, he got tired, he got bored just waiting. Not that he would tell God that he was bored. God probably knew anyway, so why bring up the subject? God may know all, but he was busy like everybody else, what with all those stars out there full of beings grunting for attention, and he probably pushed the things he knew around in his almighty mind so that while he knew all, all his business didn't necessarily get his attention all at once. Of course it was in areas of mind temporarily unoccupied by God where the Devil could do his work. But the Devil, too, was overbusy—as evidenced by the unspeakable evil of the world—and, like God, he couldn't be everywhere there was an opportunity, either. Thus it was that most men, even ones such as himself who were marked both by God and the Devil, spent most of their lives waiting for God to speak and the Devil to act.

The latest pursuit had started early in the day, which was odd because usually the Devil preferred the night shift. Ollie had been studying Willow's tracks in the snow. He was certain that if the tracks could be read, Willow could be understood. So far Ollie had been unsuccessful, but there was something about the way the tracks paused here and there, turned back on themselves briefly, and then leaped back into the path—that is, into the appearance of purpose—that led Ollie to believe that Willow was mocking him. The pursuit came while he was on his knees examining some suspicious lumps of snow. It came as it always did these last couple of weeks, with a whisper, *out there.* He had never been able to figure out whether the whisper was a warning from God or merely incompetence in his pursuers. He knew from the start that the pursuers were agents from the Welfare Department, but it took several nights of deep head work to determine that his true enemy was the Devil himself, that the Welfare Department was just one small agency of the Devil.

The thing to do now was to remain calm. If he ran, they would hear his panic in the snow, for such was the way of the Devil's military men. On the other hand, if he pretended to be unaware, they would sweep over him because he was weaker than they. He must stay on the move constantly, keep out of the darkness, remain alert. He had made his way to the road, skirting St. Pete's to keep the pursuers away from his home. He was fairly certain that Willow was in cahoots with the Welfare Department, in fact that Willow had betrayed him, taken his charm. Still he worried about the boy. Although he could fear his son for what he had become, he could not hate him. Indeed, his love for him was greater than ever, if the wound from the loss of love from Willow was any evidence. When he got to the highway, Ollie relaxed. They wouldn't dare attack along a public road. Ollie figured he had the upper hand now. His plan was to keep moving, to stay in the light. He knew from experience that they would tire and call off the chase. Soon he was able to hitch a ride to Keene.

He hurried to Railroad Street, a fishhook-shaped lane that left Main Street and twisted onto Church Street, where Ollie had lived for several years as a boy. He headed for a great red brick building that once had been the Princess Shoe Company. Here the Witch had worked before she discovered she could make more money on her back than on her feet. Ollie could see himself now as a small boy standing outside the shop on a summer night waiting for her to get out of work, fearing that someone would make him go inside to face the heat, the noise, the smell that made him think of tortured flesh, the darkness even among the light, like a dream-curse, the slamming of metal parts that reminded him of the sex acts of adults that he had witnessed as a child, the *whirry, whirry, whirry* of great belts on spinning shafts that he believed then were the thinking parts of a huge evil being. Even then he had a mind that thought too much, a mind that recognized that there were evil forces moving across the earth sure as weather. But the shoe factory had changed. Somehow the evil had been driven from the building. In place of the shoe factory there now were small stores, crafts shops, and silent businesses. The smell of sweat and tormented leather was gone. The machines themselves were gone. It was so quiet in the building you could hear echoes and the padding of your own feet. Good had come to the Princess Shoe Company, he thought. And he looked for his main piece of evidence at the northwest corner of the building where now there was a state liquor store.

To Ollie this plain box of a room, white and blue with neon lights, was like a greenhouse with the bottles so many flowers blooming from the shelves. What he liked best was the color of booze, the soft, clear pools of vodka and gin, the browns of whiskey like morning light on tree bark, and the sweet reds, the silly greens, the medicinal yellows, and even the snobby pink of wines. He pushed aside in his mind his fear of pursuit and spent a good long time browsing in the liquor store, touching this bottle or that, marveling at the design of the labels, sighting through the liquid—long drink for the eyes.

Actually, he knew beforehand what he was going to buy— two quarts of Uncle Fred's Vodka. Ollie Jordan might like to admire, to dream, but when it came to getting his liquor he was a practical man. He might not know arithmetic too well, but he knew that the best buy in booze could be determined by a never-fail formula that included relationships of amount, proof, and price. Once he had said to his friend Howard Elman, before Elman had skipped to the other side, "Some stays and some goes, and all of it you got to respect like the mad daddy that beats your behind, but ain't none of it got the wherewithal of Uncle Fred." Elman had argued that he liked the taste of good bourbon, and Ollie had only smiled, as one smiles at a child. He knew that taste means nothing. If it was booze, it tasted good.

Ollie left the liquor store with a quart of Uncle Fred's Vodka in each of his overcoat pockets. He was now almost broke, and still he had not bought any food. Nor did he expect to have any more money soon. True, he could work a few days for Elman, but that would leave him open for attack from the Welfare Department. Elman was part-time evil, part-time crazy these days, and it was impossible to know when he'd snap. He didn't hold it against Elman. He didn't hold anything against anybody anymore. He had just recognized that the world of men was a battleground controlled by other beings. Most people were drawn into the struggle without their knowledge. They believed they were working for themselves, when actually they were unwitting soldiers of the Welfare Department. Others lived good lives under the blessing of God, but usually they were praying all wrong to begin with and were blessed only because of God's good graces, or perhaps his sense of humor. Hard to tell which. Ollie figured that his own advantage—and the reason he was being pursued—was that, in the purity of the forest, he had stumbled upon some basic truths that men were not supposed to know. He was a threat to the evil forces, and perhaps even to the good forces. He was himself a third force. If he could reclaim the loyalty of Willow the two of them might be able to wield some of that force. But as things stood now, Ollie felt like a halved man. Without Willow he was, literally, not quite all there. Indeed, without Willow, Ollie was not even certain of the nature of the force within him. Oh, they were so clever in getting to him through Willow. In a way, he should feel flattered. They had been trying to destroy him for years, most recently with the onslaught of winter demons, but he had always withstood them. Even now, in pursuit, he was confident of escape. Never mind that his hands shook, that they had sicced him with a fever. He had kept moving, and now that he had his booze, he would be free of them for a while. They would not have pursued him with such vigor if they didn't fear him. Of course in the end they would win. That was determined when they had gotten to Willow. Still . . . still . . . you never knew. Maybe he had a chance. Certainly, his new and daring use of booze had strengthened his mind.

All his life Ollie had been a beer drinker, afraid of falling victim to the perils of hard liquor. What a fool he had been. Winter had come and changed him, changed how he must live. Without a vehicle it was now a day's work just to get down and back up The Folly and hitchhike to and from Keene. It didn't make sense to go to town but twice a week. Climbing the hill was difficult enough carrying groceries, never mind two cases of beer. He knew. He had tried it. Impossible. Necessity had made him face reality. It was a peculiar feeling for him, and it had summoned the memory of a similar feeling from long ago, a million years, it seemed: He was with his daddy in a canoe, and he could hear a rushing noise that he thought was in his head, and his daddy had said, "Those are the rapids below"; or perhaps he, Ollie, was the daddy, and he had spoken the words to Willow. He didn't know. The memory was all broken up, as impossible to put together as a shattered bottle. He needn't have worried. Booze was good. In fact, he had discovered that a cocktail of booze and hard-winter loneliness opened the door to certain truths. He scoffed at beer now. Beer was for common folk and trolls, which in Ollie Jordan's mind was a derogatory word for an ordinary fisherman. You made a septic tank of yourself when you drank beer. The beer drinker was nothing but a mouth and a tired bladder. With beer, to get the proper effect, you had to drink constantly. The better way was with booze. But you could not drink booze as you drank beer, a little at a time all the time. It would make you alternately drunk and sick. Slow death. The way with booze was to lay off it for a few days, put up with the dreary passing of time, and then drink steadily for two days straight. The trick was to get past the drunken stage. You had to drink yourself sober. It was only then that you could see the true shape in the true light of the things inside your mind.

He meandered up Railroad Street, his hands in his overcoat pockets clutching the vodka bottles, like some outlaw of old enjoying the comfort of the guns in his belt. The problem now was to find a safe, comfortable place to drink. He figured he'd start at Miranda's. He'd order a draught beer, like any troll, and pull on the vodka during trips to the bathroom. "Hail, hail, the gang's all here . . ." he half-sang, half-mumbled, staggering down the street as if already under the influence of alcohol.

Ike Jordan was parking his new Dodge pickup in the city lot between Railroad Street and Roxbury Plaza when he heard the voice of his half-brother Ollie. He barely recognized the man. Ollie Jordan had grown gaunt and bent. The stubble of his beard was a dirty gray and brown. His overcoat was in tatters, and he hunched down inside it like a man hiding out from himself. At one point he removed his hat, inspected the insides, and returned it to his head. His hair resembled a nest constructed by a messy bird. He looked ten years older than the last time Ike had seen him, and it was evident from his complexion that he was sick. There was something comical, yet frightening, about his eyes, his movements. He looked like Harpo Marx with cancer. Ike Jordan thrilled. It was clear to him that Ollie had failed in his life, and from that failure Ike now found himself drawing strength. He decided to greet Ollie. He wouldn't demand his beer back, or anything like that. He would just make small talk, tell him about his new truck, about the vacation he and the missus planned to take to Bermuda, about his son enrolling at the technical school in Nashua. Not that Ollie would show any jealousy. He was too clever for that. But Ike figured his achievements would grow in the grubby earth of Ollie's mind and, Ike hoped, blossom

into painful boils of envy. He got out of the truck, slamming
the door. He decided now that, after all, he would demand the
beer that Ollie had taken from him.

Just then Ollie turned toward him, and Ike was looking full
into his face. The face shone in the sunlight like a knife blade;
it was a terrifying, even murderous face. It was a face up from
hell. Ike could not look upon it. A moment of panic swept over
him. Had Ollie seen him? He didn't think so. The mind behind
the face was preoccupied. The eyes were focused beyond him.
Ike reached behind him, slowly opened the door of his pickup,
slowly got back in, and slid his body down out of sight. He
waited a couple of minutes and peeked over the window. He
could just see Ollie walking up the alley between Goodnow's
Department Store and Junie Blaisdell's Sport-O-Rama. Now
that Ollie's back was to him, Ike felt his courage rejuvenating.
Perhaps he would holler out to Ollie, call him on his crimes.
But what if Ollie ignored him? What then? Chase after him?
Ridiculous. Let it pass, he told himself. Swallow your pride. It
was only beer he took from you. You've got more important
things to consider. So he had. Ike Jordan was laying plans to
burglarize the Clapp place in Darby.

At the alley, Ollie Jordan paused, listening for a moment for
evidence of evil forces in the area, such as muffled voices or
radio music. He heard only the automobile traffic behind the
buildings. He uncapped Uncle Fred and drank. The booze
went through his system like electricity, and he was hearing
the traffic again. The noise, like breathing, reminded him of
the sound of being in his mother's arms. The emotion, the
gentleness of it, made him laugh cynically. "Almost got me
there," he said to the Devil. Gentleness came from your
mother, and he had never had a mother, had come out of the
dirt like a weed, determined to grow, if undeserving.

He walked up through the lot beside Blaisdell's to Roxbury
Street and turned left. It wasn't until he had reached the very
steps of his favorite bar that he realized his pursuers had
gotten here first. The yellow sign, rusting red at the edges,
that said "Miranda's Bar" was gone. Miranda's itself was gone.

In place of the dirty window-front, with the broken statue of the half-naked Indian sitting on a stump and thinking, there was now a new store displaying peculiar objects—little wicker baskets, a hunk of cheese, fancy crockery, a stuffed doll that made him shudder when his eyes fell upon it. In the next moment, he could feel the perspiration coming out of his skin like slimy worms, the panic rising up right through the calm of the booze. He must think. He forced himself to think. Had they actually evicted Miranda's and moved in this strange business as a front to serve their evil purposes, or were they projecting false images into his mind again? He shut his eyes and opened them again. No change in the image. He touched the window glass and its solidness against his fingertips reassured him slightly. "Glass is glass. The same glass. Ah-hah," he said. He must go inside to investigate this place. Then again, they would know that he would want to go in. They would be waiting. He had to take the risk. He had to find out whether what he was seeing was what he was seeing or a projection. They would know that, too. He had to admire the cleverness of the construction of the predicament they had put him in. The plan was too good to come from the Welfare Department. It had to come directly from the Devil himself. He had to admire the old boy. He was damn clever, stimulating in his cleverness. When the mind of God split, the evil part that was the Devil made off with the sense of humor.

"You put the joke on old Ollie this time," he said. The edges of the things he saw shimmered from his anxiety, but his voice was steady, and he bravely headed into the store. Everything that was once known as Miranda's Café was gone, even the smell of piss and greasy dust. They had taken down the walls, building new ones of Sheetrock here and there, but in one place leaving bare the brick of the building itself. He took this architectural touch as a mockery of himself. He touched the brick. Real. He walked around, carefully imitating the slow-motion daffiness of a browsing customer so that he could touch everything. Everything appeared disturbingly real. He spotted a young woman stocking shelves. She had straight blond hair, and the sleek but firm lines of a maturing red oak tree. He should touch her to see if she was real, he said to himself. That idea was foolishness. Of course she would be real. The Devil always used real people as agents. It was much easier to spread evil among a kind with the same kind. The truth was, he wanted to touch her because he wanted to touch her. Get that out of your mind, he said to himself. They wanted him to touch her. The trap in this place was the woman. That settled, he found himself a bit easier inside. But don't relax, he said to himself. It was possible that there were other traps besides the woman. He continued to pretend to browse, seeing nothing really, his mind blank, waiting for something to happen, as it must.

Finally, a thought leaped at him snarling: It was possible that there had never been a Miranda's, that they had planted that idea in his mind long ago, only to confuse him later. He recognized this thought for what it was, another trap; only this time he had been caught, for he knew that the doubt would stay with him for days. Luckily, these confusion-traps did not kill, although they could wear away your confidence in what is. All right, all right, his wiser half said. You stood up to it, now get out. Stay here longer and they'll get you. But he did not leave. He had to know how the Devil had pulled off this stunt, this transformation of businesses, this weapon of assault upon his memory. He remembered now that he had never known the true circumstances of his eviction from the property under the great sign. Come to think of it he had rarely known any of the circumstances of anything important that had ever happened to him. Had he invented Miranda's? Had his family life with Helen ever existed, or had he always lived up there on Abare's Folly, his idea of the past a dream? It was possible that the Devil's biggest trick against him had been to rob him entirely of memory at an early age, not just of the time that obviously was lost but of all things past; but thanks to God, he had constructed a past to keep from being crushed by the loneliness of being a stranger in time. Why would the Devil want to make him hurt so, and for that matter why would God want to lift his hurt? Perhaps the answer was the hurt itself. For every hurt that the Devil could inflict, the Devil hurt less. Still, that didn't account for the apparent need for conquest in both God and the Devil. If he could judge from the assaults from the Devil that he had beaten back and the assists from God that he had accepted, he could say that they both had at heart the conquest of his soul—whatever that was. He wasn't sure. But "soul" was the closest word he had to whatever it was they wanted. He could not know any of these matters for certain. Indeed, it was possible that hurt, which was the issue as Ollie Jordan saw it, in truth was no more than a pimple on the ass of Ultimate Purpose. Ollie started to hum a private dirge, until the clerk-maiden was standing before him, glistening like a rock in the sunlight after a rain.

"May I help you?" she asked.

The clerk suddenly caught the nervous smell of the man who stood before her. He was bearded and disheveled, not like the men she knew who cultivated such a look, but the real thing: an old tomcat too weakened from battle to care for itself, too vain or stupid—too something—to know that he already was defeated. His eyes, also, shone like a cat's, squirming and strange—Christmas gone crazy. The next thing she knew he seemed about to fall toward her, as if he were fighting an impulse to touch her. She gave no ground, remaining still, unthinking, unfeeling, fascinated, like that split second when you realize you are about to crash the car; and then the movement toward her dissolved into a sort of half bow, and the man turned and left the store. She did not know whether to feel fright, revulsion, or pity. Minutes later she closed the store for the holiday.

They were after him now. He couldn't hear them or see them, but he could feel their presence. The thing to do now was to keep moving, staying in public areas until he could find a place where he might drink his booze unmolested. He returned to Central Square. The Salvation Army sister was gone, and in her place was a man in an overcoat. They had made the switch to confuse him. He was in grave danger. He needed a drink and he needed to remain in public; yet if he drank in public the police would put him in jail, and then the Welfare Department would come and take him away. A public men's room would do. The trouble was there were few such places left these days. They had even closed the toilets in city hall. Maybe people just didn't piss as much as in the old days. He supposed he could try the rest room in the new transportation center on Gilbo Avenue, but he had never been in there, and his good judgment told him to stay away. Strange people who rode buses great distances could be found in the transportation center, and who knows what sort of mischief they might be planning? The idea of traveling any other way but by automobile seemed vaguely communistic to him. Another problem was that if he went to any of these places he might be seen, reported, and the Welfare Department could catch him out of view of the public, for a public toilet could be private. Oh, this was difficult.

He'd have to risk sneaking off somewhere, hoping that he wouldn't be seen. He had a place in mind and headed for it. He walked south of Main Street, and turned left in an alley called Lamson Street. After half a block, he reached another alley that cut underneath the Latchis Theater. Here he found a comfortable, protected spot among some garbage pails. He paused for a moment, listening. The traffic sounds could be heard, and they were rather pleasant, muted by the brick fortress of the theater. He sensed that here, for a while at least, he would be safe.

He found a narrow opening between some crates and decided that here would be his nest. He rummaged about the garbage cans, coming up with a foam cup and a bonanza of newspapers. He lined the nest with the papers, sat down, rearranged the papers until his back and bottom fit in place, then covered his legs and lap with more papers. No one ever handled a newspaper more lovingly than Ollie Jordan that day. Soon he felt warm and secure, and, thinking that newspapers might just contain properties that protected one against the thoughts inserted in your mind by the Devil, he filled the cup with vodka. "Home," he said in a whisper, and sipped from the cup.

He was feeling good, and he was a little sad that his stay at this mental way station in his passage would be so brief. He didn't like what was down the path—drunkenness—the obstacle that he had to drink past before he achieved a new level of sobriety. He imagined that he was in a valley meadow in the summer as the butterflies escaped from their cocoons. He giggled with mirth. His mind began to shape cocoons of its own making. He pictured a cocoon of newspapers and foam cups, decorated with bottles of booze, until it took on the qualities of a Christmas tree. Inside was a sleeping human being.

Nudge him, wake him, said the voice, surfacing into his conscious from the depths of the lost years. The voice gathered strength, took hold of him, and dragged him down into a darkness. He was spinning, falling down the shaft of a well. He was going back in time. He hit the bottom of the well and there was a great splash rising up, like the spreading wings of a butterfly, and he had burst through the well into a different world. There in the cocoon was Willow, sleeping, gathering his colors. There was himself, a young Ollie, except that he resembled the grown Willow, and he had blazing eyes. There was the Witch, all in colors. And there was a man, slouching, with his face obscured by hazy light. This world had a pond and vegetation and a stone wall that snaked up into a black sky. The man was holding roses in the cups of his hands. "They are mine," he was saying, moving menacingly toward the cocoon, until his intent was clear: He wanted to steal the colors from within. And he, Ollie in Willow's body, was telling the man to keep away. Then there was a gap in time, and he and the man were dancing slowly toward the wall, the motion producing something in his stomach like car sickness. They fell. The man vanished, and Ollie was holding the roses, and the Witch was tugging at him, as if trying to wake him up. He said to her, "The roses are mine."

Ollie realized now that he was speaking aloud, and he

thought he could feel the vibrations of his voice amidst the garbage cans. He strained to remember something of the vision, and he was able to summon the image of a meadow and butterflies struggling to be free of cocoons, which reminded him now—quite suddenly and delightfully—of women wriggling out of tight clothes. And he was seeing women with butterfly wings flying off into the sky.

The sound of an automobile horn on Main Street plucked him from his thoughts, and a second later the vision was gone, forgotten, replaced by a vague yearning. What had he been thinking about? Something about the Witch and a dance. He tried to reach back into his mind and discovered his brain power had diminished, a sure sign he was getting drunk. He sipped from his cup, knowing the drunkenness would come swiftly now. He wanted to get it over with, get past it. He refilled his cup and downed most of it in one gulp. Moments later the cup in his hand duplicated itself. "Seeing double, double, double," he tried to sing, but couldn't think of any more words. "Double, double, double," he sang. There was some meaning here, and he labored to find it. "Double, double, double." He needed words to go with double. Um. Trouble. "Trouble, trouble, trouble . . . double, double, ble, drouble, rubble, ble, ble, ble, b,b,b, b b'bum, dee-do, bum, bum, bum-a-roodoo, dum-bum, bum-bum, do-deerodee, bum." Let's see now, what was he thinking about? Not that it made any difference, he admitted to himself. In his present state, he couldn't think about what he was thinking about anyway. He heard himself giggle. God, he was drunk. Fart drunk. He held the neck of the bottle and attempted to pour some vodka in the cup, but the bottle was empty. How drunk was he? An interesting problem to ponder. The fact that he could ask himself a question showed he was not totally drunk. He was where? Behind the Latchis Theater. The weather it was cold and dark. He was who? He was Ollie Jordan, daddy of Willow Jordan, idiot. "Willow," he breathed the word. "Willow, your daddy is shit-face."

Go to sleep, angels said. No sleep. Sleep and you wake up

cold. The door opens during sleep, and in comes the Devil. Keep drinking, drink to get sober. He opened the new bottle with some difficulty, fished around his newspapers for his cup, failed to find it, sulked for a moment, and drank from the bottle. The cup turned up when he stood to take a piss. It was lying between his legs. He bent for the cup, fell, and found himself looking toward the lights of the Keene Transportation Center. Here the buses came in from Boston and New York, and here working stiffs labored at second jobs as taxi drivers. But all Ollie saw were large shapes swaying amidst the Christmas lights, as if he were on a ship in a stormy sea and he was getting a glimpse of land.

He was walking on Main Street. Time had passed. It was ten p.m. by the clock on the big white church at the head of the square. He didn't know exactly how he'd left his nest and gotten to walking, but he knew he hadn't slept. Not strictly slept, that is. He had just passed from one state to another, in between which there was a period of forgetfulness. He knew he had tossed his cookies—indeed, there were still traces of vomit on his shoes. He knew that he had gotten past drunkenness. He was no longer seeing double. He was steady on his feet. He could think. Not that he was fooling himself into believing he was sober. He was not sober. He was outside it all, outside booze, the earth, even his own skin and bones. This body, this soiled man in a soiled suit (face it, he was never the snappy dresser he sometimes thought he was), this hunted face hiding all, scared behind whiskers, this constipated, shit-pile brain—these were not his. They were merely old parts from a junkyard that God had put together as a temporary vehicle of flesh until he was ready to take possession of his real self. Willow, he thought, and laughed aloud. God had given him Willow's body to live in, but something had gone wrong and he had never taken possession. Meanwhile, some poor spirit of an animal that he had learned to call Willow was inhabiting his own self. What a joke. Poor Willow, no wonder he was so screwed up. Wonder what he is? Maybe a cricket, or a god-damn hound. A hound? Wouldn't that be something: Willow a dog, a stubborn, lovable, dumb mongrel dog stuck, yes, stuck—as dogs get stuck in sex—in a human body, his, Ollie Jordan's own body. The idea delighted him. He wanted to laugh. He wanted to tell somebody, and he was speaking his mind: "The man I am ain't supposed to be in this bag of bones but in that one there, call him son, and the man in him ain't a man at all, but a stray mutt that strayed too far."

In the next moment, the sound of his own mad laughter snapped him out of his thoughts. He found he was standing in front of St. Bernard's Catholic Church. He looked back toward downtown Keene. The lights were like gunfire. He sensed that the Welfare Department was on to him. A few more minutes and they would be around him, crazy birds suddenly appearing out of a dark sky, crazy, starving birds pecking at his mind. He dug his hands deeply into the pockets of his overcoat, clutching the remaining bottle of vodka by the hard neck, and then he walked up the church stairs. He felt safe as soon as the door shut behind him. He was alone in the church. The only light came from burning candles whose flickering comforted him by reminding him of small boys whispering from a hiding place. The very air here was differ-ent, God's air. "Hush," it said. "Hush." Down front the Christ-man could be seen in shadow on his cross. The shadow shimmered like a fern in a gentle breeze. Ollie walked slowly about the aisles, looking for a place to rest. He rejected the idea of approaching the altar. The area seemed too holy for the likes of him. Besides, the Christ-man frightened him.

On one of the side altars he discovered a manger. There was a barn about two feet long, lined with straw. Inside were little statues of a man and woman in bathrobes, as in movies he had seen long ago at the drive-in theater. He studied the figures in the manger. The Christ-man looked a little old to be just born, but he supposed that was to be expected from the son of God, if that's what he was. People thought it was a pity that the Christ-man had been born in a barn, instead of a hospital, but

Ollie didn't see anything wrong with that. Lots of creatures were born in barns. Barns were pretty places, full of old wood beams intimate with one another, like so many fellows drinking together. Barns were comfortable places. You could put your feet up, scratch your ass, spit, holler, and nobody would think of complaining. Not like a hospital. No sir. In the hospital, they made you wait and behave like children in school, which to Ollie was another horrible place. Christ had known what he was doing getting born in a barn. He was no dummy. The couple in the bathrobes beside the child were the parents, Mary and what's-his-name. Ollie knew that Mary was regarded as a virgin by the worshipers here, and this idea seemed not only peculiar to him but lacking in purpose. He couldn't see how virginity could aid and abet worship. Oh, well, he supposed they knew something he didn't. It also struck Ollie as odd that the husband, what's-his-name, took on so little importance in the story. He admitted he didn't know that story well, hadn't paid much attention to the explanations, but it was clear that what's-his-name had brought up the Christ and then faded out of the picture. Never got credit. Well, that's the way it goes with the man of the house, he thought. He bet that Christ fellow gave what's-his-name an awful hard time. He knew what it was like trying to raise these special ones. Well, for what it was worth, what's-his-name had his warm regards.

In the barn with the Christ family were statues of three other men, standing together like three jacks in a poker hand. He remembered now: They were the three wise men, fellows who from the backs of camels tracked a star. Amazing. The whole thing, the fact of the birth in the barn and that it had been written about and remembered all this time—amazing. Of course there was no Welfare Department in those days. Good thing, too, or else there would have been no Jesus Christ. The three wise men were carrying fancy items for the baby that Ollie couldn't identify from the statues. A nice gesture, but pretty goddamn useless when you thought about it. What use would a baby, especially one that was half-god, have for a hunk of something from Mrs. McGuirk's parlor?

Outside the barn were sheep standing around, all looking kind of dumb and pleased with themselves, like folks playing bingo. Here and there knelt shepherds with bowed heads, except for one guy who was looking up at a gold star that Ollie could see was dangling from a wire. The wire reminded Ollie that this arrangement wasn't necessarily a true representation of the true facts, but merely someone's idea of what had happened. But, what the hell? It was an honest effort. What else could people do to reach the face of God, but try lots of different things?

Off to the side was a grandstand of candles in little red bottles just a bit bigger than booze shot glasses. He wanted to get a better look at the barn, so he pried one candle out, lit it, and held it inside the barn. One slip and he could ignite the straw and burn down the barn, maybe even the whole church. He toyed with this idea for a moment. He was half-thinking, half-mumbling now. "Well, God, what would you do if I burned down this church? I bet you wouldn't let the Devil take me, then. I bet you'd want my ass for all your own to kick from one end of heaven to the other. But don't you worry. I don't intend to burn down no church. I may be a lot of things, but I ain't no fire bug." He felt called upon now to perform some holy act, but he couldn't think of one. He asked himself what the good people did in a situation like this. The answer came to him: They knelt. So he knelt. It was an uncomfortable position, and it seemed foolish to him to attempt contact with God while you were uncomfortable. So he sat. Now, I suppose I ought to pray, he thought. "Well, God, here I am," he whispered, but could think of nothing more to say. Face it, he didn't know how to pray. So he remained sitting there on the floor of the side altar, his mind wandering where it would.

After a while, Ollie got bored. He found himself looking around the church. The ceiling was very high, which he supposed gave the place the feeling of busy air and which was probably a delight to God, who, if he was a fellow at all, would be a tall fellow. But Ollie couldn't justify a ceiling that high. It must be ungodly expensive to heat this place, he thought.

Also, he figured there would be a thriving colony of mice up there. For some reason, mice loved the high places of buildings. He remembered the "boodwar" shack he had built underneath the great sign. It was the third building that he and Helen had built, briefly providing them with privacy they had never had before and never would again, for soon Willow began to act up and it became clear that his place was at his father's side, even in sleep. (Ollie now realized that it was when Willow took a place on the floor beside their bed that he and Helen had begun to part as lovers. Perhaps even then Willow was the Devil's man, whispering tales of anger in their ears at night. Or was it the mice, chirping madness in the dark? Or was it the fibers from the insulating itself that had gotten into their systems?) Like most women, Helen complained constantly of being cold. She would say that one of the benefits of pregnancy was that it warmed the blood. She bitched about the house being too hot near the stove and too cold everywhere else, but then again she bitched about everything so that it was impossible for him to tell the important bitching from the sporting bitching. So he ignored her. He lived on the principle that if you could ignore a problem you should, that problems came and went with the inevitability of weather. Also, somehow, he couldn't get it into his head that she really hurt, that any woman could hurt. Evidence to the contrary was an act to get their way, which was fine with him as long as he didn't have to furnish the labor.

One day, God knows how, she learned about insulation. The next thing he knew she had a hammer in her hands and she was taking down the inside boards of their home, the boards he had salvaged from a chicken coop and painted white, and she was insisting that he go find insulation to put up. He complied because it was more trouble not to. Lo and behold, but didn't it make a difference! The house was warmer, less drafty, and they burned less wood. He had to hand it to her. He had to hand it to womanhood. Deep down, he knew they were more cunning than men, if less conjuring. What bothered him was that she couldn't just accept her ascendancy over him. She had to remind him constantly when she was right and he was wrong. She had a wonderful memory for the moments that he failed her. Of course, now that he thought about it, he had failed her a lot. He had failed everybody, and everybody had failed him. So it goes, from one generation to the other, he thought, everybody fails everybody else. She made a point of insisting he insulate the new bedroom shack, and that angered him because he had intended to insulate it all along. He built as he always did, without a plan, the structure taking shape as he salvaged what he could from this dump or that. He swapped a pistol and a snow tire with Ike for some good 2-by-8 western stock, which Ike must have taken from a job site, and it occurred to him in a comic way that he could hide the evidence and do some good for his house by using the 2-by-8s for rafters and insulating between them.

All went well for a month or so, but then Helen started complaining of hearing scratching noises on the roof. Soon he was hearing them, too. Mice, he had thought, late-night mice. Jordans usually didn't have mice in their homes, because so many half-starved cats lived with them. But the cats avoided these mice, as if the sound coming from above bore danger. Ollie set traps, and now and then caught a small, dirty-white mouse that had taken to its death a look of pure hate. Traps or no, the mice multiplied, every night scratching and squealing from the rising of the moon until an hour before dawn. It was Helen who first noticed that the mice were not on the roof but inside, between the rafters in the insulation. This new information bothered them in a peculiar way: It made them distrust each other. He felt desperate to rid the place of the mice, and so he bought some poison. Helen refused to let him use it, saying he'd kill the kids. He wanted to hurt her then, not because she was right but because she made him realize that something in him wanted the kids dead more than the mice dead.

In a moment of fearful knowledge, it had struck him that the scratching of the mice was warring and the squealing was breeding, the two married in a single ceremony of survival.

Then came a strange odor that reminded him of dead animal, crotch, perfume, an old woman coughing up—all these things. Mysterious stains began appearing on the inside of the plastic against the insulation. He was having bad dreams, bad thoughts, bad feelings. He wanted to burn down the building and walk away, but he was paralyzed from doing anything at all. They were both paralyzed. They marched to their bedroom at night like prisoners obeying orders from a hidden warden who sent his commands to radio receivers grafted onto their brains. Sometimes when the breeding squeals of the mice reached a peak they themselves embraced, full of lust but meanly, like strangers copulating to spite other lovers.

One night Helen began to tease him as a child teases another child. This was not his woman. Someone had stolen her, and now was mocking him with this person. He hit her in the face with his open hand. And then everything was happening in slow motion. He had left his body and he was in the other room watching, judging, snickering over this fool who was stacking the dresser on top of the bed, then climbing like some clumsy monkey and ripping down the plastic and insulation. He could see Helen, her face buried in her hands like a kid who doesn't know any better playing peekaboo on Judgment Day; he could see mice raining from the rafters. The sight had reminded him of a vague memory he had of a story that the Witch told him when he was a boy, something about God punishing the wicked with a downpour of locusts, which he had taken to be grasshoppers or crickets and which upset him because these were among his favorite creatures and he didn't like the idea of them being used as a tool of divine justice. The mice soon vanished and were never seen or heard from again.

The rolls of insulation lying on the floor revealed a world—a network of tunnels and shelters constructed by the mice in the fiberglass quilt. There were caverns where seeds were stored for food; there were nursery stations where offspring sped from infancy to adulthood in a moon's age; there were toilets pressed against the rafters, now stained with mysterious markings in mouse urine. He lugged the insulation outside, laying the batts one upon the other until they made a monstrous hill. There the insulation stayed, untouched, surrendered to the weather.

It seemed to him now that he could hear mice overhead, scurrying about. Ah, he thought, church mice, agents of heaven, perhaps the souls of men and women who had screwed up and were sent back to repeat a former life closer to the bone of the earth. He listened. No, he wasn't hearing mice; he wasn't hearing anything except the air in here which spoke of the restlessness of God himself. He was reminded of his own loneliness. It nagged at him like a woman. He reached for his bottle, but only for the comfort of holding its hard neck. He would not drink until he found a place in the church that felt right.

He wandered. Against the walls were big pictures every eight or nine feet. Some light from outside came into the church through the stained-glass windows, but not enough to allow him to see the pictures clearly. He stood on a pew for a closer look, discovering that the figures in the pictures actually came out round from the flat surface like carvings, so that they could be touched, enjoyed, understood with the hands. It took him a while to realize that the pictures told the story of the death of Christ. Seeing was a strain, but touching was easy and it gave him great pleasure. He was, he thought, like a man who has devised a method to touch the characters on the TV screen. Slowly, he worked his way from picture to picture, fourteen in all. He could feel the fear and uselessness in the friends of Christ, the weeping of the women, the intoxication from shedding blood among the tormentors, the suffering and—yes—the conceit of the Christ-man himself. The tormentors were Romans, those villains of old he had seen in movies in the 1950s. The Romans were, let's see, olden-time versions of the soldiers of the Welfare Department.

He touched the Christ very carefully, discovering something unusual on his head. At first it seemed like some simple hat such as his cousin Toby Constant had worn before they sent him to Pleasant Street in Concord. But after testing the hat with the tips of his fingers, Ollie determined that it was made of something like barbed wire strung tightly around the skull, an instrument of torture. He pondered this evil. These Romans, they liked to hurt the head. So did the Welfare Department. However, there was a difference. The Romans only wanted to dish out some pain, probably just for the droolly fun of it. The Welfare Department wanted you as stove wood to keep stoked the fire in their own private corner of hell. They made hats so pretty you would *want* to put them on, and they put things in those hats—devices—which removed information from the mind, planted ideas and clouded memories. He figured that Christ had pulled a fast one on the Romans, getting himself killed all spectacularlike, knowing his death would serve as a kick in the ass for his followers, that for him to die was to live forever through them. Christ never could have pulled off that trick with the Welfare Department. They would not have allowed a public execution. They would have knocked him off in an alley somewhere, or more likely bribed him to save themselves the trouble, gotten him a cushy job in a liquor store or something. Through his fingertips, Ollie Jordan followed Christ up that long hill. The cross on his shoulders brought Christ down three times, and each time Ollie winced. "Don't go on," he whispered. "Make 'em lug you." But Christ did not listen. He continued onward and upward. It began to dawn on Ollie that Christ wanted to climb the hill, wanted the pain, wanted the abuse because at heart he had some damn fool idea that his pains would help make a better world. Sad how some people deluded themselves.

Temporarily having lost respect for Christ, Ollie found his curiosity turning toward the cross itself. It must have been made of wood. In those days, all they had for materials were rock, wood, wool, leather, and maybe some metal for spears, but not plastic or aluminum, or even shingles. The roofs must have leaked. Christ being a holier-than-thou fellow would have preferred a holier-than-thou wood for his cross, say, oak. Then again, he wouldn't have been able to lift an oak cross, let alone haul it from here to hell and back. But Christ was no ordinary man—had to give him that. Maybe he was knotty enough to carry an oak cross. Still, the Romans who hanged him on that cross thought he was ordinary, else why would they have hung him with two other fellows? It was doubtful they would have supplied a valuable wood such as oak or yellow birch for even the fanciest of criminals. It was more likely that they used a wood that was cheap and easy to carry, say pine or hemlock, so that the fellow put on a good show. Also, it was well known that they had nailed Christ's hands and feet. You could drive a spike through bone and flesh all right but it would be difficult to continue to nail on into solid oak, or any hardwood, without bending it. Of course you could drill some starter holes. But why bother just to hang a man dead on? A spike would drive nice and easy into pine. Furthermore, the fellow who had to drive those spikes in front of all those people would look good working with pine. He'd probably fix it so they had to use pine, knowing that the people in charge could be influenced in such matters where they knew little, cared not. All the evidence was on the side of pine, or at least some softwood.

Another question that popped into Ollie's head was whether the Romans finished the crosses with anything, some kind of varnish or stain, or whether they left the wood raw. Certainly, they would have to season the crosses because a green cross of any wood would be too heavy to carry. That raised some interesting questions. Was a cross used only once, perhaps buried with the man who had been hung on it? Or was a cross used over and over again until it just wore out? The latter idea excited Ollie. He could imagine nothing grander to look at than a cross that had been up and down countless hills, laid across the backs of countless Christs, the wood aged by the sun, stained with blood, sweat, tears, and dirt. If such a cross could know, it would know everything. No wonder these Christians hung their imitation crosses everywhere.

The cross was a story of a human pain revealed in the beauty of wood. The Romans must have put fellows in charge of the crosses—crosskeepers—men who picked the wood right from the tree, cut it down, shaped it, dried the wood so it did not split or check, and then fashioned two pieces in a cross with wooden dowels and glue. Course now and then a fellow would cheat, as workmen will out of anger or boredom or laziness, and join the pieces with a mahaunchous bolt. The crosskeeper would store his crosses in barns when not in use, keeping them away from moisture so the rot wouldn't get to them. Later, when the crosses were retired from active duty, the crosskeeper would buy his old crosses at auction from the state, or maybe steal them if he could, cut them up and make them into coffee tables, selling them to the rich who lived down-country, or whatever they called down-country in those days. He bet those crosses lived long lives, longer than the poor bastards who were hung upon them. He concluded that the Romans had been wise to use wood for their crosses and Christ had been equally wise to arrange to have himself die on one.

After Ollie Jordan had completed his round of the pictures, he figured he had a pretty good understanding of the way Christ died. Not a sweet death but a showy one, its meaning formed by the minds of the crowd. He had to admit, though, that there was something missing in his knowledge. He had the potatoes and vegetables, but not the meat. He tried to recall what he knew about Christianity. Not much, and what he had came no thanks to the Witch. She was full of weird powers and crazy ideas and spooky talk that might have passed for prayer, but that was just to get her way. In truth, she was as godless as a government man. Still, he had picked up a few things about Christianity. Christ had claimed that he had died for the sins of mankind. If that was so, why had mankind kept on sinning after Christ died? And if he had died for sins of the future as well as for sins of the past, wasn't he giving an excuse to those of the future to sin, so a Christian man could say, "If he died for my sins, why I better rack 'em up on the board so he can say he done his job"? Maybe Christ was just another disguise of the Devil. Maybe. Yet, there was something to the Christ business, and he wanted to know more. What it came down to was that Christ, if he truly had the power, could take Willow away from him so that he could be his own man or join him to Willow so that they were one. There was nothing else that could be done for the two of them, even by the son of God, which he doubted that Christ was.

Ollie heard the mice again, the mice that he knew were not there. He wondered whether the Welfare Department had found him here and now was working their evil on him. He couldn't imagine that they would dare enter the church, but it was possible they were sending invisible rays through the stained-glass window. It was possible they had arranged to have the windows installed for just that purpose. Yes, he was under attack. He could feel something like a wall of hate in the darkness. He must find a protected place. He must drink his booze.

He stumbled upon the oddest closet in the oddest place. It was in the rear of the church opposite a side aisle, at the other end of the manger. There was no door on the closet, just a heavy purple drape that ran to the floor. Inside the closet was a seat. How convenient. He fancied that God—Christ, somebody—had prepared this place for him. With the drapes drawn the closet was black as his own smile; the darkness unsettled him, for he could feel himself losing his sense of upside down and right side up. He went back to the front of the church to fetch a candle. He returned, sat upon his seat, and saw now that on each side of the little closet was a slide panel. He opened one to reveal a window covered with a screen. He poked his head outside through the drapes and discovered that the windows opened into two other tiny closets, both with their own draped doors. What could these windows be for? They did not open to the outdoors. Why would you want windows in a closet opening into other closets? Certainly not to let the light, for there was no light. Certainly not to keep out the black flies or the mosquitoes, for a Christian hardly would object to the small pains insects dished out. And then the answer came to him: rays. The windows were vents; the screens allowed air to come through but blocked the rays. The word "rays" had jumped to his mind, and he struggled to give it meaning: rays—"conjuring gases sent through windows by the Welfare Department." It was as if, having defined the word, he had sent it out into the world of actions. Perhaps the rays could penetrate doors also, but not apparently these purple drapes. He touched them—they felt like a woman. He sniffed them—they smelled like cave air. They must be very old, old as Christ's cross. As long as he kept the drapes drawn, he would be safe here. If the air went bad, he'd just open a window. The screens would keep out the rays. He tested the safety of this place by sitting still, allowing the barriers in his mind to slip down for just a moment, inviting attack. There was no attack. There could be no attack. He was protected here. He could drink in peace. He thanked God, uncapped his bottle of vodka, and enjoyed the burning of the throat.

The candle was burning low; the bottle was nearly empty—these were clocks, telling him that time had passed. Without clocks, nothing happens, he thought. It's quarter to two, we say; it's going on three-thirty, we say; it rained and now the sun is shining, we say; time must have passed for my face is uglier, we say. He was drunk again. Not really stinko. Just a little bit outside of sobriety. He suppressed an urge to sing. He wished Helen were here. She could sing pretty when the spirit moved her. She used to sing such songs as, "My Heart Is Pushing Up Daisies Since You Gunned Down Our Love," and "Where Home Used To Be They Put I-93." He liked music, especially fiddlers playing at a contredanse, but he didn't like the words to songs. Most went on and on about how so-and-so had got gypped, or shot, or lost his girl. Seemed like nobody in a song could do anything right. Still, he had liked listening when Helen sang, although he never told her so. He'd always held the idea that if you showed a woman you liked something about her, you were making it easier for her to hold something against you at some later date. Maybe he had been wrong in not telling her, wrong about a lot of things. Not that there was anything special about being wrong. Everyone he knew was wrong all the time about everything. Of course you ought to treat a woman right, but what was right? Nobody he knew knew. He remembered that the Witch one fine day told him all would be well in his next life. She had given him comfort then, but now he wanted to ask her, "How come with all that experience, thousands of years' worth in thousands of bodies, nobody ever learns anything?"

He was brooding on this matter when he heard a noise. The mice? In a few moments he realized that he was hearing someone rummaging about the church. He blew out his candle. The sounds were disturbingly familiar. They reminded him of Ike as a boy practicing his sneaking-up on poor old Toby Constant; they reminded him of Willow browsing at the town dump; they reminded him of his own mindless putterings. An unsettling idea came over him that in this closet somehow he had been thrust back in time and the sounds he was hearing were those of his own self an hour or so ago. He was swept simultaneously with the urge to rush out into the church and embrace that self or kill it. And then there was light creeping under the drapes. How bony and red his hands looked. Whoever was out there had put on some lights in the church. Was the Welfare Department coming to get him? Was his own ghost prowling about? Had they sent his own ghost to haunt him? He had to know who was out there. Carefully, he poked his head through the drapes. He saw the back of a man wearing a black garb that resembled a woman's dress, reaching almost to the floor. A priest, a goddamn priest. What else in God's name did he expect to find in a church? For the moment, he was relieved, but then it occurred to him that there was no good reason for even a priest to put the lights on in a church in the dead of night.

Ollie Jordan did not know it was Christmas Eve and that in half an hour midnight mass was scheduled to begin. People were filling the church. He could not see them, but he could hear them and feel them, the way you can feel a storm coming. Perhaps these were troops massing for an attack upon him. He thought about Christ, dragged and kicked and spat upon and wept over, in the end dying with his hands outstretched. He felt oddly comforted by this thought that came to him as though it were a memory of his own experience. He pulled the drapes aside and peeked again. The seats in the church bulged with the backs of kneeling Christians. They made him think of gorged largemouth bass. A few people were standing in the rear, all of them men, he noticed. Apparently, women were not allowed to stand. This made sense to him. He smelled booze on someone's breath. A kin. He wanted to pat the fellow on the back. A daring idea came to him: He might mingle with the people and not be discovered. He stepped out into the body of the church. The people were looking toward the front and no one noticed him. He was almost disappointed that he was not attacked. There seemed to be no interest in him whatsoever. He was insulted. It hurt him to think that they did not care. Their inattention made him feel dead, a ghost who hadn't caught on to the idea of otherworldliness. He wanted to speak, to slap one of these fellows on the shoulder and tell him: God plays cruel games. But he remained quiet. Something here enforced a silence.

The priest, accompanied by a couple of boys who might have been his nephews, came out dressed like a bird in mating feathers and began the ceremony. Ollie could not tell whether the priest was the same one who had turned on the lights earlier. He was short and fat and rosy-cheeked and white of tooth, and he muttered his holy words with an affectionate growl, a man not at all like himself; yet Ollie saw something of his own ways in certain movements of the priest, especially the way he motored about his altar. He wondered whether the souls of some men pirated parts from other souls. Had this priest found him out, stolen something from him, left him lame in a limbo whose numbness would set in only later? Perhaps a priest actually could sense the presence of his own soul and therefore could command it about; or maybe it was the other way around, the soul bossing the mind, a priest as much a robot of God as a soldier of the Welfare Department was a robot of the Devil. Ollie could not say for sure. He wasn't even sure whether there was such a thing as a soul. It was just somebody's word for the unexplainable craving in a man to touch the stars. The fact was he wasn't even sure whether he had ever had contact with his own soul. Unless it was his soul that was waging a war within him at this very moment. But no. He could not believe such a thing. The evil was *out there*.

Ollie Jordan watched the ceremony carefully. Things made more sense to him than they had the last time he had been in the church. The priest told the story of the holy family being refused admission at the local motel, and how Mary had to have her baby in a barn. Then the priest put the book down and gave the people a piece of his mind, telling them they ought to be goddamn grateful for what they had, and to get off their asses and help those less fortunate. Later a couple of fellows circulated among the crowd with baskets on the ends of poles and people put money into the baskets. Ollie gave a quarter. What the hell, it might not get him into heaven, but it wouldn't hurt either.

The bells rang and Ollie knew that it was time for the important part of the ceremony to begin. The priest said something about bread and wine and Christ's body and blood, and the people bowed their heads as one. Apparently, the body and blood business was very important, but damned if he could make any sense of it. A deep—almost menacing—quiet took hold in the church. It was, he thought, like being in a dark cave full of sleeping bats. Bells rang now and again, many thanks to one of the boys helping out the priest. A choir upstairs in a small balcony blasted out some hymns that even Ollie had heard before. Accompanying the singers was a moaning pipe organ. The choir gave him the willies, but the organ was pleasant enough. The people got up from their seats now and stood in line, while the priest and a couple of helpers handed out those little white wafers. He was tempted to try one. He could stand in line like anybody else, and it was clear by now that nobody here meant him any harm—if in fact they could see him. (He couldn't get it out of his mind that he was invisible.) But something stopped him, the same force that kept him quiet before. So he stood there, lulled by the shuffling sounds of the communicants of St. Bernard's Church approaching the rail. They all look so sleepy, he thought.

His mind started to wander. A vision of summer came to him, like a windowpane blown out of its casing by a hurricane. He could feel the warm air, could hear laughing and big talk over beer, could watch the acrobatic displays of Willow, could catch the smell of cooking, could enjoy children fooling around in trees, could stir to Helen humming. Good things. There had been some good things in his life. They couldn't take that from him. And then he was thinking about a certain day long ago. There were ducks on a pond, and a man swimming in his underwear way way out, maybe half a mile, and there was a woman on the shore and a boy, just old enough to be getting his chin whiskers, and the boy was lying beside the woman and he was breathing her in and out, as though she were the very air of his life. Then, as he knew it would, the scene faded and his mind started to empty. He felt freed from the bounds of earth. The stars drifted by. He floated in space, like a bather lolling in an inner tube on a quiet lake. Here there was no loneliness, no fear, in fact, no importance attached to existence and therefore no chores to do, the pleasure of marking the passing of time was enough.

When Ollie came out of his revery, the priest was wrapping up the ceremony. Ollie felt older, more worn. He remembered something the priest had said, something about a lamb and the shedding of blood. The idea seemed wrong, strange. He had seen no blood. He thought hard. Finally, he realized what a fool he had been. They had killed something up there on the altar, and he had not seen it. Right before his eyes: a death. And he had not seen it. They had shielded it. Things happening right under his nose. Evil things. They had bamboozled him. He could trust nothing, not even the actions reported by his eyes and ears and touch. Spinning. The world was spinning away. All at once, the booze caught up with him. The priest became two, the altar helpers four. One part of him went thisaway, the other part thataway. He heard strange noises—children wheezing, old men breathing like dying, gunshot deer, women hissing prayers in hopes of getting some enemy broken by heaven. For a moment he was afraid he would puke in the church. He staggered outside, almost falling down the concrete steps. He found a tree to hug and he threw up. They shed the blood because it is demanded, Ollie thought. He had the dry heaves and he was cold.

The Appointment

February: the third day of a thaw. Ollie had put too much wood on the fire earlier and now it was hot and stuffy inside the shelter, but he didn't care. He could hear the tiny rivulets of melting snow rolling off the boulders and the trees outside. He decided to take a nap, listen to the melting as he drifted off to sleep. He didn't mind the nightmares anymore. Once you recognized that everything was a nightmare, the fear was gone. Everything was gone; the difference between life and death, hate and love was no greater than the difference between one snowflake and another. He crawled from his place by the fire to Willow's nest. The boy lay there, his eyes open and frightened; he knew something was up. Ollie had hobbled him with a chain around his ankles. "Daddy wants to nap now," Ollie said. "Daddy wants to listen to the melting. You sleep, too." And he breathed in the smell of his son and crawled off. Willow was silent. Soon he shut his eyes. Perhaps he slept. Ollie lay in his own nest. He felt weaker than ever before. His fever raged and his body ached. It was a good thing that this was the appointed day or else he wouldn't have the strength to do the appointed chore. He shut his eyes. The image of the easy chair he had salvaged took shape in his mind. It was outside at this moment, covered with snow. He concentrated, and in a moment he had left his body and was outside, looking at St. Pete's. The wind had torn its plastic skin, the snow had caved in the roof, the wooden framework had fallen down. (Poor design, and Ollie knew it.) St. Pete's had been reduced to a crude tepeelike structure that Ollie had built by leaning a few poles against the stove pipe, covering them with layers of plastic, newspapers, and hemlock boughs, all sewed in a crazy quilt held together with clothesline rope (shoplifted) and granny knots (his very own). There was no door as such, just a flap. There were no windows. The sunshine filtered through from about ten a.m. to two p.m., leaving bits of wandering green light that reminded him of troublemaking insects, and then it was dark in St. Pete's. The floor was littered with clothes, newspapers, empty bottles, and dozens of items that Ollie had picked up: bird nests, pinecones, oddly shaped sticks, rocks with white in them, and junk from the sides of roads. Whatever use these things might have did not interest him. What pleased him was their unusual shapes, which made the pity in him well up inside when he touched them. It was difficult to walk around inside of St. Pete's without tripping in the mess, so he crawled.

His home was a dream gone bad, and it was Willow's fault. Not that the boy was to blame, not strictly—the Welfare Department was to blame. If he could just escape from this dying body that he was imprisoned in, he might yet do some good for himself and his kin. He would try soon. The day had come. He would take possession of his true self, held now by the Welfare Department, through the creature they had set up as his son. He had no son; he had instead a sorrow: He still loved Willow. He imagined that the Welfare Department had stolen a mind somewhere, a poor ghost—perhaps the ghost of a child—and stuck it inside the body that was rightfully his own because they knew they could command the mind inside and because they knew that he would feel the need to be near the body, not only because he believed it to be a son but because of something else—a kinship of self that was there but which they never expected him to discover, only long for—and thus they could keep an eye on him and destroy him when he weakened. But he had fooled them. He had exercised his mentality.

Ollie Jordan lay in his nest, half-asleep—that is, pretending to himself to be half-asleep—and he imagined himself rising on a current of warm air, up, up, far above the trees until St. Pete's below resembled just another boulder that a traveler from another planet might feel kindly toward; up, up, until all that remained of Abare's Folly was the purple of a forest viewed from far away; up, up, into the high-beam glare of the sun, right on past into the night and the stars. "How peaceful, Willow," he whispered. He started his return to earth, working on the sensation of tumbling until he actually could see the stars spinning away from him, and then the darkness of the earth. And on he went, for hours it seemed, although he knew it was only a moment in earth time, spinning from light to dark to light. Very pleasant. But then the idea went bad on him. He was falling toward a city all lit up. He was spinning from light to light; he could not tell true light from made light, up from down, earth from sky.

"Frankly, Willow, I'd sooner fall onto the rocks of Abare's Folly," Ollie said, surprising himself with the sound of his own voice.

The boy's eyes opened. It was possible that the eyes were little television cameras, the purpose of which was to transmit images of earth as entertainment to outer-world beings sitting in their easy chairs. I'll give 'em something to get excited about, Ollie thought, and he looked at Willow with a malicious smile that tried to convey something of his plan without giving it away. He wanted to show that they couldn't conquer him. No, that wasn't it. He knew they could—would—conquer him. They knew, and they knew he knew. Rather, he wanted to show that he could surprise them, that to the end his mind was fresh.

Ollie stood. It took him a while to get used to the sensation of being on his feet. He should have something to eat, but what the hell, he didn't want to eat. Then, deliberately, he spoke aloud in Willow's direction as if addressing an unseen listener over a microphone: "I don't want nothing." It was true—food held no meaning for him. Not that it mattered; there was little to eat at St. Pete's anyway. It was just that he desired to put his pleasure before God and the Devil in the manner of one making a choice, even though there was none to be made. Once, before he had wised up, he would have felt vaguely guilty about not eating, believing that it was a man's duty to keep his body strong. But now he knew that eating was a trick by the Welfare Department to cloud the mind. They poisoned the food to prevent you from seeing the shape of truth. He had learned that if you stopped eating, the hunger went away, the mind became clear—well, clear enough—the senses more acute, and the pathfinder began to see. So what that he was starving. He had no obligation to this body, this face. This was an old man's body with raw, wrinkled hands that shook all the time, with a beard gone gray overnight and the eyes of a rabid dog. He had seen those eyes staring at him from shop windows, from various pictures of the Devil that passed as mirrors to the common folk. This sick thing was not his body. His body was there, and he stumbled over to Willow and handled the strong arms, the thick, powerful neck.

He caught, then, the look of the boy's eyes, like drops of pond water kicking with life. Ollie embraced his son. For a moment, he was swimming with affection. Then he pulled away. This was no good. He was confusing in his own mind just what it was he loved. Himself, the boy, the two of them together, some third party—a stranger striding away—whom did he love? Who loved him? He was shaking again. He needed some booze to calm down. He reached for his vodka. There was almost an entire bottle left. He must not drink too much, else he'd be late for his appointment. He heard himself cackle at this joke between himself and whatever was out there advising him. He must drink just enough to remain steady. He took a nip; another. The magic worked fast, warming him with silk handkerchiefs and rabbit fur. So it went when you were hungry and sick—the booze was kindlier, quicker.

He could think now. Thinking was the only thing that he had ever been good at. He bet that if they gave out prizes at the Cheshire Fair for thinking he'd get one every year. The problem was, thinking was no good. You couldn't make a living at it; you could only suffer with it. The Devil had invented thinking. Still, he was a thinker. He had to think, sure as Mrs. McGuirk's dog pisseth against walls. He should think about the appointment, for there were certain details to be worked out, but he was afraid to, afraid of the sting, the confusion. The fact was he hadn't been able to consider the act itself until he had come up with that word "appointment." Other words seemingly more accurate—"sacrifice," which was what the church people called it; "killing," which was what it was, really—prevented him from thinking about the act at all. Not that he felt that making the appointment was wrong. It was absolutely right, commanded by God. He had learned how God worked—away from words. The sounds in his head—such as the whispers of the female voice, calling *Ollie, Ollie, be kind*—were mainly from the Devil, not even directly from the Devil, either, but from the clutter the Devil left in the mind even after he had departed, like bombs dropped from airplanes that did not go off but blew up years later for no apparent reason. No doubt about it—words were the invention of the Devil. The truth was obvious when you thought about the matter: Before man got ahold of words, he was doing as fine as any common critter. God did not speak. God was mute as Willow himself. God did not say, "Listen up. Got an idea how you can get yours and his, too." God powered a man like a battery, charging his arms, legs, eyes, mouth, sex organs—oh, yes, those especially—so that he acted on command, often against his so-called better judgment, afterwards feeling sick and confused. All those years he had beaten his dogs, beaten his children, beaten his women (when they had let him), he had felt ashamed, quivering in fear at what he thought then was a nameless evil driving him. Now he realized, it was not evil but good that charged a man, drove him to do what he must, and evil that left him ashamed. He had been right to give in to his impulses. God had meant him to beat his loved ones for reasons that he likely would never know, could never know. It didn't matter what he thought personally about plunging a knife into the chest of his own son. God would see to it that he kept the appointment. He merely would be doing God's bidding. He was blameless as a pig gobbling up the young of a nearby sow, his young. He wouldn't be able to help himself . . . help himself. He started to shake with the horror of what he planned to do. "Please, I don't want to keep no appointment," he whispered. God comforted Ollie by directing him toward his bottle of booze. Ollie drank and was calmed.

The boy was crying, mocking him probably, but maybe suffering, too, suffering to beat the band. Who could tell? How long had he been crying? Two minutes, two million years? Was Willow crying, or was Ollie hearing himself crying? It was all the same—he was beside himself with desperation. He'd always been beside himself. Ha, what a good joke! He laughed aloud mirthlessly, stirring Willow into a weak, imitative cackle. Or was it his own laugh that was weak, and Willow's reproduction of it merely accurate? The whole situation—idiot son and crazy father, both doomed—suddenly struck Ollie as worthy of some notice. If only there was someone here to see, to appreciate all this—this body and blood wreckage of St. Pete's. Willow cackled again. Ollie waited for God to compel him to slap the boy, but no command came. Maybe there was no God. Maybe there was no anything anywhere that cared for anything anywhere. Whatever—he was grateful that there was no alien force in him at the moment. He didn't want to hit anybody. There was no anger in him. No anything in him. Never had been really. If there was anything, he was sure of it now, it was the fact of his own emptiness. It was possible that there were people out there who had been filled like a warm mug with beauty, love, knowledge—even riches—and had remained warm and full, but he doubted it. The human soul required fullness but it was full of holes. You could fill a soul with good, but it was like water and drained out in five minutes. Hate, being like tar, stayed in the system longer and thus was greatly favored by the population, but eventually it too dribbled out and got hard to find toward the end. Now Harold Flagg—there was a man who could hate. Ollie had to admire him, even though he knew that he himself was the tar in Flagg's soul. Maybe by hating him, Flagg felt less empty. Maybe he had done more for Flagg than he had done for any other human being. At this point, Ollie formed his mouth into the silly "o" of a carp's feeding-suck and he rapped himself on the head with his knuckles so that he could hear the hollowness in himself. Willow did the same thing, and Ollie walked over to him and slapped his face.

It was warm in here, Ollie thought. He shucked his coat and went outside. The sun was huge in the sky, perfuming the air like a woman's breath—warm, inviting, false. It was a good day to be alive, if alive was what you wanted to be. He laughed aloud at that idea and the echo of the laugh returned. It was a scared but not unfriendly echo. It had more character than Willow's imitations. He liked the echo. He wished to converse with it, test it for wisdom, but he laughed no more, said nothing. The idea of talking to an echo not only was crazy, it was undignified. If God and the Devil—or whatever was out there—were going to scorn him they would do so because of his probably wrongheaded attempts at doing right or because of their own plans, not because he was a fool. Gods, devils, employees of the Welfare Department—what the hell was out there? He wished he knew for certain whose wicked ass to kick, if that could be done, and whose holy ass to kiss, if that's what it was all about. He had tried everything: thinking, drinking, praying, cursing, pissing in the snow at midnight under a horny moon. *Ollllllie,* a familiar voice whispered in his head.

"Damn you, if you got something to say, say it," he said. But he knew the voice would not answer. It was a female voice, not like the Witch's, softer. It was even tender. And it had something of himself in it. Sometimes he imagined the voice belonged to the ghost of his mother, if he had a mother. The idea of a mother had become clouded in him. She was part of that time that was lost. No one spoke of her. He did not think of her, as if there was danger in such thought. Still, she came to him in dreams sometimes, leaving him fearful yet oddly rested . . . He was fooling himself. He knew he had a mother, even knew her. He chuckled at that one. He pushed the knowledge away . . . He didn't have a mother. He was an orphan. His mother was dead. His father was alive somewhere—of this he was certain. But so what? He would not know his father if he saw him, and his father would not know him. A longing made no difference, for they would never know each other. They were strangers for all time. What bothered him, made him jealous as a matter of fact, was that his father had gotten away, and he hadn't, being stuck here with an idiot son—if idiot he was. Ollie still had a vague doubt. The boy still might be a genius, ready to crawl out of the cocoon of St. Pete's and fly away. But no, but no. It would not happen. Could not. The fact was the boy was not a boy. The boy was himself. He, Ollie Jordan, was the boy. He was the boy. They were the same person, yet not the same person. They must be separated, they must be joined. Today.

"Nice day for it, hey, Willow?" he asked, wondering whether the boy heard inside St. Pete's. He must be getting hot in there. It was already warm as french fries outside. He took off his shirt, pausing before the sun as if before a mirror or an admirer, and walked down to the pool to bathe, knowing that the water was frozen. It was pleasant down there. He paused to listen to the stream gushing under the snow and ice. It was said these little streams joined rivers and went all the way to the ocean. And why? Why for no better reason than that God insisted that water flow downhill. Stupid reason. He listened some more, and then thought he sensed danger. Willow was getting away! His friends from the Welfare Department had gotten up here and were freeing him at this moment. He rushed back to St. Pete's. Willow was on the floor, still tied but wiggling.

"Your buddies in the Welfare Department seen me coming and got scared of my scorn, eh?" Ollie said.

He attempted to hoist Willow into a sitting position, but failed. He was so weak and the boy was so strong. Why was the boy so strong? Why did he allow himself to be chained and slapped?

"Why, Willow, why?" he asked and slapped the boy. And again. Ollie felt the blows himself, even as he inflicted them.

It was time. He couldn't delay any longer. A man must be on time for the important things. It was getting late in the afternoon. This must be done by daylight. He drank some more vodka, as much as he could get down. He gave the boy something to eat, all he had left, actually. But Willow refused to touch the food—the remains of a rabbit Ollie had trapped days ago and a can of sardines. He tried to eat the sardines himself, but they had frozen and thawed, frozen and thawed, and they smelled bad. The rabbit, unrecognizable in a stew, looked appetizing enough. Too appetizing. His suspicions were aroused. Somebody had put something bad in the stew. What did that matter? What could they have put in? Something to kill him? Something to drive him crazy?

"Ha, Willow," he said. "They can't hurt what's hurt to death already."

Time passed. He didn't know how much. He had blacked out. It was later in the day but the air was still warm. Too warm. Had they shipped Abare's Folly to the southland? Pure meanness—that was the mark of gods, or whatever was out there. The bastards, they controlled everything from the seasons of the year to the urges in a man. All you had that was your own were your thoughts. He looked up, seeing the same old sun. He looked down, seeing the altar stone. It was whisked clean of snow, the mica crystals on its pitted surface shining like the hardened tears of the earth herself. He saw that his hands were bleeding. Apparently, it was he who had scraped the snow and ice from the altar stone. He was reminded now that he had an appointment to keep. The job ahead was to get Willow on the stone and figure some painless way to take from him his blood. There was a butcher knife (salvaged) by the altar stone. Where was Willow?

"Willow," he heard his own voice calling. "Willow, where are you?" The voice was cunning, but weak. There was no answer. Ollie returned to St. Pete's. Willow was not there. He was chained and could not have gone far. Ollie walked around St. Pete's in a widening spiral. The warm air had loosened some of the crust on the snow and now and then one of his legs plunged through. It was hard for him to get his foot out and continue on. He was getting so weak. He probably never would have found Willow, except that he heard the chain rattling. Willow was in plain sight of St. Pete's high up his favorite maple tree. At this moment, the sap would be running. It would be sweet.

"Well, I'll be—that boy always did have a fine sense of humor," Ollie said in a whisper to himself. Then he shouted, "Willow, you get your ass down here."

". . . ass down here," answered the echo.

"Down here," Ollie said.

". . . here," the echo said.

Willow said nothing. He was standing on a branch and he was looking to the west. Ollie figured he could see the Connecticut River from his vantage point.

"Willow."

". . . low."

"If all you can do is trail after me, I don't want to hear from you no more," Ollie said, addressing the echo.

As for Willow, he was not in a conversing mood. After taking in the view, he settled back into a branch-seat near the center of the tree. Ollie stood back to watch, to behold. "Willow," he called, but did not expect an answer. The boy folded his arms, looking beyond, ignoring his father. Soon, he was standing again, making his way out on the limb. The sound of water moving everywhere on the hill and the jangle of chains high up in the tree mingled in Ollie's mind to make music. A bird flew out of Willow's hand and dived into the snow at Ollie's feet. The bird was Willow's right shoe. Seconds later the second shoe dived earthward. Then came the coat, shirt, undershirt, fluttering like great, dying moths. Willow struggled to get his trousers past the chain, discovered it could not be done, and gave up. He sat, his bare ass on a branch, pants hanging from his bound feet.

An hour or so passed, Ollie wasn't sure exactly. He had swooned for a moment, coming to in the snow. He pulled himself up to a sitting position, took a few breaths, and rose. It took all the strength he had left to pull some boughs from some young hemlocks and make a bed on top of the snow. He lay down, leaning his head against a tree. He knew now the boy had saved him from madness and murder, if not from doom.

The afternoon was wearing on, and yet the golden light that gave all objects their own halo seemed to deepen. Ollie could see what he had made and unmade these last few months. There was St. Pete's, a wonderful idea that had failed for lack of care, just as he himself was the failure of some tinkering god. There was no pain in this realization. It was enough for Ollie now merely to understand. The refuse he had strewn about St. Pete's, like grass seed, was beginning to poke up through the melting snow. He could see the altar stone, bare and solid. It reminded him of the Witch, lying with her arms upraised.

"It wasn't your fault, Witch, or his fault, or my fault," he said. "It was the fact that we didn't know any better. I forgot out of hurt. You must have hurt, too, and Daddy, too. All except Willow. Lucky Willow. Too dumb to hurt. Poor Willow. Too dumb to know."

Ollie could not tell now whether he was actually speaking or whether he was thinking only. But he knew that his mind was free from false ideas. He could see now into the deep past he had forgotten. He had done right to forget. To know, until this moment, would have killed him with torment. It was the booze that had brought on the evil, the booze and fear and jealousy and just plain stupidity.

"You knew all along, Witch, didn't you?" he said.

He would miss the fire on the altar stone. He would miss booze, even though that was the start and end of his troubles, of his life itself. He was sorry that he had never been able to listen properly to God; for he believed now, sure as he was dying, that there was a God, a God who cared for him and who was weeping for him now and whom he had let down and who would forgive him. He thanked God for making him see that a sacrifice of Willow was not necessary to make him see his own madness. He shut his eyes, and when he opened them he found that the altar stone had been moved and now lay before him, a bright burning fire on its belly. "Willow," he said, but his voice was only a whisper. He shut his eyes, and opened them in what seemed like a moment. There was moonlight through the trees. He shut his eyes, and opened them. The sun was high and bright. He could see Willow up on the branch. The boy was still, apparently at peace, as he was at peace. The wind, which before had been from the south, now came from the northwest. It must be very cold, he knew, and yet he felt warm and comfortable. The melting had stopped, and now the only sound was the wind clacking through the dry leaves of a beech tree. He shut his eyes, and opened them. His mother and father were dancing in the snow in front of him. They came to him and kissed him. He shut his eyes, and opened them, and it was night. He could see Willow high up, blue in the moonlight. "Willow," he said, and found that by uttering the boy's name, he could lighten the burden of his own flesh until he was floating in the air. "Willow," he said, and he was rising now. He thought about the butterfly that comes out of the cocoon and leaves the grimey earth forever. When he got to Willow, the boy reached out to him and said, "Father." Ollie took him into his arms, and they flew off.

The Charcoal Burners

When the storekeeper returned from the funeral of Old Man Dorne he felt a need to work in the open air, so he decided to chip ice from the hardtop in front of the store. There had been a few warm days and some rain, but although it was April the ground remained frozen and the trees were still bare of leaves. Cousin Richard had said that New Hampshire did not have a spring. Now the storekeeper knew what he meant. Winter hung on here. What the natives called spring was really winter, South Carolina-style.

Gloria hadn't gone to the funeral. She didn't like matters to do with death. That morning he had been putting on his tie in front of the bedroom mirror, which he rarely looked at and which revealed a certain slouch that he had believed was peculiar to his father, and he had blurted out, "Gloria, everybody has got to die. Death is as natural as . . . as, ah, . . ." And the door had slammed, and she was gone. When he went downstairs, she was doing the dishes. She had put on the radio and she was humming with the music. So he had gone to the funeral alone.

The ice chipper had come with the store, one of the many tools that the Flagg family had accumulated. It had a long handle and a flat blade. It was nice to use because you didn't have to bend over to operate it. No one had wept at Old Man Dorne's funeral. These Yankees are stingy with their feelings, he had thought. Then he realized no tears were called for. Dorne had had a good life. He had left shining likenesses of himself in the memories of those who had known him. There was no reason to weep for him. The storekeeper wished he could explain that to Gloria.

The ice chipper made pleasant sounds, much more congenial to the thinking man than the music Gloria liked to listen to. The funeral had attracted a large crowd of family, friends, and acquaintances like himself. All these people had the look of the county, the women with out-of-date hairdos, the men with work-dirt creased in their hands. The exceptions were the piece workers at the textile mills, who were pale, bent, but neat. "A good weaver learns to keep his web clean and in so doing, himself," Old Man Dorne had said.

A woman in the back row of the church caught the storekeeper's eye. There was something out of place about her. For one thing, she was alone. Unwritten law of the land: Ladies do not attend funerals alone. She had long, straight black hair, a few strands of white showing. Her face was coarse, hard, masklike, and yet there was something about her eyes that said, "Come along, sailor boy." She looked like an old whore, the kind that hangs around bars whose doors open directly onto the street. Here in Cheshire County—a semiretired pro? No, he didn't believe it.

The casket was closed. That disappointed the storekeeper. He wanted to see Dorne in death. Dead people looked serene, hinted that there really was such a thing as eternal peace. The dead soothed the fear of death. He wished somehow he could explain this idea to Gloria.

During the ceremony, the storekeeper tried to remember some of the stories Old Man Dorne had told on those mornings at the store, but none came to mind. He could not even remember clearly what the old man had looked like—the color of his eyes, the shape of his nose and mouth. He could hear that voice, though, slow-talking and soft, yet penetrating, too, so you didn't have to concentrate to listen. And now as the ice kicked up around his feet, the work-sounds of the ice chipper lulling his mind, the storekeeper again was hearing Old Man Dorne's voice . . .

"It wasn't always so that the trees were here. There's been times when they were cleared, and sheep grazed in fields—and not so long ago, either. I can recollect when there were fields even on The Folly, although not all the way to the top, of course. Even before, in days gone by, there were three times as many people in Darby as there are now. There even was industry, as you can see by the stone foundations and brick litter down by the falls of Trout Brook. Nonetheless, the farmer was king. When I say farmer, I don't mean just the harvesters of vegetables. I include the keepers of sheep, which roamed these rocky slopes. There were no commuters then because there was no place anyone would want to commute to. Keene was only a town amongst towns. The railroad made Keene the city in the county. But it wasn't the railroad that changed these hills. It was the steamboat.

"You laugh. How could the steamboat change the face of Darby, you ask? If my Granduncle Evvan was here, he'd explain it so you could all understand, as he explained it to me on his deathbed. 'Leave the room,' he said. 'A dark man is coming to get me, and I don't want you here when he arrives.' Course I didn't leave the room. I was a boy and curious, and I'd just as soon take my chances with the dark man if it meant I could hear a story.

"Uncle Evvan, he didn't really want me to leave either. He wanted to talk, uncommon for him. He had come to live with us when the arthritis got so bad he couldn't pour water into a cup. Those were the days when you took care of your own. Never mind that Granduncle Evvan was Evvan Jordan, and after he died we'd lie about owning up to him as a relative. Long as he was alive and couldn't do for himself, we—his own—did for him.

"It seems as if in his youth Uncle Evvan had been a helper to a charcoaler. See, back when Mr. Fulton invented the steamboat, he says you going to have to run these things on charcoal from hardwood trees. The forest that grew around here suddenly came into demand. A trade developed, as it will when there's demand. These fellows would cut the trees down and build these mound-type structures with the logs, maybe forty feet through and eighteen feet tall. I suppose they resembled domes. These were skill-made things, with passageways inside. The charcoaler would make a smoky fire in that green wood. I don't know exactly how—lost art, you know—but anyway the idea was to drive the moisture out of the wood and combust everything but the pure charcoal, which then could be shipped south to feed the appetite of the steamboat. Anyone who has tried to burn a pile of brush knows that any open fire is difficult to control. You can imagine the dangers involved for the charcoaler.

"Granduncle Evvan was not one of those babies born of woman. He came out of the belly of a fish in Nova Scotia, made his way here as a boy ('Got no memories before age twelve,' he claimed), and hooked up with this charcoaler. These characters weren't welcome, and you can see why. It was a depression time in these parts then. The charcoalers would contract with some land-poor old fart, cut down all the trees, leaving smoke in the air for days and stumps on the land for years. Nothing to show for the visit but a few dollars and scars, scars, scars.

"Think of these fellows coming into town, exhausted so they moved like sleepwalkers, their skin blackened from exposure to smoke, their very being smelling of fire. They must have been a fearsome sight. Granduncle Evvan on his deathbed, in the hoarse voice of a man strangling in his own coughup, said it was the kind of life that broke a man's spirit or made him permanently mean. As he spoke, I'd have sworn that I saw the dark, greasy tan of a man whose skin was altered by years of exposure to heat—in short, a demon. Course that was just the imagination of a boy.

"Granduncle Evvan was pretty coherent until he got to the part about the accident. Somehow, one day—the wind had been blowing: bad sign—the fire in the mound roared up out of control and incinerated Granduncle Evvan's mentor. He staggered out of the mound, looking like a hunk of burnt toast, and then, for reasons unknown, he went back in. There were no remains. Granduncle Evvan hunted through the ashes for days, trying to find some evidence of a body. He found nothing. I guess he blamed himself for the fire, and maybe justly so. It was hard to tell, as he explained it, whose fault, if anyone's, the fire had been.

"The upshot of the charcoal burners is that with the forest denuded, another group came on their heels and created, from the stumpy land, rough pastures. Here they raised sheep. Out of the ugly, pocked hill came green meadows. The place was beautiful in a way that it had never been before, in a way that even the Indians could not have imagined. For this you can thank the steamboat. Then the market fell out on the sheep business during the bad times of 1890 and again in 1910. Over the years, the farmers started heading west. I imagined they dreamt of warm sunshine, soil without stones. Later still, along came rayon and the like, and the wool industry all but expired. Finally, somebody invented the big tractor, which was just dandy for the plains states, but useless on these rocky, slanted hills, thus furthering the advantage of the western farmer. More and more New Hampshire farmers left, and their pastures did what this land does best when left alone—grew trees. All that's left of the pasture life are the stone walls you see today in every woodland. Except for some sporadic logging, these forests have been untouched for seventy-five or eighty years, and this part of New Hampshire is wilder now than it has been since the Indians were here.

"Granduncle Evvan he saw all this, saw the forest that he had cut down grow back up. That day on his deathbed, he led me to the window, and he said, 'See in the woods, see that man

in black? I'll be leaving with him by and by.' The next day
Granduncle Evvan died. The upshot to me is that I believed it.
I saw that man in black that day, I see him still on occasion.
You won't catch this soul walking no woodsy paths."

The storekeeper came out of his reverie satiated by his
memory of Old Man Dorne's tale. Odd, he thought, that even
though Dorne was from the heart of the county, there was
something of an outsider's wistfulness about him. Such had
been the kinship between himself and the old man. The storekeeper realized now that he was slightly overwarmed by his
labors. He looked up into the hills and beyond at the sun, and
then to his feet. There was a pile of ice chips lying there, a
streamlet forming from them on the blacktop. Perhaps spring
had arrived. "Nice," he said aloud. A peculiar sense of opti-
mism took hold in him. He got the crazy idea that one of these
days everything everywhere was going to be fine. And then it
struck him that he was settled down in Darby town at last. He
rejoiced. Now he had something he could talk about with
Gloria.

Where Willow Went

She could feel herself coming out of the fog. Always an exciting time. Brain power increased. Awareness quickened. Colors of the world brightened and shook. Memories came on like cooling thunderstorms on a hot August evening. She was seeing Osgood's canoe coming round from the point on the pond—that gawd-awful, bug-ridden pond. There he had built that terribly primitive shack that he insisted on calling a camp, which bothered her because it was uncharacteristically imprecise of him. The only neighbors were beavers that slapped their tails on the water, as if in criticism, and then vanished before you could answer. She must have loved Osgood mightily to put up with that place. Year after year, she had nothing to do but knit. At least she had the comfort of her own easy chair. No thanks to Osgood. He had tried to talk her into sitting on something he built out of birch sticks. "Rough it, Amy," he would say, as though he were Teddy Roosevelt. "You rough it," she would answer, and turn on the radio; and he would go off, paddling around on the water with his fishing pole, hooking countless tiny fish and occasionally shooting some poor creature that could only be eaten in a stew treated with tomato and oregano. "Osgood . . . Osgood . . ." She was speaking aloud now. She might be deaf, but she could feel the vibrations of her own speech. "Osgood, why this black pond covered with green scum? Why not a blue lake with neighbors that feed ducks?" The canoe was coming round the point. The fog was clearing. The canoe was empty. She shrieked. A moment later, Miss Bordeaux appeared in her room with the new night LPN. They were blathering away—about her, she imagined—and she was glad she could not hear them.

"Mrs. Clapp, I want you to meet our new night nurse," said Miss Bordeaux. Then, turning to address the new nurse: "She can't hear us. She's deaf as a footstool, but we try to act natural around her because this one can lose contact on you real fast. Poor soul. Lost her husband a while back. We're not sure at this point whether she's senile or just depressed. It's a quiet night. Why don't you give her a back rub—gentl'er down, so's she sleeps well and doesn't wake up the others."

Mrs. Clapp found herself shaking hands with a lanky, sallow-faced woman with a blank expression. Mrs. Clapp liked the face because it told no stories, requested no sympathies. She liked the hand that took hers because it was warm. So many of these girls they hired were cold-handed. She especially didn't like Miz Coburn, or Coldbuns, or something like that. You could see that she was revolted by old people, but she faked a big smile and babbled constantly and she was cold-handed. Mrs. Clapp had derived some pleasure from telling her to go boil her nose. This new LPN—if that's what she was—had good hands. She squirted the lotion in her palm—not like Miz Cummerbun who shot the stuff cold right onto your spine—and she rubbed deeply and firmly into the back, but with no rush. Mrs. Clapp liked this one, all right. She would be ignorant as a pickle, of course. All the good ones were. The smart ones really didn't like the work. They liked the idea of the work.

"A lot of these old people," said the widow Clapp, "a lot of these old people, a lot of these old people, a lot of these old people . . . they don't. Oh dear, forgot my lines, as Osgood used to say. He also used to say, 'Crimey—Amy, where'd you put my crimey blue suit coat?' It's hell being old. You don't remember where you are half the time, and you worry the other half where you went. It's like a fog. I don't mean like the never-never land of fog that the high school kids are in, day-dreaming and all about pretties. I mean fog where you understand that everything is out there but you can't remember what it is . . . Um. What is your name? I said, 'What is your name, nursee?' "

There was a pause in the kneading strokes of the woman. She must be speaking. The widow Clapp turned over on her side, and said, "Am I shouting?"

The nurse mumbled something, but her expression remained unchanging.

"I can't hear," said the widow Clapp. "You know I can't hear. They must have told you."

The woman nodded.

"Your name is what?" said the widow Clapp. "They told me, but I didn't get it. Say it clear. Don't mumble like some teenager, and I'll know it."

"My name is Helen Jordan."

"Helen, you do a good job. You know how to give a back rub. Some of these nurses don't know how to touch."

The widow Clapp turned her head into the pillow, and the back rub resumed.

"I imagine you've got children," said the widow Clapp, and she could sense Helen Jordan nodding. "Of course you do. I know in your touch. I have children, all grown and wishing I'd pass away. I guess I can't blame them. I've been hard to get along with since I lost my Osgood. I used to be sweet. He'd call me sweet Amy. I imagine your husband has got a nickname for you too."

Mrs. Clapp could feel a momentary stiffening in the fingers rubbing her back, and she immediately jumped to the conclusion that the Jordan woman, like herself, was widowed.

"I know, I know," said the widow Clapp. "These men exercise all the time, and they get all that fresh air, and then they die, leaving us alone. It's not alone that I minded, up until recently, that is. It's the not being able to do for yourself. These men do for you for so long, and then they die. You'd think the sons would do for you, too, but they don't. Husbands do everything and give nothing. Sons give everything and do nothing. You don't know about such because your boys aren't old enough. But you'll find that the little boy who picked the flowers for you but wouldn't clean the sink still won't. They're all the same. I'm not bitter. Just being realistic. In fact, I'm grateful, because in my old age, I was delivered a boy like a woman dreams of, at least an old woman of my turn of mind. You don't believe me. Nobody does. All for the best, I suppose."

Mrs. Clapp began to drift off. She was grateful that the new nurse did not stop her kneading, did not try some phony comforting routine. She did not want to be comforted. She wanted to be touched. The fog had cleared and she was seeing the boy in her mind, remembering that first day when he came to her. Soon the fog would return, and she would forget. She tried to concentrate on her memories. She felt like some desperate god who was losing the power to open flowers.

She had just put a Table Talk pie in the oven. A woman knew she was sliding into the pit when she stopped baking her own pies and started buying them. Nevertheless, you had to eat. She couldn't bear to eat pies cold out of the carton. She opened the box, threw it away, and popped the pie in the oven, as if she were baking it. Sometimes her mind wandered, and the pies stayed in too long and were burned, and she would think about the Devil. She had been looking out the back window at the garden. It was early summer, and the vegetables that the Shepard boy had helped her plant were taking hold— but so were the weeds. She was too weak to weed, too weak to harvest. Looking at the garden made her angry, but she courted the anger because anger was preferable to the alternative—fear.

"Nursee? Nursee? I didn't hear him or see him at first, but smelled him, the scent of him like evergreen boughs and young manhood mixed coming through the screen door. I went outside in the yard, not knowing what I would find, but quickened by that scent. Boy who sleeps in trees: That's where I saw him first—in the crook of the maple in the backyard, just as at home as a bird. I'd like to tell you that he was a nice-looking young fellow, on the lines of the Shepard boy, but he wasn't. He was homely as a dog bone, and you could tell he was retarded. I wasn't scared of him. I said to myself right then and there that I was too old to defend myself, and therefore there was nothing for me to do but make the best of the situation. Besides, I could see he had no evil intentions. You know how it goes, nursee: No mind, no malice. 'Down out of that tree,' I says, and like a good boy he did what he was told. I soon figured it was the aroma of the pie that brought him, so I gave him a piece, and he ate it, and I gave him some more, and he ate that. Pretty soon there was no more pie. I says, 'Well, you've got some appetite.' He grinned a yard wide, but I could see it wasn't what I said that tickled him but his gratitude over the pie. Five minutes later he was gone, darting up in the woods, removed just as quick as a kiss from a nephew. I called the store and ordered some more goodies. Next day, same hour, my boy shows up for his pie. This time he stayed longer and kept me company. We got along fine, the two of us. It didn't matter what I said to him, because he couldn't understand, and it didn't matter I couldn't hear because he had nothing on his mind to spout off about.

"I'd strongly promote the idea that a young couple not speak to each other—ever. A couple should not cackle, but couple. You know how it goes, nursee: He says you don't clean the toilet bowl regularly; you feel hurt and sprinkle the Ajax on his head; he says and you says and he says and you says. You both say too much, and you say it all wrong. Trust the hands, I say. Let the hands speak . . . The boy would take my hands in his and hold them to his cheek and shut his eyes. I don't think anybody ever touched that boy. I touched him often, sometimes for his sake, sometimes for mine, and sometimes to lead him to the chores. Oh yes, ma'am, I made him earn his pie. There's a little la-di-da in this old lady, but some practicality, too. If I can get work cheap out of a fellow, I will. I showed him how to weed the garden, and if he pulled a carrot instead of the witch grass, why I'd bat him in the ear. Hands across the head speak, too. He stayed at first only for the pie, and then I touched his cheek one day and he stayed on deep into the afternoon like young summer sol himself. He liked to show me things he found in the forest—clumps of leaves, old bird nests, twisted branches and stones. He loved the mica shining in the stones. He loved patterns of things. He was a good boy in that he brought home no crawlies.

"Osgood was obsessed with slimy creatures. He would take me down to the pond and show me green, living nets throbbing to be born. They were his idea of adventure and discovery. He had other habits I had a hard time forgiving, such as squirting the eggs of fish into a bowl of scrambled eggs, and then saying—optimisticlike—'Amy, I got a treat for you this morning that will knock your socks off.' As if a woman likes her socks tampered with at breakfast.

"The summer wore on. The boy stayed nights sometimes, sleeping in the tree. Fall came and the night chill settled in me in a different way than in past years. The cold stiffened spirit and body. The boy came out of the tree and slept in the house. He didn't like the house after dark. Something in there bothered him. Night dust, house lights, house darkness—I don't know what it was. But he didn't like where he came from either, so most nights he stayed with me, up at all hours like a cat, and napping through the day. He liked to sleep in the living room chair, so the sun through the window touched his face. His cheek was warm. His cheek warmed my hands. He never stayed more than three nights at a time, although I tried my best to keep him. I wanted to steal him from the people he belonged to, whoever they were. They did not love him. I loved him. I deserved him. He always came back at pie time and usually left after pie time. Often, he left with provisions, vegetables from the garden and even food from the fridge. I probably should have stopped him, but I could see he was taking the food to someone, someone perhaps even less able than himself. It was important to him that he did this turn. I let him take what he wanted; I even bought extra food so that he could take it away, but I did it for him, not for his secret someone.

"Fall wore into winter, and with each cold morning there was less of me. I was shriveling like an autumn leaf. One morning I went outdoors and noticed that the trees were bare. I ran inside in fear and hid under the kitchen table. I felt put upon by a terrible immensity. There was something going bad with the boy, too. Day by day, he grew more nervous, confused, and sad. It would take a hot, soapy bath to calm him. This old woman will say no more of that. He tried to tell me things with his hands. Someone was hurting him in some way. He got worse. I got worse. I must save him I thought—I cannot save myself—but no solution came to mind. I never had the experience of saving someone before.

"I knew our time together was going to end when he brought me this thing, a piece of carved wood the size of your hand. I thought he'd taken it from the Elks Club, or someplace like that, and frankly I was insulted. But he made me look at it closely, and I could see that it was too crude to be anything but personal. He was trying to tell me some tale with it, or he hoped that my having it perhaps would do something beneficial for him. I don't know. This was puzzling, confusing. This was not one of those gratifying displays of love. Around Christmas, the grandchildren and the great-grandchildren came from Keene. Louisa found the carving. I made her put it back on the shelf. After that I felt disagreeable. The chirpings of the children set me on edge. Even then, I think I knew that, as this carving was lost, so was I. Time passed. I forgot. Remembered. Forgot. The boy did not return. I bought pies. Off to the dump they'd go in Mr. Elman's truck. I hated the waste. One afternoon, my daughter-in-law took me to the clinic for a checkup. When we came back, we found the clock collection gone, the house burglarized. Before getting sick on the spot—in direct contradiction to the proclamations of that stupid doctor, I might add—I think I said, 'Osgood has taken his damn clocks.' It wasn't until they took me out the door on a stretcher-bed that I saw the pile of stones that the boy left, stacked round like a pie, his way of saying, 'Thank you, ma'am. Good-bye.' I reached up and grasped the arm of one of the fellows carrying the stretcher. He was shocked by my strength. 'The stones,' I said. 'The stones have been rained on and the ice is on them like a topping.' He looked at the stones, and said. 'Don't worry lady, we'll clean them.' Then they shoved me into the ambulance . . . Osgood, Osgood, the fog is descending . . . Bring the boat in; get off the pond. You will be lost. You will drown. Don't go, I have something to tell you."

"She's asleep. You put her to sleep," said Miss Bordeaux.

"She takes good to a back rub," said Helen Jordan.

"You like this work, don't you Helen?"

"I like the old people. They are so cute."

"Did Mrs. Clapp say anything?"

"She talked about this and that."

"No, I mean was she coherent?"

"She just talked on."

Miss Bordeaux could see now that her new night attendant did not understand the meaning of the word "coherent."

"Did she say anything you could understand? Did she make sense?"

"I don't know what she said. She talked to her pillow and I weren't listening."

"If you had been listening, could you have understood her?"

"If she was talking to me and she was making sense, why I would have understood her."

"Therefore," said Miss Bordeaux, "she was not coherent, or else you would have paid attention."

"I guess you'd say she wasn't coherent," said Helen Jordan, wondering what in the world difference it made.

Statues

It was Howard Elman who found the bodies of Ollie Jordan and his son Willow. Elman had watched Ollie head for destruction. It was as if Ollie believed he were strolling onto the grounds of a picnic sponsored by a sportsman's club, whereas Elman could see him walking to the edge of a cliff. Another man might have tried to do something for his friend, talk to him or trick him into going to see a counselor or try to turn him from the way of doom, but Elman was not such a man. In Elman's code of friendship, you did not interfere. So he watched as Ollie became less and less able. Elman gave him work, pay, and companionship, but he did not interfere. When Ollie failed to show up for work after that brief February thaw, Elman suspected trouble. He didn't like these spells of warm rain and happy sunshine in the middle of winter. He liked winter. Winter was something hard a man could get used to, unlike, say, rejection by someone you loved. (He thought of his son Freddy.) Every December, you would say to yourself, surely this year winter will kill me, and then you found it was really Christmas that was the pain in the ass, and you went out in the woods and shot snowshoe hares and realized just how goddamnly awesome the woods are without all those leaves and mosquitoes and black flies and hikers tromping from place to place for God knows what purpose. By March, you hated to see the spring come—until it came, and then you marveled that you had borne up under yet another winter, and you went fishing, making sure to stay in the wind so the black flies wouldn't have your ass for supper. But a thaw was not spring. A thaw was a lie.

Elman began his search for Ollie Jordan on a Sunday morning. He should have set out on Saturday, but that was a work day. Work came before everything with Elman. He outfitted himself with a rope, cigarettes, matches, hunting knife, and his .308 rifle. Howard Elman never went into the woods without being armed. It was a crisp morning, the sky blue, the temperature well below freezing, with a couple of inches of good tracking snow that had fallen during the night. The sun was bright and it did something exciting to the snow; Elman looked forward to the hike. After some study, he chose his pickup to drive, the most reliable—if least comfortable—in his current stable of vehicles. He headed for Abare's Folly. Ollie had a camp up there somewhere, although he had been careful not to divulge the exact location. Still, Elman had a pretty good idea of where he would find Ollie. There was a spot on that nasty, ledgy hill that was relatively flat and that caught the southern sun. Elman remembered how he and Ollie had stumbled upon it while hunting years earlier. The place wasn't exactly paradise, but compared to the rest of the terrain on that hill, it looked mighty inviting.

Elman hoped that he could drive up the logging road of The Folly, but he soon found that that was impossible. The thaw may have wiped the old snow from the valleys, but there was still plenty on the hill. Besides, the road itself was in terrible condition, probably just barely passable with a four-wheel drive vehicle in the dry season in the summer. Furthermore, someone—probably Ollie himself—had felled trees along the trail to make access impossible even by snowmobile. The only way up was to walk.

Elman was feeling vaguely uneasy. He was afraid that he would stumble upon Ollie, hale and hearty. Elman did not flinch at the possibilities of Ollie's wrath, and it did not disturb him greatly to violate Ollie's wish for privacy. However, he could not bear the thought that Ollie would think him merely nosey. Still, he walked on up the hill for about an hour before he came to Ollie Jordan's truck. Out of habit, he lifted the hood and looked at the engine, discovering quickly that the block was cracked. "Ollie," he said to the sky, "you stupid bastard. You didn't even have enough sense to put antifreeze in your radiator." The truck had gone as far as possible. The road ended here against some ledges rising above. It was years ago that Elman had been here, but he figured that the garden spot had to be just over the ledges. He climbed. When he reached the top, he got a glimpse of the Connecticut River valley far below, and for a moment he could imagine himself catching smallmouth bass on a warm summer night. Immediately below, Ollie's camp site was visible. Elman could just make out some sort of plastic, man-made object through the trees.

The moment he stepped down from the ledge, he felt a difference in the air. It was less windy, quieter, warmer; he could smell evergreens. There were no tracks in the snow, not even of mice or birds. The place had a kind of near-perfection about it, like an expensive shotgun that you could admire but didn't want to own because you might mar it. Whatever errors of God or man were here, they were covered with new snow. Elman wished he could glide above the surface of the land, so that he wouldn't disturb the snow with his footprints. A short way from the shelter he found firewood, covered with plastic and neatly stacked between trees: Willow's work. The boy might be an idiot, but he could do some things well, if he felt like it. Ollie never had the patience for neatness. He always threw his wood into a big pile without cover and complained when it got wet, as though it were somebody else's fault.

Beside the shelter was a table-shaped rock. Very pretty. Elman could see that the shelter once had been more elaborate, although it was difficult to tell just what the original layout was. What was left had no form, no stamp of individual mind. It was strictly shelter, as if made by an animal. Inside, Elman saw many of the items that he had helped Ollie Jordan gather. There was a clock, its face pointed toward the wall, empty cans of food lying about, a radio on the littered floor, and bits of junk everywhere. The place disturbed him. It was in such contrast with the outdoors: objects were not in their proper place, but strewn about like bones in the den of a beast; the air itself smelled sick inside the shelter. Elman was happy to get out of there.

He found Ollie and Willow beside a tree. The snow had covered the bodies, but Ollie's face was visible. The eyes were closed, the expression placid, the skin deep blue. Elman was gripped by what seemed to him a powerful realization: Snow was blue, pale blue. Water was blue and snow was one-twelfth water and therefore one-twelfth blue. Bits of sky fell with every rain, every snow. He wanted to say, "Ollie, thanks to you I now know that snow is blue." He whisked away the snow from the bodies with his cap. The boy was naked in his father's arms. They were half-sitting, half-reclining, as if on a chaise longue. They were both frozen solid, interwound so they could not be separated. Blue statues formed by some master craftsmen. They were beautiful.

Elman sat down on a log to smoke a cigarette. He didn't know what to do next. By law, he should walk down the mountain, call the cops, and lead them back up here. But he knew that Ollie hated the authorities and would not want his body or the body of his son in their hands. Elman imagined Godfrey Perkins, the town constable, spreading it all over Darby that Willow had been found bareass in his father's embrace. He would make a dirty thing of it. Howard Elman decided right then and there that whatever he was going to do, he wasn't going to turn these bodies in. He sat smoking, looking at the bodies, feeling oddly elated. He should be sorrowful or angry or revolted. As it was, he felt clean and bristling with life. The statues (he was thinking of them as statues) had put him in touch with his own life. They were, he thought, concentrated sky come to earth, and he could feel their power settle into his body. The things he saw were brighter, the smoke he drew into his lungs sharper, the quiet around him peaceful as a house after company has left. Elman basked in this mood until it began to slip away, and then he began to think, considering the bodies as a problem. He could not leave them here. Spring would come and soften the statues until they were again merely dead flesh, and dogs and wild animals would devour them. That was certainly a better fate than falling into the hands of Godfrey Perkins; but it was hardly desirable. Elman believed he had a mission to give these bodies a dignified resting place. He touched them. They were hard as stone, even the eyelids. It would be easier to move them one at a time, but difficult to chisel them free from one another without damaging them. He decided he would move them as one.

If Howard Elman was vain about anything, it was his ability to deal with mechanical problems, and he had no doubt that he could solve this one. He put his hands behind his back, like some brooding college professor, and paced in the snow. Without conscious thought, he then began to dismantle the shelter. He knew that he had solved the problem, but as yet the solution hadn't surfaced in his mind. When the idea finally burst forth, he smiled for the pleasure it gave him. He wrapped the bodies in plastic and rope from the shelter, and he fashioned a sled from its collapsed poles. He put the bodies on the sled, then paused a moment to admire his work. Even underneath the layers of plastic the beauty of the shape of the bodies interwound came through. Elman hitched a rope to the sled and tugged it. "Um, heavy," he said aloud. "But we'll get you on home, Ollie. Have no fear, Howie's here."

Howard Elman was a large and powerful man, but his burden was heavy and by the time he dragged the sled up over the ledges he was winded. After that, most of the going was downhill, and he knew he'd make it. Still, it was almost three hours before he got the bodies to his pickup truck. He levered the bodies, with sled, onto the bed of the pickup and covered them with a brown tarp. He headed for home, tired, hungry, thirsty for beer, and absolutely delighted with himself. He felt as if he had stolen some rare statues from evil forces and was bringing them to some fancy museum, which would show them off for the ages, with a plaque underneath that said, "Delivered by Howard Elman." But there was more to the feeling than just that. He was spiritually uplifted, joyous, full of wonder. He couldn't explain the feeling, even to himself, and he didn't try. He just enjoyed it.

When he got home, Elman walked into the house (he called it "the house," even though it was a trailer), and he said to Elenore, "Whoopie-do! Give me a beer."

"Get your own beer, you. You. You. What right . . ." and she could not go on, for her anger was in the way of her ability to bring form to her thoughts.

She was angry because he had been out a long time and she had worried, Elman knew. He searched around in his own mind for a means to apologize, but the best he could do was say, "I guess I'm late."

"I wish you'd call. You never call. You'd rather scare me," she said. "I don't want you to have a heart attack or get hit by a car." She said these things as if such misfortunes would be his own fault.

"I wasn't near no telephone—I was in the woods, er, hunting around," he said.

"Shooting dogs again," she said.

"Nope."

"For the life of me, I don't know why you men have to go out in the woods and shoot things."

"Crazy, crazy, crazy. We're all crazy," he said, and burst into laughter. There was such mirth in his voice, such mystery, that Elenore found it difficult to hang on to her righteous indignation.

"Well, you are in some kind of mood," she said.

"Indeed, I am."

"I imagine, then, you must have brought home some game. A rabbit? Are you going to clean me a rabbit?"

"In a manner of speaking, I brought home some game," Howard said, and laughed again.

He drank a couple of beers, and they ate supper—meatloaf with boiled potatoes and canned peas. Afterwards he said, "Elenore, that's the best meal I've ever had in my entire life."

Elenore ignored him. He always said his last meal was his best.

All that night, Howard Elman could not get over this giddy feeling. A man was not supposed to be this pleased. It was dangerous. It was the kind of thing that made you trust your fellow man—dangerous stuff.

"I tell you Elenore, happiness is as dangerous as misery," he said, right out of the blue as they were watching television.

"Then you're in trouble," she said.

Elenore didn't know what was happening, didn't care. Her husband's glorious mood was infecting her. At bed time, he took her hand. They both knew there was romance in the offing.

The next morning, Howard Elman stood outside looking at the bundle in the back of the pickup truck. Crazy, he thought. His friend Ollie was dead, and yet he couldn't help rejoicing.

"All these years, and it's only now that I realize the snow is blue," Elman said, addressing the bundle.

He lifted a corner of the tarp and looked at the bodies. The boy's face was buried in his father's bosom. Their arms were around each other.

Elman went back into the house. He didn't quite know what to do next. He couldn't leave the statues on the truck. Warm weather would come eventually and raise a stink with them, or some kid would be intrigued by the package in the bed of the truck and would steal it. This thought made Elman chuckle. He could rent freezer space at Horland's in Greenfield, Mass., perhaps visiting the statues from time to time, taking a peek at them and saying, "Hello—good-bye," which was as close as Elman could come to conjuring a prayer over the body of a friend. The freezer plan wouldn't work. Eventually, one of the employees would get curious and discover the statues. He sat in the living room of the mobile home with his coffee and some toast, and he watched part of a show on television that Elenore was following. It was on the educational channel, and he felt uplifted by that very fact. The fellow on the screen said that everything, from rocks to teardrops, was made of molecules, which he demonstrated with the help of models of little colored balls in clusters. "Chains of being," he called them. The idea of chains of being thrilled Elman and triggered something in his mind, and he was seeing Willow doing some stupid-ass thing and hearing Ollie saying, "My, what a sense of humor that boy has got," and his knowledge of the Jordans came together. In a moment, he understood the kind of love that had welded Ollie and Willow.

"Goddamn," he said.

"What is the matter with you?" Elenore asked.

"I got a secret," he said.

"Get it off your chest," she said.

"If I was to tell you, you'd wet your pants," Elman said, roaring with laughter.

"Tell," said Elenore.

"Nope."

"Not fair. If you got a secret, why tell me you got a secret and tease me? You should have shut up to begin with. But since you didn't, then tell."

"It ain't pretty," said Elman, getting serious now.

"Nothing you say is pretty. Tell."

Elman considered for a moment. He knew he couldn't keep the secret of the Jordans bottled up forever. So he told.

"That ain't a secret," Elenore said. "That knowledge is as common as dandelions."

"I know, I know. People say that, I know. But I know for sure. I tell you I know. I know it all now."

"Well, I didn't wet my pants," said Elenore, and she rose from her chair, limped toward her husband, and punched him on the shoulder.

Elman laughed and set her on his lap. "There's more to

tell," he said, and he spun his yarn about finding the bodies.

"You do what you want with Ollie and his boy, just get them out of here," she said. She should have been upset, but Howard's mood was so buoyant, it floated her somehow.

Howard Elman transferred the statues, still wrapped in plastic and a tarp, into his dump truck. It did not bother him that the corpse of a friend lay amidst trash, because Elman had no more ill feelings toward trash than an average person would have toward sawdust or earth itself. He left Cooty Patterson behind today, and set off on his trash route alone. As the morning wore on he realized the nature of his responsibility toward Ollie and Willow, and he knew where he was going to take them. He finished his work first. Work came before everything. He completed the Keene leg on his route by eleven a.m. Amazing that he could work faster alone than with Cooty. Actually, he needed Cooty—and Ollie when he was alive—to slow him, keep him from burning up his energy with work. The statues were now surrounded by piles of refuse. All his life, Ollie Jordan had been a dump rat, living off the discards of others. He must be happy now, Elman thought, and he headed the truck for Dubber, N. H.

The trailer where the old whore lived sat in a lonely spot by a swamp. The sky was huge here, and Elman took a moment to look at it. He thought of that color blue, which in concentrated form had settled into his friend. "Blue sky, I got your friend— your friend and mine," he said. The swamp itself was silver and blue with snow and patches of ice revealed by the wind. Here and there were coffee-colored stumps, decayed signs of a past age like signs of a business gone broke. In winter, it would be cold as iron here; in summer, hotter than a stray piece on a Friday night. Still, he liked the swamp, liked its isolation. He imagined that it would be a wonderful place to fool around in. The trailer was old, ugly, and small, and it tilted slightly to one side because the concrete blocks it sat on were sinking into the ground. There was some kind of hippie beads hanging in a window. He didn't have to knock because the woman came right to the door, opened it, stood there looking at him, and held her ground, making it clear he was to state his business but not come in. She was no spring chicken, but she had long, black hair and there was something undeniably alluring about her. He wanted to break the news to her kindly, but he never had the knack for kindliness, and he heard himself say next:

"I got your boys out here."

Estelle

If it hadn't been for Old Man Dorne's funeral, Estelle Jordan never would have recovered the Kinship Charm. She had known Dorne, as the Bible would say. He was a half-way decent man, even if he was a hypocrite. But they were all hypocrites. Hypocrisy rose and fell in a man just like his prick. She had learned to forgive hypocrisy—and all the other sins—when she realized how pathetic men were. She ranked Dorne as decent because he was not cruel and because he paid in cash, without quibbling. She went to a lot of funerals. She would say to herself that she should "pay her respects." In fact, respect had nothing to do with it. Estelle Jordan long ago had lost the very idea that human beings deserved respect. She liked funerals because there she could almost regain the feelings that she had lost so long ago. She would take on the emotional shimmer of widows and children, occasionally being able to draw from them just a hint of what true grief must be like. She had been so long without feelings, so hungry for feelings, that she was willing to settle for the worst, because they were the easiest to come by.

She hadn't bothered to bathe. Now if she were going to Hiram Lodge's funeral—which she hoped some day she would—she would bathe, because Lodge liked it clean, liked it neat, liked the room itself and even the bed neat and clean. Dorne wasn't like that. He was common stuff, liked it common. She sprayed on some Evening in Paris, which was what she called any cheap perfume. She dressed slowly in front of the mirror—black undies, black stockings, black dress, black veil. If she could not feel pleasure, at least she could remember what once pleasure had been like. She spent a long time looking at her breasts. Even at her age they were firm. She was glad that she had never allowed any of her children to feed from them. It angered her that nature seemed bent on destroying a woman's beauty with birthing, destroying beauty with beauty. Before she went to the funeral, she smoked a weed. Marijuana was the best she could do by way of capturing bliss.

After the funeral, Estelle had troubles with her car. She detoured to her son's place, Ike's White Elephant. Ike was not home, but Cousin Irv was, and he fixed the car. While Irv was working on the engine, she browsed about in the great warehouse where Ike stored the things he got, who knows where. Out of curiosity, she opened a big box marked "Connecticut," and there she found the Kinship Charm. She had no idea how it had gotten here. She doubted that Ollie had given it to his halfbrother. The two didn't get along, and anyway the thing held no value for Ike, since its maker, Oliver, Ollie's father, was not Ike's father. Somehow, through sheer accident, Ike had acquired the charm and now planned to sell it. Well, it don't belong to him, it belongs to the heir, she thought, and she plucked it out and put it inside her dress against her bosom.

April: the weather had begun to warm. Growing time. Changing time. Love searching. The bodies must be buried. She telephoned Elman. She liked his type: blunt, not stupid, if stupidly loyal. He suggested a fitting burial, saying, "He'll love it—be enough picking for him for all eternity." Of course he was talking about Ollie, his friend. It didn't matter about

Willow because Willow had never had a self. She remembered that both Ollie and Willow had been hard to birth.

When she and Elman arrived at the landfill in the dump truck, Elman drove up beside the operator of a pay loader. The two men seemed to know each other.

"I got some bulky objects," said Elman.

"White goods?" asked the operator.

"Statues—they won't mash down too good," Elman said.

Estelle Jordan could see in her mind's eye now the bodies buried in refuse, the pay loader driving over them to pack them, then distributing dirt across the refuse until a layer was formed. She saw layer after layer, no beginning, no end. The universe itself.

"Statues?" asked the operator. "We don't get too many of those. What kind of statues?"

"Religious stuff. People praying. Saints—jeez, I don't know," said Elman.

"Who'd throw something like that away? It's disgusting," said the operator.

"You know how it goes," Elman said. "If a man makes it, eventually it's no good and winds up at the dump."

"Put 'em in that corner," said the operator, pointing. "There's a low spot there, and they'll sit comfortable; and you can dump the rest of your stuff on top, and the saints will be happy."

"As you say," said Elman, and drove off.

Elman started the dump on the truck, and Estelle Jordan could hear the hydraulic lifters underneath pushing the load. Elman motioned her out of the truck. She watched him guide the statues—she too was thinking of the bodies as statues—into a hollow of trash. Then he walked down to the statues and pulled back the tarp. A moment later he said, "Well, I got my last look," and he walked away.

Estelle Jordan did not know she wanted a private moment with Ollie and Willow until Elman had left to give her that moment. She was wearing boots but it was hard walking in all that trash. The place stank of garbage once she got down out of the wind. She looked at the face of Ollie, blue and oddly calm, certainly calmer than it had been in life. Willow's face was turned away from her, into the bosom of his father. That was best, she thought. She remembered the day Oliver died now and she envied Ollie's ability to forget that terrible moment. Of course, in the end, he had paid. Ollie was a good boy. She had not seduced him. He had not come after her. They had just fallen in together after drinking, as was the way with the kinship in those days.

It had been a warm summery day when Oliver died. She was playing outside with the baby, Willow. Ollie was there, too. He was just sixteen himself, just as she had been sixteen when Oliver had taken her out of a shack in Sullivan town. Ollie liked playing with the baby. He was, she thought, more like a mother than she was. Then Oliver had come on the scene, drunk as a skunk. After that it was unclear in her mind just what had happened. There was an argument. Oliver threatened the baby—he never liked the baby; he knew where it had come from. Or, perhaps, Ollie thought that he threatened the baby, for Ollie had been drinking too. She remembered that Oliver had said, "He's an idiot. He'd be better off dead." She didn't remember them as fighting exactly. Oliver had grabbed Ollie by the shoulders, as a drunken father will, and they began to turn and step lively, like dancers, until they fell and Ollie was bashing out his father's brains on the stone wall near the family shack. She told the cops Oliver had fallen from a ledge.

Then Ollie forgot, and she ceased to feel. For months Ollie walked around like a zombie, knowing not even his name. Then one day he said to her, "You're the Witch." He recovered his memory, but not all of it, not that part that would hurt. It was she who had the hurt, so much of it that she had nothing. The name "Witch" stuck with her. She realized that that's the way it was with men. They did evil, and then they blamed women. Ask Eve. Call me Witch: woman who cannot feel, she thought.

She removed the charm from the inside of her dress, looking at it for a moment before surrendering it. Oliver had made it as a gift for her. It was the closest he ever came to telling her he loved her. He could carve pretty well, but he needed a model to work from, and he used to get angry because the final product never looked exactly like the model. Still, she could not imagine how Ollie could have seen a butterfly in the carving. She saw no such butterfly. The charm was what it was, nothing more. Oliver had carved the charm by copying the label from a bottle of Four Roses whiskey. She tucked the charm into a nook between the faces of Ollie and Willow. "Good luck," she whispered. The day was getting warmer. She could feel the sun stroking her cheek. She could feel a breath of air sweep down into the hollow and cleanse it. It was spring air. She could feel it. She could feel a great welling up inside of her. These boys, as statues, had released her.

"My sons, my sons," she said, and wept.